MW00898456

SINFULLY DELICIOUS

A TWO BROOMSTICKS GAS & GRILL WITCH COZY
MYSTERY

AMANDA M. LEE

WINCHESTERSHAW PUBLICATIONS

PROLOGUE

12 YEARS AGO

"The day your mother was born was the worst day of my life. Do you want to know why? I'm going to tell you."

My grandfather worked behind the huge industrial stove, his eyes meeting mine next to the order wheel. He was cooking today rather than holding court at the coffee counter, because my uncle had called in sick. Days when my grandfather mastered the griddle were both the worst and best days to work.

They were the best because he insisted waitresses not wash dishes so they wouldn't dirty their uniforms. When my uncle was in charge, everybody had to help with the dishes — and it sucked. My grandfather, however, believed in looking professional above all else. That was a minor treat, though. In exchange, the days were the worst because he told endless stories (and occasionally threw bread when things didn't go his way). I couldn't have a single moment to myself as he insisted on spinning yarns that I'd heard at least fifty times each during the course of my sixteen years. I'd heard at least thirty variations of this particular story.

"It was the worst day of your life because it also happened to be the first day of deer season," I answered without thinking. "It was snowing just enough for you to be able to make out tracks, but not so cold you would've frozen your nuts off — which was probably a good thing for all your other kids, huh?" I flashed a smile that I didn't really feel. "And, of course, she was a girl and you wanted a boy. Missing deer season for a girl is simply unacceptable."

Grandpa met my gaze with a dark one of his own. "I'm going to tell you the story the way I want to tell it," he snapped. "And, just for the record, I was fine with your mother being a girl. If she says otherwise, she's lying."

I knew better. Grandpa had gotten drunk a time or two and admitted that he had melted down about missing deer season for the birth of a girl. Apparently he would've been fine missing it for a boy, but a girl was something else entirely. I liked to think karma was listening that day, because the baby that was born the following December — forcing him to miss another deer season opener — was also a girl.

"Uh-huh." I tapped the counter next to the ticket I'd given him minutes ago. "Do you have my eggs and bacon?"

Grandpa's eyes narrowed. Charles Archer hated being rushed. "I'm working on it." He turned his back was to me and focused on the griddle. It was a busy morning at the Two Broomsticks Gas & Grill in Shadow Hills, Michigan. The leaves were just starting to fall, signaling our busy season was right around the corner. Given our location in northern Lower Michigan, we had exactly two seasons to make money: summer, when all the golfers came to town to hang out at the neighboring resorts, and winter, when the skiers and snowmobilers flocked to the surrounding hills and trails. Sure, people visited in the spring and fall, but two seasons could make or break every business in the area.

"You know what your problem is?" Grandpa called over his shoulder.

"Yes, I've been waiting for my bacon and eggs twice as long as necessary," I drawled, rubbing my forearm against my forehead and glancing at the clock on the wall. My shift ended in an hour. I had a paper due for English class and I hadn't even started it. I should go straight home after my shift and hit the writing. That wasn't going to happen, though. My boyfriend Hunter Ryan was picking me up so we could hang out for a few hours. I had been looking forward to that more than anything else all shift, including no longer smelling like a grease trap thanks to my proximity to the deep fryers.

"Your problem is that you're exactly like your mother," Grandpa shot back. "Why do you think she named you Stormy Breeze Morgan?"

I'd been wondering that very thing for most of my life. "I think she secretly hated me for twenty-five hours of labor and that's how she paid me back," I replied without hesitation.

"Wrong. She was always going to name you Stormy. I tried talking her into giving you a normal name, but she was having none of it. Do you want to know why?"

He was big on asking questions to which he provided his own answers. It drove me insane at times. "I just told you why."

"And I told you that's not why. Listen." He reached through the order window and flicked the spot between my eyebrows before I realized what was happening, earning a yelp and a glare for his efforts. "Your mother named you Stormy Breeze to irritate me."

Oh, well, this was a new variation. "Really? She saddled me with this stupid name because of you? How so?"

He looked around, perhaps to see if anybody was listening, and lowered his voice. "She's a hippie."

I pressed my lips together, unsure how to respond. "She's a hippie?" I asked, amusement and annoyance warring in my busy brain. Seriously, why couldn't he just cook the eggs and bacon? Why was I being forced to listen to this when I wanted to think about other things ... like homework and Hunter (although not necessarily in that order)?

"She's a hippie," he confirmed, bobbing his head. He said it in a manner that indicated he thought it was a big deal. "She left the family business. You know that."

I was thrilled about that little development. Working with my grandfather, aunts, uncles, and cousins was difficult enough. Working with my mother on top of everything else would've sent me over the edge. "I'm well aware she left the family business," I said dryly. "She didn't like being a waitress."

Grandpa's expression darkened. "Yes, even though that business is the reason she had shoes on her feet and clothes on her back the entire time she was growing up."

And here it was. He just wanted to rant about Mom quitting the diner. No matter how many shifts we worked together, the conversation always turned to Mom and her lack of appreciation. It was frustrating — and sometimes funny, because I enjoyed complaining about my mother almost as much as he did. "She doesn't want to be a waitress," I said, tapping the open ticket again for emphasis. "Cook my eggs."

"I'm doing it." He glared at me. "What's wrong with waitressing? You're a waitress and you're happy."

"I'm not happy being a waitress," I argued. "I don't mind the money. And I can tolerate smelling like French fries five days a week because Hunter thinks it's better than perfume. But it's not as if this is my dream job."

"Oh, really?" Grandpa folded his arms across his stained apron. "Just what is your dream job?"

That was a good question. "I think I want to be a writer."

Grandpa looked horrified at the prospect. "A writer? Like, a reporter?"

I shook my head. "I want to write books."

His expression twisted. "That's not a real job."

"Says who?"

"Um ... everybody who has ever tried to be a writer. I don't like the idea of you sitting around writing sex scenes for those stupid bodice-rippers all the women read."

Now it was my turn to frown. "You know that women can write different sorts of books, right? Just because Grandma likes her romance novels on the kinky side doesn't mean there aren't other things to write about."

Grandpa straightened his tall frame and looked around to see if anyone had heard the tidbit I'd dropped about my grandmother. When he lowered himself again, his expression was dark. "First off, your grandmother doesn't read filth."

I rolled my eyes.

"Second, nobody needs to know that your grandmother reads filth," he hissed, extending a warning finger. "That's a secret."

"I'm sorry that Grandma reads filth," I said dryly. I knew the books he was talking about. She had a whole stack of them next to her bed. I had a few theories about why, but I figured that was a conversation I could never share with my grandfather if I didn't want to die of embarrassment. "Not all women read romance novels. And not all women writers write romance novels."

"Of course not. That's ridiculous. Some authors write westerns ... and war books ... and biographies. Those are good books."

I knew what he was saying without saying it. "You mean male authors."

He pretended an air of innocence. "I didn't say that." He focused on the griddle, where the bacon hissed and popped. "Why do you always jump to the men-versus-women thing? It's ridiculous and, frankly, a little insulting. Not everything boils down to ovaries and testicles."

My mouth fell open and I felt the color rushing to my cheeks. "I can't believe you just said that!"

"What?" His brow furrowed. "It's the truth. You should know by now that men and women have different plumbing."

He had to be joking. "Of course I know that!" I was scandalized. "I don't even understand how we got on this topic. I know about the different parts."

Grandpa's shoulders stiffened. "How do you know about the parts? You haven't seen them, have you?"

I couldn't believe we were having this conversation. "Cook the bacon and eggs!"

He ignored the demand. "It's that Ryan boy, isn't it? Hunter. That's his first name. You two have been joined at the hip of late. You're not joining anywhere else, are you?"

I couldn't find the words to respond because I was certain my cheeks had burst into flames.

"Maybe I should have a talk with the boy," Grandpa mused. "He's big and sturdy, like a maple tree, but if I catch him off guard I might be able to get the drop on him."

"You're going to get the drop on him?" I couldn't believe he was still talking. "This isn't some cop movie, and you won't do anything to him. He hasn't done anything wrong. You need to just ... stop talking about this."

I don't care how enlightened you are — I was raised by a loose-lipped mother who thought we should talk frequently about absolutely everything, including menstruation and the female body's erogenous zones — there are some things you should not discuss with a grandparent. It should be outlawed.

"I'm not trying to embarrass you," Grandpa fired back.

"Well, you're doing a great job of it."

He pretended not to hear me. "If that boy is putting the moves on you ... ."

"Who even says that any longer?" I challenged. "You're showing your age, Grandpa."

"Yeah, that doesn't work on me." He was blasé. "Your mother can be manipulated by the age thing. Even though she's a hippie, tree-loving, pain in the keister, she's vain. You can tell by how often she looks in the mirror. I don't care about the age. I believe in being who you are no matter your age."

I was over this conversation. "Well, great. Finish my bacon and eggs. I've probably already lost this tip."

"I said I was working on it." His eyes flashed with annoyance. "You get more and more like your mother every day. You know that, right?"

He meant it as an insult, and that's how I took it. "I just want my bacon and eggs," I complained. "Why can't you just give me my bacon and eggs?"

He smirked. "Your mother does that whiny thing, too."

He knew exactly how to irritate me. "Okay, listen here, Grandpa." I lowered my voice to barely a hiss. "If you don't get me my bacon and eggs, I'll tell Grandma you've been reading her books for tips but not using them."

It took him a second to realize my threat. "You wouldn't dare!"

"Try me." I'd had enough. "I just want my bacon and eggs, for crying out loud. I want this shift to end. Then I want to leave with my boyfriend and spend a few hours hanging out without worrying about anything.

"You know what I really want, though?" I'd learned how to rant from him, so I was a pro. My talent was on full display today. "What I really want is not to have to work with family anymore. I mean ... is that not the absolute worst?"

"I like working with family," he fired back. "It's fun."

"No, it's not." I couldn't let it go now that I'd started. "It's not fun at all. It's loud ... and annoying ... and everybody always fights. When someone calls in sick, family has to cover. When you're in a bad mood, family knows exactly how to make it worse — and they enjoy doing it. Strangers wouldn't even know where to start on something like that."

"Working with strangers is highly overrated," Grandpa muttered. "Working with family is the best of both worlds. You say it's annoying because family members always know how to make your day worse. They also know how to make it better, and if things are really bad, they go out of their way to make it better. Strangers don't do that."

He had a point. "I still hate it. The only thing I can say with any degree of certainty is that when I get older I'm not working with family. That's all there is to it. I'm going to do something else, be someone else."

"Like your mother?" Grandpa's expression darkened further. "You really are like her."

"I'm not. I don't want to be like her either. I want to be my own person."

"Well, I hope that works out for you." His slapped the eggs and bacon on a chipped plate and slid it to me. "Just remember, family is people who have to take you back when your dreams fall apart. Something tells me you're going to need to remember that."

His jab wasn't lost on me. "I'll remember. But I'm never coming back here. As soon as I graduate high school, I'm heading to college and never looking back. Mark my words, Shadow Hills will just be a place I visit every five years or so."

Grandpa snorted, disdain on full display. "Adulthood rarely turns out the way you think it will."

"Oh, I'm going to make it happen. I promise. This is not going to be my life. You have my word."

"Good luck with that. You're going to need it."

ONE

PRESENT DAY

"Stormy, you have three orders stacked. Get a move on."

My uncle Brad peered through the window between the order wheel and spice rack and caught my gaze.

"Did you hear me?" he pressed when I didn't immediately respond. "All of these are your orders."

I glanced at the jumble of plates and sighed. They claim you never forget how to waitress; it's like riding a bike. They're right. I remembered all of my shortcuts from when I was a teenager. Unfortunately, I was severely lacking in the speed department, and it was beginning to show. Apparently that was going to take some dedicated concentration.

"I'm on it." I transferred the first two orders to the same tray and shifted it to carry with my left arm. "I'll be back for the other order in a second."

"Hurry up." Brad's gaze was serious as he regarded me. "It's not even the lunch rush yet. You need to get it together."

"I said I was on it," I snapped, agitation coming out to play. It was my first day on the job — er, well, it was my first day *back* on the job — and I was still bitter about the turn my life had taken. That wasn't my uncle's fault, of course. That didn't mean I wasn't keen to lash out at someone, though, and turning my frustration inward was no longer an option because I was already bruised and battered from all the internal loathing I'd unleashed on myself. "I'll be right back."

I swung through the double doors that led to the cafe side of the restaurant and headed to my table. Two women, both in their thirties and with sleeping babies in car seats propped up next to them on booth benches, stopped talking as I approached. It was obvious they'd been gossiping and didn't want me to overhear. I was fine with that. There's little I hated more than gossip.

Okay, that's a lie. I love gossip. Still, I didn't recognize the women, and it's only fun to gossip if you know who is being talked about behind his or her back.

"Grilled chicken salad, no croutons, and ranch on the side," I announced, delivering the first plate. "Toasted tuna on rye, two extra pickles on the side," I said to the other woman as I slid the plate in front of her." I kept my smile in place, even though it was a chore, and glanced between the women. "Do you need anything else right now?"

"I think we're good," the brunette replied as she unfolded her napkin. She was slim, had the sort of glossy hair I always dreamed about, and cast me a cursory dose of side eye. "You look familiar. Do I know you?"

"I don't know." I'd been dreading this part of my day. When people started realizing who I was, the questions were bound to start flying fast and furious. "Who are you?"

"Sarah Bollinger, but that's my married name. I used to be Sarah Harris."

I did a double-take. "Seriously?" She didn't look even remotely the same as when I'd left. She'd been four years ahead of me in high school, which meant we didn't hang out or even really know each other. She'd been popular, though, a cheerleader, and everybody knew her. "I thought you were living in East Lansing these days."

Sarah's nose wrinkled as she looked me up and down. "That's where I went to school."

Right, on a volleyball scholarship. Shadow Hills wasn't known for producing world-class athletes, but Sarah was one of the few who managed to parlay meager talent above the net into a full education. She was essentially the epitome of the standard Shadow Hills teenage dream. That didn't explain what she was doing back here now. "And you're back here visiting?" I was hopeful that was the case.

She shook her head. "No. I went to school in East Lansing and then returned home. I worked in the feed and seed with my parents for a year or two before meeting my husband."

And that's when my hope fled. "You married Danny Bollinger?" That was disappointing. He'd been hot when I was in middle school, quarterback of the football team. All the girls threw themselves at him. Shadow Hills was basically one stereotype heaped on top of another stereotype, and Danny hadn't escaped the curse. Now, fifteen years after his graduation, he was fifty pounds overweight, about a pound of hair lighter, and he spent all his time sitting at the front coffee counter talking about his glory days with the other men who lived and worked in town. He'd been parked in what I assumed was his regular spot when I showed up for my first shift.

She nodded and smiled. "Yes, he's the love of my life," Sarah said blandly, her tone telling me she would happily pack up and run should the chance arise. Danny was apparently nobody's happily ever after, which was probably to be expected. "I still don't know who you are."

The time I'd been dreading had finally come and I wanted to find a hole and crawl inside to hide. I'd made a promise to myself, though. I wasn't going to run from this. It was only a temporary solution after all. I wasn't back in Shadow Hills forever.

Except you are, a weak voice whispered in the back of my mind. *You know that as well as anybody. You took your shot, made it for five seconds, and now you're back. There's no escaping this town.*

I brutally shoved the voice out of my mind and pasted what I hoped could pass for a friendly smile onto my face. "Stormy Morgan."

Realization dawned on Sarah and I didn't miss the hint of triumph that managed to push through even as she wrestled to hide her glee. "Right. I should've recognized you. I saw you on television when you were doing the rounds on all the news shows years ago for that book you wrote. What was it again?"

"*Death of a Small Town,*" I gritted out. She darned well knew the title. Heck, everybody knew the title. It was set in Shadow Hills, for crying out loud. The book put the town on the map for a full year — before everyone forgot about it and I faded into obscurity.

"Yeah, that was a big hit, right?" Sarah's expression was encouraging, but I knew better. She wanted to hear the sad tale of my fall from grace. She wanted to hear how I got one book contract and sold hundreds of thousands of copies and then flopped with my second book and the publisher dropped the option on my third. That was the reason I was back in Shadow Hills. Everybody was going to want to hear that story.

"It did okay," I replied evasively, shifting the tray. "I really need to deliver this order. I'll be back to see if you need anything else."

Sarah beamed at me. "Maybe when you come back we can catch up. I'd love to hear about the time you spent in New York."

I had no doubt that was true. "I really spent only a few months in New

York. I was in North Carolina after that ... and Savannah ... and New Orleans." *Basically anywhere I thought I could find inspiration for my second book*, I silently added. "I have to get back to work. It was good to see you."

I was grateful that the women on the other side of the cafe, the dinner side that boasted salad and soup bars, were older and didn't appear even mildly curious about who I was, or why I was delivering their cheeseburgers and fries. They were in their sixties and deep in conversation, talking about some incident that occurred at the senior center the previous day.

"I'm telling you she's a cheat," the woman with the platinum blond curls hissed, barely sparing a smile for me as I delivered her food. "She has hand signals she shares with Marla. That's how they always win the weekly euchre tournament."

The other woman gasped in surprise, which quickly turned to outrage. "That makes so much sense."

I checked to make sure their beverages were full and then disappeared back into the kitchen to claim my last order. Brad was busy talking to the dishwasher, a kid from the local high school I didn't recognize.

"The Democrats want everyone to be on welfare and the Republicans want everyone to starve," Brad explained to the hapless teenager, who looked confused by my uncle's filibustering. "You have to decide which one you believe in more and then go with it."

I'd barely spent any time with my uncle before reporting for my first shift, but one of the first things I'd noticed about him was he'd suddenly developed an interest in politics. When I was a kid, he was all about peace, love, and understanding. Now he was all about political shows and arguing simply for argument's sake. As far as I could tell, most of what he said was complete and total nonsense. He couldn't even pick a side to land on when it came to these arguments. He bagged on both sides.

"You should leave him alone," I instructed Brad as I collected my plates. "He's a teenager. He doesn't want to hear your bitter old guy shtick. He's still dreaming of getting out of this place."

"Oh, I'm going to get out of this place," the teenager intoned, his eyes lighting with excitement. "Two more years and then I'm out of here. I'm going to college at Central Michigan and then I'm going to find an actual city to live in."

"One that has more than one stoplight and actually has a fast-food restaurant, right?" I asked, thinking back to the things that were important to me when I was his age.

He bobbed his head excitedly. "Exactly. I want a Taco Bell, people. Is that too much to ask?"

His enthusiasm made me smile — and then frown. I'd wanted a McDonald's. Who doesn't love those fries? I'd been so excited when I got to college and could eat fast food regularly. That lasted only a few weeks, though. Then I missed the food at the cafe. Of course, I wouldn't admit that to anyone.

"Well, good luck." I swooped out of the kitchen just as my uncle was explaining proper military strategy from the Republican point of view, and I delivered the food to a corner table in the cafe. The men waiting on their burgers started inhaling the food, as if they hadn't eaten in weeks, and I left them to it. I saw Sarah trying to catch my attention and flashed her an apologetic smile before crossing over to my grandfather. He sat at the coffee counter, alone, reading his newspaper as he ate chili over a bed of onions — with a fork.

"How can you eat that?" I complained as I moved behind the counter and grabbed the pot of coffee to top off his mug. "I mean ... that's like all-day heartburn right there. It's gross."

Grandpa glanced up from his newspaper and regarded me with unreadable eyes. In the years since I'd left, his hair had thinned some and grayed at the temples. His face had a few more lines. Other than that, he looked mostly the same.

He also acted the same.

"Do I comment on your meals?"

I shook my head. "No, but we haven't had many meals together since I got back. I expect that to change because you comment on everything."

He chuckled. "You haven't been around for any of the family dinners," he countered. "You even missed last night's meal, which was a welcome home dinner for you, so that was a ballsy move. Your mother was mad, by the way."

As far as I could tell, my mother was angry about everything these days — especially the fact that I was working in the family restaurant again. She couldn't understand why I didn't get rich off the one book that sold well, enough to live comfortably forever. When I explained that's not the way it worked, her response was that I should've tried to sell a second book. I told her I did, but it didn't sell. Her response? "Well, you should've tried harder."

That was two weeks ago and we hadn't spoken since. I'd made my move to Shadow Hills, taken over the apartment above the restaurant, and seen almost everybody in my family during the intervening days. There was still no sign of my mother. It was too much to hope she wouldn't speak to me for the rest of her life. She would be back, there was no doubt about that.

"Isn't my mother always ticked off?" I asked, grabbing a rag from the small sink and wiping down the counter. I felt the need to stay busy. If I didn't, my mind would start to wander, which was the reason I was living on four hours of sleep a night these days. I couldn't stop running what had happened through my head. *How could I get everything I ever wanted and then lose it in a few short years?* It would've been easier if I'd never been published.

"It seems so these days," Grandpa confirmed. "She told me to fire you, by the way."

I was stunned. "What? Why does she want you to fire me?"

"Why do you think?" His eyebrows hopped with amusement as he dropped the newspaper. He was one of the few people I knew who still insisted on regular delivery even though the local newspaper was so thin you could read it in five minutes. "She believes that you'll write another best-selling book if I fire you."

"Yeah, unless I starve first."

He smirked. "She doesn't understand what happened. I think perhaps that's because you've never taken the time to explain what happened to her."

Oh, well, of course he would think that. "Why is everything always my fault?"

"You make an easy scapegoat," Grandpa replied without hesitation. "No one is at fault in this particular situation. You got lucky with that first book. You didn't get lucky with the second. Maybe, after taking a little downtime and getting some perspective, you'll get lucky with the third."

I narrowed my eyes to blue slits. "What makes you think there will be a third book?"

"We didn't raise you to be a quitter. Your mother may be a hippie-dippy freak, but she's a hard worker. She owns her own real estate business now, which is something to be proud of. Your father is a hard worker, too. You always worked at the restaurant, even when you hated it. I don't expect you to suddenly give up on your dreams now that things have gotten rough. You'll put it back together."

He sounded sure of himself, which only served to annoy me. "It doesn't feel like anything is coming together right now," I argued. "It feels as if everything has fallen apart and I'm sitting on the edge of a cliff, ready to fall off at any moment."

"And people say your second book lacked dramatic tension." He shook his head.

I glared at him. "You're not funny."

"I think I'm hilarious." He patted my wrist and then turned back to his chili and onions. "You need time to absorb what happened to you, Stormy. You're still young. You haven't lost the dream forever. You've simply misplaced it for now. You can get it back."

That felt unlikely. "I don't know many literary agents willing to accept submissions from waitresses," I muttered.

"Then don't tell them you're a waitress. Tell them you're a princess or something. I know, tell them you're a witch. Witches are everywhere now."

"A witch? Stormy the witch? That's just ... way too much."

He smiled. "And somehow I think it fits." He inclined his head toward the swinging doors, to where Brad's head poked between the opening. "I think your uncle wants you."

I scowled as I turned my gaze in that direction. I used to think the worst thing in the world was working a shift with my grandfather. I would gladly take it today if it meant I didn't have to listen to Brad's nonsense. His political conspiracy theories were starting to give me indigestion. I was running on caffeine and nerves as it was. "Do you need something?"

He nodded. "I'm out of pickles."

I waited for him to continue. When he didn't, I shrugged. "So what do we do?"

"They're in the storage building behind the restaurant," he replied. "You need to get them."

"Why do I need to get them?" I was feeling petulant, in no mood to be ordered around. "Why can't you get them?"

"I'm the chef, which means I'm in charge of the kitchen today. As my underling, it's your job to do as I say."

I wasn't a fan of the word "underling," but when I turned a questioning look toward Grandpa, I found he'd already disengaged from the conversation and was again reading his newspaper. Apparently I was on my own. "Fine. I'll get the pickles."

I muttered a series of nasty words as I cut through the kitchen and headed for the back door. There were two exits, one close to the steps that led to my apartment and the other by the industrial-sized freezers. I sidestepped two of my cousins smoking by the steps and went out the other door.

I was lost in thought, my mind jumbled with my new reality, and made the mistake of not watching where I was going. I stepped in a puddle, skidding a good two feet before I found pavement again. The alley between the restaurant and storage building was wide enough for a semitruck to park for deliveries, but that wasn't a benefit now as I stumbled four hard paces to keep myself upright, stopping only when I crashed into the storage building.

"Ow." I rubbed my elbow as I turned to see where the water had come from. The first thing I realized as I studied the area was that it wasn't water I'd slid in. It was something else. Something red.

My mouth went dry as my eyes drifted to the crumpled form resting in the puddle. The older man in mismatched socks wasn't moving.

I opened my mouth to scream for help but I couldn't find my voice. I tried again but nothing.

All that time I stared at the body, willing it to move. This had to be a mistake. Perhaps my uncle was explaining his political views on crime. After a good three minutes, I realized this wasn't a joke gone awry.

It was something much, much worse.

TWO

I stood there for a long time staring at the body. Then I forced myself to move, as if I was walking on an uneven surface because I kept stumbling as I circled the body and made my way back into the restaurant.

My fingers felt numb and I had to grasp the door handle twice before I managed to get a firm grip. I tripped on the step as I went inside, smacking into the freezer. The noise drew my uncle's attention.

"Did you get my pickles?" he asked, giving me a long once-over. "It doesn't look like you did."

I pointed at the door in response.

"Yes, the pickles are that way," he intoned. "I'm well aware. You have to get them. I'm in charge of the kitchen. You're my subordinate. As my subordinate, you do what I say."

"That could be taken in a really gross way," a new voice supplied. It belonged to my cousin David. Close to my age, I'd yet to see him since I'd returned. He was one of the few cousins I would've been happy to see ... at least under different circumstances. "You probably shouldn't get off on using the word 'subordinate.'"

Brad rolled his eyes. "I'm not using it in a filthy way. Don't be a disgusting pervert." He flicked David's ear and smirked. "How was your vacation? I can't remember the last time I got two weeks off work. Do you want to know why? Because I've never had that much time off in one go."

"The vacation was great," David replied. "We went to Mexico."

"Yes, I heard. It's unsafe to go to Mexico these days. You know that, right? I didn't want to tell you before your trip and ruin your fun, but it was a bad idea."

"Says who?"

"Anyone with a brain," Brad replied. "I heard it from Rush Limbaugh. The Republicans want to close the border."

"Oh, geez." David shook his head. "Can we get through one conversation without mentioning politics? That would be great." He focused on me. "I'm sorry I wasn't here when you arrived. I'm sure your reintroduction to the family couldn't have been easy. I met a girl, though."

That was David. He always had a new girl. He went through a new one about every six months. They were all much younger than him. He was almost thirty, but his dates had rarely reached the age of twenty. I'd spent a long time thinking about it — mostly when trying to plot a hit book — but I'd come to the conclusion that he felt his life was out of control so he dated younger girls because he thought them more malleable. He simply couldn't take a woman who knew what she wanted.

That was a discussion for another time.

"We need to call the police." I squeaked as I tried to maintain control of my emotions.

"Because I went to Mexico?" David furrowed his brow. "I'm perfectly fine. Don't listen to Brad. He's always been something of an alarmist. You know as well as anyone that if he sees something on television — whether it's fiction or news — he extrapolates it to everyday life. He's ridiculous."

"Not that." My throat felt dry and I gestured toward the alley again. "We need to call the police."

"Is this about the pickles?" Brad pinned me with a dark look. "I told you that I'm the boss. That means you have to wrangle the pickles."

"That could be viewed as sexual harassment," David said, starting for the door. Unlike our uncle, he seemed genuinely curious to see what had shaken me.

"She's my niece," Brad argued, scandalized. "I can't sexually harass my niece."

"You could, but then we'd have a whole other problem to deal with." David pushed open the door and poked his head outside.

"Sexual harassment is something the left drummed up to hurt the right," Brad said. "Of course, the right used it against political figures from the left for a time. Wait ... maybe I need to give this one more thought. There could be something here."

It's hell having an uncle who is a conspiracy theorist and yet can manage to side with both political parties in the same breath.

David flew through the door.

"Call the police," he barked, causing Brad to stand up straight. "There's a body out back."

"A body?" Brad's eyebrows drew together.

David nodded, grim. "It's Roy Axe."

I frowned. I knew that name. "Grandpa's friend?"

"I don't know that friend is the right word, but yeah, he knows Grandpa."

"He's dead?" Brad couldn't seem to wrap his head around the concept.

"He's definitely dead," David confirmed. "Call the police. Get Hunter out here right now."

My heart skipped at the words, but Brad was already moving. "Wait ... Hunter? You can't call him here."

David shot me an impatient look. "He's one of three police officers in this town. We have to call him."

"Yeah, but ... I'm all greasy from working in the kitchen." What a ridiculous thing to say, and yet I was bothered by the thought of Hunter seeing me after the hectic morning rush.

"I think the dead body takes precedence over your hair."

Obviously he didn't grasp the etiquette of seeing your ex for the first time in a decade. "I'm not ready."

"Well, you'd better get ready. We need help and he's our only option. Suck it up." He clapped his hand against my shoulder hard enough to rock me to the side. "There's a dead body outside. Your issues with Hunter aren't important right now."

That showed just how out of touch he really was with reality.

HUNTER RYAN LOOKED THE SAME.

Actually, he looked better than he had in high school, and that was saying something.

I watched his arrival from the area by the freezers, David and Brad with me, and felt my heart give a long, slow roll. Why did he have to look the same? It would've been easier if he'd let himself go. Instead, he'd filled out in all the right ways.

His shoulders were always broad, his waist narrow. His arms were powerful, just like in high school when he liked to brag about how much he could bench press when competing with David. They would play off each other, compete, and yet they were always friends. Apparently they still were, because David detached from our small cluster and went out to greet him.

"Hey, man." David offered a smile that didn't make it all the way to his eyes. "Sorry to call you out here, but, well ... ." He gestured toward the body.

"That's why I'm here." Hunter flashed the smile I remembered from high school and I had to tamp something down when the familiar dimple came out to play in his cheek. He was one of the few guys who could carry off a dimple and still look rugged. It was one of the things that forever etched his face into my dreams. "Tell me what happened."

"I'm not sure." David nervously cracked his knuckles and watched as Hunter crouched down to get a better look at the body. "I just got back from Mexico last night so I slept in this morning. I'm not even on shift until tomor-row. I stopped in to get my paycheck. That's when Stormy started freaking out."

Freaking out? I wasn't even close to freaking out. David's words bothered me. I managed — just barely — to keep my opinion to myself.

"Stormy?" Hunter jerked up his chin, surprise etching across his handsome features.

"Stormy." David gestured toward me, causing Hunter to fix his attention on the small crowd that had gathered inside of the restaurant to watch the show through the open door. His breath hitched for a moment and then he steadied himself. There was no smile of welcome on his face. "Can you come out here, please?"

There was no doubt he was talking to me. Resigned, I dropped my head and shuffled through the door, doing my best to pretend I wasn't bothered by the way our reintroduction was playing out. "Hi." My voice was a breathy squeak I absolutely hated.

"Hello." His response was cooler. "David says you found the body."

I nodded, grim. "Brad sent me out for pickles," I started.

"Pickles I never got," Brad called out.

I shot him a dark look. "I think there are more important things to worry about besides your pickles."

"Again, there are so many different ways that statement could be miscon-strued," David lamented.

Hunter shot him an amused look before turning his full attention back to me. "Go on."

He acted as if we didn't know one another, as if we hadn't spent more than two years wrapped up in each other to the point of distraction. It was irritating, but also easier because it allowed me to focus on what needed to be done. Perhaps he knew that going in.

"There's not much to tell," I replied. "I walked out this way. I wasn't really paying attention. My shoe landed in what I thought was water and I kind of slid until I hit the storage building. When I turned to see what I'd slipped on, I saw ... him."

"Uh-huh." Hunter glanced down at my sneakers. "I need those for evidence."

I balked. "They're brand new."

"That doesn't change the fact that I need them." His inflection didn't change, which agitated me. *How could he be so calm when we were seeing each other for the first time in almost ten years — and standing over a body?*

"Fine." I fixed him with a dark look. "Would you like me to take them off now or can I go upstairs to get a different pair?"

"I need them now." He reached in his pocket and came back with a plastic bag. "Just drop them in here."

I was dumbfounded. "You can't be serious. You want me to go barefoot around a dead body?"

"I want those shoes," Hunter replied. "I need them before you contaminate any evidence even further than you already have."

"And just how am I contaminating them?"

"By ruining whatever evidence you might've stepped in." For the first time since arriving, Hunter raised his voice. "Don't make me ask for them again."

Was that a threat? It sure sounded like a threat.

Clearly uncomfortable, David cleared his throat to get my attention. "Just give him your shoes, Stormy. It's no big deal. They're Skechers. You can get a new pair for fifty bucks."

I was ashamed to admit that I didn't have the fifty bucks. That's the reason I was living in the apartment above the restaurant. "Whatever." I plopped down on the ground, making sure I was nowhere near the body, and started wrestling my shoes off. "This is ridiculous."

"Thank you." Hunter dropped the bag by my feet and went back to studying the body. "This is Roy Axe. He was friends with your grandfather."

"More like frenemies," David replied, causing me to narrow my eyes as I shoved one of my shoes into the plastic bag.

"I thought they golfed together," I said, grimacing when I noticed the blood on the second shoe. That's what had caused me to slide across the alley. The white bottom of the formerly pristine sneaker was stained a horrible rust color.

"They did ... back then," David explained. "I don't know that I would ever call them friends, but they were certainly friendlier back then than they were in recent years."

Hunter's forehead wrinkled. "What caused the falling out?"

I sensed trouble. "You can't think Grandpa had anything to do with this," I argued before David could answer.

Hunter pinned me with an unreadable look. "I'm just trying to get a feel for what might've happened."

He was lying. He still had the same tell. His left eye opened wider than his right when he was hiding something back then. The same phenomenon was on display today.

"I think we should call Grandpa out here," I said to David, fixing him with a pointed look. "This is his restaurant. Has anyone bothered to tell him what's going on?"

"It's after lunch," Brad reminded me through the door. "He's taking his post-lunch ... um ... constitutional."

I wasn't sure what that meant. "I don't understand. Did he leave?"

David let loose a low chuckle and shook his head. "He didn't leave. He's just ... taking his afternoon ... um ... bathroom break."

My cheeks burned under the sudden realization of what he was saying. "Oh, I ... ."

"It's a regular occurrence," Brad explained. "It usually takes him an hour."

An hour? That couldn't be healthy. "Maybe he should try eating something other than chili and onions for lunch," I groused. Something occurred to me. "Wait, he's not doing that in the guest restroom, is he?"

"No," Brad replied, shaking his head. "He wouldn't do that to the customers."

"So, where ... ?" A horrible thought filled my head.

"Sometimes he goes home," David offered, his lips curving into a wide smile. "But his truck is still here, so I'm sure he felt the situation was more ... dire."

"That means he's in my apartment," I muttered, closing my eyes and shaking my head. When I opened them again, I found Hunter watching me with overt amusement. He was clearly enjoying himself. "It's not funny."

"I didn't say it was. I was just ... thinking." He turned his attention back to the body. "What's the deal with Roy and your grandfather? I always thought they were friends."

"Something happened about two years ago," David replied. "They got in a fight while golfing or something. That's the story I heard."

"I thought it was over a poker game," Brad countered. "He tried to cheat Dad or something. At least that's the story that was making the rounds a few weeks after."

"But they definitely weren't friends any longer?" Hunter snapped on a pair of rubber gloves before lifting the collar of Roy's shirt and getting a better look at the chaos underneath.

"Roy still came in the restaurant every day," Brad offered. "He was part of that morning coffee crew that liked to drink and gossip together."

"Your grandfather is the center of that crew." Hunter said it more as a statement than a question. "That's the way it was when I visited during high school."

His words struck a chord. "You haven't come here since we were teenagers?"

Hunter's gaze slowly tracked back to me. "I've been in the restaurant. I just don't visit very often."

I wanted to ask why, but that seemed invasive ... and completely beside the point given that we were standing over a dead body. Still, it wouldn't have hurt my feelings to know that he was avoiding the place because memories of our great high school love affair were too painful for him. What? It's not like I want anything bad to happen to him or anything. I just want to believe he had been pining for me for ten years. That doesn't seem like too much to ask for.

"Go back to Roy," Hunter ordered. "When was the last time you saw him with your grandfather? Was he in the restaurant this morning?"

"I ... don't know." Brad slid his eyes to me. "Did you see him?"

I shook my head. In truth, the morning rush had been so busy that I could barely focus on myself, let alone the other people in the restaurant. Getting used to the schedule was going to take some time. "I didn't really look. I was busy dealing with other stuff."

"Yes, like the fact that you're suddenly the world's slowest waitress," Brad drawled. "Do you think that's because you became soft while you were away? I mean ... being an author is easier than being a waitress, right?"

I pretended not to hear the question. "Isn't Roy the guy Grandpa used to call an Axehole?"

David snickered at the question. "Yeah. We all picked that up because it was a way to swear without getting in trouble. That was when they were supposedly friends. The relationship has always been a bit tempestuous."

"I'll have to talk to your grandfather," Hunter noted, his gaze on David rather than me. "He'll have to answer questions, whether he likes it or not. Roy was obviously killed."

21

"How was he killed?" I asked. "I see the blood. It's mixed with the water from the refrigerator system. He couldn't have been out here all that long. People use the back door when they're coming in before the morning shift. Someone would've seen him."

"Only if they came through this door," David countered. "Most people go in through the other door because it's more convenient. I think most of the staff ignores this door for the most part."

"So it's possible he's been out here for hours?" The notion didn't sit well with me. "That doesn't seem right."

"Right or not, it's what we're dealing with," Hunter replied, retrieving his phone from his back pocket. "All I can say with any degree of certainty is that Roy was stabbed and I think it was sometime during the night. I have to get the medical examiner out here."

"So ... what should we do?" Brad asked. "I still need those pickles."

I wanted to choke him with the pickles but I managed to hold it together — just barely.

"Go about your day," Hunter replied. "You'll have to avoid this area, but that's it. I'm not sure how long we'll be out here, but it'll be a couple of hours at least."

That was not what I wanted to hear. "Are you going to want to question anyone?"

Hunter nodded as his eyes briefly connected with mine before he turned back to Brad. "I'll try not to disrupt your day too much, but I'll need ten minutes with each employee."

"We'll figure it out." Brad flashed a smile. "The Republicans are tougher on crime. Did you know that?"

Hunter nodded, unruffled. If he found my uncle's response weird, he didn't show it. "That's great. I'll start with Stormy."

Well, awesome.

THREE

H unter had me sit at the picnic table behind the restaurant. He waited to join me until the medical examiner arrived and had taken control of the body.

"Test these, too," Hunter instructed, handing over the bag that contained my shoes. "One of the waitresses was leaving the restaurant and stepped in the blood."

The medical examiner nodded and absently took the bag. He was already focused on the body, and it seemed Hunter's presence was an annoyance to him.

I was still fuming about being dismissed as nothing more than a waitress when Hunter finally deigned to join me.

"How long have you been back in town?"

The question caught me off guard. "Two weeks. But I've been going back and forth between here and my old place on Harsens Island, so I only spent a few hours here between trips."

"I didn't realize you were back in the state already." He looked put out. "I guess your family failed to mention it."

"I wasn't on Harsens Island very long. I was trying to get information for a book, but it didn't pan out."

He eyed me for a moment, his expression unreadable. "I'm sorry about the book thing. I know how important that is to you."

"I don't know if I would say it was important," I hedged. It was a ridiculous lie. If anyone knew how important writing was to me, it was Hunter. He'd sat around watching *SportsCenter* for two years while I scrawled hundreds of story ideas on napkins and in little notebooks I insisted on carrying around with me. Denying it now was bad form, but I couldn't stop myself.

"Right." He held my gaze for a long beat and then heaved out a sigh. "I know you didn't have anything to do with this, but I have to ask you some questions."

"Then I guess you have to ask them." I rubbed at a food stain on my apron. "I didn't think you wanted to be a cop. I mean ... after your father and everything I just assumed you were going to follow your dream and be a sportscaster. That's what you always wanted."

His gaze was contemplative. "Not everybody gets to live their dreams, Stormy." His voice was soft. "You got to, which is nice, but it was never a reality for me. My parents didn't have the money to send me to an expensive school. I had very few options up here. One of the more reasonable ones was the police academy."

On the surface, that made sense. Still, it hurt me to think about what he wanted compared to where he'd ended up. "That doesn't mean you had to stay here. You wanted to live in the city like me. You could've been a police officer anywhere."

"This is home."

"Yeah, but ... ."

"You had big dreams about living in a city, too," he countered, his eyes firing. "You're right back here with me. You better than anyone should realize that some dreams aren't meant to be."

The statement, however true, grated. "I'm still working on my writing. This is just temporary until I can figure things out."

"There's nothing wrong with waitressing."

"That's what people who don't waitress say." My temper flared. "It's a hard job. Really hard. That's why I wanted to do something else."

"You wanted to be a writer because you couldn't keep your head in one place," he corrected. "You liked visiting a million different locations, even if it was only in your dreams. You didn't want this life. You wanted something more. I'm sorry it didn't happen for you."

I wanted to argue that it still could, but it seemed like adding to a conversation going nowhere. "What do you need to know?" I rubbed my forehead to ward off what I was certain would flower into a raging headache.

"Has your grandfather said anything about Roy since you've been back?"

The question caught me off guard. "You can't think he had anything to do with this. My grandfather is many things, but he's no murderer."

"I don't have a choice but to follow the clues." Hunter was firm. "Your grandfather had a relationship with the victim. Now, granted, Roy had a particular personality. People everywhere hated him because he was a cranky old pervert who said inappropriate things to any female he crossed paths with. I have to start somewhere."

"I don't know what his relationship was with my grandfather," I said. "I wasn't around for any of that. I've been ... busy."

"You mean you tried to separate yourself from this world," Hunter countered. "I get it. I understand. You separated yourself from me, so I get it better than most. You were still in touch with your family, though. Did they mention your grandfather arguing with Roy?"

I shook my head, my heart pinging at the naked emotion that briefly took over his features. He shuttered it quickly, which was to be expected, but it wasn't fast enough that I could stop the guilt from bubbling up and grabbing me by the throat.

"I didn't want to leave you." The words were out of my mouth before I thought better of them. "I wanted you to come with me. You wouldn't."

"I couldn't," he said, looking away from me. "I didn't have the money to leave."

"And I couldn't stay."

Briefly, his eyes filled with sadness. Then he collected himself. "Try to think if you remember your family telling you any stories about Roy while you were gone. It's important. Someone obviously cared enough to kill him — and in a hard way."

"You still haven't told me how he died."

"Someone stabbed him at least three times."

"Okay. I'll let you know if I remember anything."

"Thank you." Hunter pushed himself to a standing position. "I need to talk to the other workers. We're done here."

And just like that, I'd been dismissed. If I was hoping things between us would thaw, at least be friendly, our brief interaction was enough to dissuade me of that notion. We weren't going to be friends, or even friendly. Whatever we had years ago was long gone, and it was time to accept that.

MY FAMILY IS BIG BUT CLOSE. I was an only child, but I had a bevy of cousins, all of whom might as well have been siblings given the way we were raised. My Aunt Lottie always joked that it didn't matter which kids you took with you after a family event, you simply had to leave with the same number. Most of the adults in the family took that to heart. Of all my cousins, I was closest with Alice. In addition to being David's sister, she was close to me in age. We spent a lot of time hanging out while growing up. It didn't surprise me that she was the first to darken my doorstep once the restaurant had closed for the night.

"I brought whiskey," she announced, brandishing a bottle as I opened the door.

She was small, not even five feet, and had one of those ski-slope noses that made her face look young and pixie-ish.

"Whiskey, huh?" I took the bottle and studied the label as she pushed inside the apartment. "I could use a shot — or three."

"I figured you could." Alice was all smiles as she glanced around. "Where's all your stuff?"

I followed her gaze, frowning at the three boxes in the corner. "That's all the stuff I have."

"But ... that's nothing."

"Yeah, well, I spent years moving around," I reminded her. "It's better to pack light when you're doing all that moving. Over the years, I learned that things were a bad idea."

"I love things." Alice threw herself on the couch, a throwback from my grandparents' house. Years ago, they'd bought new furniture and the old stuff had migrated to the apartment. It was orange velour — and ugly. Luckily it was also comfortable. "I can't get enough of things."

"I never would've guessed that about you," I teased, moving into the kitchen. The floor plan of the apartment was simple. The living room was long and rectangular, opening into the kitchen, which was one step up. On the far side of the kitchen was a small balcony that led down to the alley and back of the restaurant, to exactly where I'd found Roy's body. In winter, the steps were too treacherous to even consider. Bedrooms were on either end of the apartment, one with an attached bathroom. It was pretty basic, but I was grateful to have a roof over my head at all.

"How long do you plan on staying?" Alice asked, moving to the sliding glass door to monitor the activity in the alley.

"I don't know."

"Are you going to try writing again?"

"I never stopped trying to write. I just ... couldn't make it work." I struggled to keep the bite from my voice but wasn't entirely successful. "I don't really want to talk about the writing."

"Fair enough." Alice had one of those faces that reflected mayhem whether she was thinking evil thoughts or not. To an outside observer, she looked innocent and chaste. I'd known her most of my life, however. I knew better. "You do know that Hunter is down there?"

The question made me scowl, so I buried my head in the freezer searching for ice cubes to hide my reaction. "I'm well aware. He interviewed me. I found the body."

"I heard." I turned back with two glasses. Alice pursed her lips and regarded me with wide eyes. "I used to have a huge crush on Hunter when we were kids."

"How could I have missed it? You swore you were going to curse me when I started dating him."

"That's because I loved him and thought you stole him from me."

"You were twelve."

"Yes, but an old twelve."

"He was sixteen," I pointed out. "No matter how much you loved him, he was never going to love you back without going to jail."

"Yes, but you're being rational." Alice accepted her glass and twisted the cap from the bottle. "Do you have something to mix with this?"

"Diet Coke."

She made a face. "Well, beggars can't be choosers."

"Or you could go downstairs and use the pop machine in the kitchen," I reminded her.

She brightened considerably. "That's a great idea."

I was relieved for the few minutes she was gone, which gave me a chance to collect myself. I knew coming home would be difficult. I left on a cloud, thinking I'd succeeded where so many others had failed. All anyone who grew up in Shadow Hills wanted was to get away from the town. I thought I had, and yet I hadn't been happy.

I traveled. I enjoyed it. I always thought about home, though. I always wondered what might have been if I'd opted not to cut ties with my past.

And, yes, I thought about Hunter. When we'd separated after graduation it was with the intention that we would somehow make things work, even if it was over a distance. That's probably the goal of every high school romance, though. You fall so fast and so hard, and losing the other person you've made the center of your world seems unthinkable — until it happens.

It didn't happen all at once for Hunter and me. I didn't get an epiphany one day and say, "I need to break up with him." It was little things over the course of my first year of college. By the end, when we reunited in the summer, I realized we no longer had anything in common. That didn't mean the love was gone. It was there, and we tried to recapture the magic, but we broke up before sophomore year. It gutted us both. I made one last-ditch effort at the time. I wanted him to accompany me back to college. I didn't know how I was going to find a place for us to be together. I simply knew I didn't want to let him go.

He was a realist even then, tearful when he explained why it wouldn't work. To me, he wasn't trying. I was bitter ... and angry ... and that was my last summer in Shadow Hills. I refused to return because I didn't want to accidentally run into him.

Over the years, I realized he was right. We were far too young to make the necessary effort. Both of us were emotionally disabled, but in different ways. I was from a codependent family and, while self-sufficient, I'd never really been on my own. He lived with an alcoholic father and a fearful mother who never once stepped in to protect him. We were doomed from the start. Yet I often thought of him. Perhaps it was because none of the men I dated during my travels ever piqued my interest for the long haul. Ultimately it didn't matter. All I knew now was that it hurt to look at him.

"So, what's the plan?" Alice asked when she returned with her soda. "Are you just hanging out here until you write another book that sells?"

She assumed I could write another book that would sell. I wasn't so sure. "I don't know if I have a plan. Right now, I need to survive." I sank onto the couch and sipped my whiskey and Diet Coke. It wasn't exactly the drink of champions, but it would do in a pinch. "As for Hunter, well, I'll never be sorry we dated."

"But it's over, right?"

I was instantly suspicious. "Why do you care?"

She shrugged, avoiding eye contact. "Maybe I want to ask him out. I'm an adult. The age difference isn't a big thing. He might be interested."

The notion made my stomach churn. "I'd rather you didn't. Can't you find someone else to date?"

"Do you still have feelings for him?" She looked smug enough that I couldn't maintain eye contact.

"Of course not. We were in high school."

"That doesn't mean the feelings you shared weren't real."

Part of me wanted to believe that. The other part knew it was best to let it go. "So ... what do you want to do?" Changing the subject felt like the best option. "I don't have the cable hooked up yet. There are some old board games in the closet."

"Games?" Alice furrowed her brow. "What games?"

"There's that old Ouija board we used to play with as kids, the one our mothers kept catching us with and insisting was too dangerous for us to use."

Alice's expression brightened. "I forgot all about that stupid board. Where did it even come from?"

"I don't know. Let me get it." I left her in the living room and rummaged through the hallway closet until I came up with the board and planchette. When I returned to the table, Alice's eyes were keen as she blew away a layer of dust from the board.

"Man, this thing must've been locked in there for years." She ran her fingertips over the board. "This doesn't look like the one they sell in stores."

"It doesn't," I agreed, plopping the planchette in the middle of the letters. "I think it's homemade."

"I wonder who made it." Alice leaned closer and studied the letters. "Hey, this thing is carved out of actual wood."

"I know. It's good work. I bet it's worth money if we found the right collector."

She cocked an eyebrow. "You're going to sell it?"

"It's not mine to sell."

"I bet no one even knows it's up here," Alice said. "If you need money ... ."

I shook my head. "I'm not completely destitute." Close, but I could still feed myself — as long as I had access to the restaurant. I had no intention of selling family belongings until I hadn't eaten for at least a week. "Let's ask it a few questions."

"Okay." Alice was agreeable as she sipped her drink before moving her fingers to the planchette. "What should we ask it?"

I shrugged.

"Maybe we should ask if you're ever going to write another book that sells."

I glared at her. "Or maybe we should ask if you'll ever stop going after the men I've dated."

Her eyes narrowed. "I know. Let's ask if you and Hunter will get back together."

I moved to withdraw my fingers from the planchette but she anticipated the move and grabbed my hand.

"You can't pull away now," she argued. "We just started. You can ask it an embarrassing question about me next."

"Why do you get to start?" I was reticent as I rested my fingers next to hers. I didn't want to ask the board about Hunter. I feared my subconscious would somehow force me to move the planchette and answer in a way that would embarrass me.

"Because I said so." Alice sucked in a breath and closed her eyes. "Okay, here we go. Spirits of the other world, we beseech you," she started in dramatic fashion.

"Spirits of the other world?" That sounded ridiculous.

She ignored me. "We call upon the higher power," she offered. "We call to the four corners of magic. We call upon the Goddess."

I was confused. "How do you know there are four corners of magic?"

"I saw it on television."

Oh, well, that explained it.

"Close your eyes," she ordered in her most authoritative voice. "I'm serious. I want to know what's going to happen with you and Hunter."

"Nothing is going to happen."

"I don't believe that." She was insistent. "Will Hunter and Stormy make it two weeks before they tear each other's clothes off, or will it be longer?"

My eyes snapped open. "I can't believe you asked that." I jerked my fingers from the planchette. "You're not playing right. I don't want to ask that question."

"You're just afraid of the answer," Alice countered, keeping her hands on the planchette. "In fact ... ." She trailed off, her eyes moving back to the board. Her expression changed such that I couldn't force myself to look away.

The planchette was zipping across the board at a fantastic rate. I wished I'd found the strength to keep my eyes focused somewhere else. Heck, anywhere else would do.

"What's happening?" I asked, my mouth going dry.

"I don't know." Alice looked around, bewildered. "Are you doing that?"

The look I shot her was withering. "Um ... obviously not." I wiggled my fingers for emphasis. "I'm not touching it."

"Someone has to be doing it." Alice was firm. "That's not normal."

"Oh, you think?" My heart rate ratcheted up a notch when the planchette increased its speed. "What is it doing?"

"I don't know. I ... ." Alice didn't finish as the planchette flew off the board and smacked into the wall, a small puff of light emanating from the contact point. It almost looked like purple sparkles, gone as soon as it appeared.

"What just happened?" Alice's voice was barely a whisper.

"I have no idea. I don't know what that was."

"Should we try again?"

"Are you crazy?" I almost screeched. "We have to get rid of the demon board and never play with it again. You don't keep messing around with something that moves on its own."

"Hunter moves on his own and you want to mess with him."

I extended a warning finger. "I will kill you if you don't stop saying stuff like that."

"I think the board might kill me first," Alice argued. "What should we do with it? You won't be able to sleep if it's in the apartment after what it just did."

She had a point. "We could hide it in the storage shed once Hunter leaves," I said.

"That's a good idea. What do we do until then?"

I inclined my head toward the whiskey bottle. "One guess."

She exhaled heavily and then nodded. "I guess I've had worse offers. Drinking it is ... just as soon as we lock this board under a blanket so the spirits can't crawl through and get to us."

I'd never heard anything more ludicrous. "Good idea."

FOUR

I woke with a raging hangover, wanting nothing more than to roll over, bury my head under the covers, and spend the entire day wallowing in misery. That wasn't an option, though. I had the breakfast shift with Grandpa, which meant I had to get up and, more importantly, get moving. Reporting late wasn't an option. There was no excuse he would buy.

Scenes from the previous evening flitted through my head as I showered. I remembered sneaking down to the storage building with Alice once we were certain Hunter had left. When we realized the shed was locked, we had to go back inside to find the keys. Neither of us wanted to be left alone with the Ouija board, so we did everything together. It took us almost a full hour to stash the board. I couldn't even remember what hiding spot we'd finally selected.

I applied only minimal makeup before throwing my blond hair back in a bun and heading downstairs. Grandpa had already done the majority of the prep work. The look he shot me as I headed for the coffee pot wasn't difficult to interpret.

"Late night?"

I nodded, almost groaning in delight at the scent of fresh coffee. "Later than I planned."

"Hunter?"

I almost coughed the coffee through my nose in surprise. "No. Why would you think that?"

He shrugged, amusement lighting his dark eyes. "Just wondered. You two were attached at the hip for a time."

"Something I believe you hated."

"I didn't hate it. I just thought you were young to be so attached to one boy. You had dreams that were always going to take you out of Shadow Hills."

I regarded him for a long moment, unsure if my head was in the right place to get into a heavy discussion. "He said something similar yesterday."

"He always was a pragmatic kid. I guess he would have to be, growing up the way he did."

He'd opened the door, and I had a few questions that needed answering. "What happened to his father?"

"He's still alive, if that's what you're wondering."

"I'm sure I would've heard if he'd died. It's just ... when I left town, he was chief of police. I very much doubt Hunter would be okay working for him."

"You're right on that. Hunter came in after his father lost his position."

"And when was that?"

"About five years ago. Before that, I think Hunter was working over in Hemlock Cove. He spent a few years there under someone named Terry Bradshaw. I think they grew close. It was Terry who came in and ultimately relieved Greg Ryan of his position."

This was all gossip I'd missed while out of town. I wanted to ask about Hunter when I'd called my mother, but I feared she would tell him about my interest. Even worse, I feared she'd figure out why I cared. He was the one thing I could never shake about Shadow Hills.

"Why was he removed?"

"Because of the drunk driving. And beating his wife, though he denied that to the bitter end. And she helped. The cops here overlooked it for a long time. Hunter stepped in to save his mother a few times as a teenager, getting a beating or two himself for the effort. That's why he went to live with his grandparents across town before graduation."

"I know about all of this." Hunter had confided in me a time or two, mostly when he was at his most vulnerable. "I don't know why his father was finally removed."

"It was the other chief. Hunter must've let a few things slip, because that guy came in guns blazing. He had friends in high places and there was enough evidence on Greg to oust the entire department. Terry served as interim chief until a new one could be appointed, a guy who used to work in Detroit and wanted away from the city. Things have been quiet ever since."

"And Hunter came in sometime after?"

"Weeks after. Terry eased the transition himself."

"You know a lot about the situation."

"Terry had coffee in here every day when he was in town. We got to know one another. He's a good guy. He still stops in about once a week, when he needs a break from the antics of Hemlock Cove. It's only a twenty-minute drive."

Hemlock Cove. It was known as Walkerville when I was growing up. Then, about the time I was going to college, they rebranded themselves as a tourist town for witches. Everyone in the area thought it was a terrible idea, but it turned out to be a stroke of genius, because the town has thrived as others in the area struggled.

Witches. That made me think of the Ouija board. I was about to ask my grandfather what he knew regarding its origin when I thought better of it. He would think Alice and I were doing more than drinking if I told him what we'd witnessed. Besides, under the hammering of my hangover, I was starting to question what really had happened. Perhaps we imagined it, or somehow made it happen without realizing what we were doing.

"Do you think Hunter is happy?" I really was curious as I watched Grandpa turn on the grill.

"I think he grew into a good man who is still figuring things out," Grandpa replied. "Life was never easy for Hunter. Things are better now, though his father is still around, making things difficult sometimes."

That was another thing I'd been wondering about. "What about his mother?"

"She stayed with her husband. He doesn't talk to Hunter, which is exactly how Hunter probably wants it, but she won't talk to him either. They tell anyone who will listen that it was some sort of dastardly plan by Hunter to wrest control of the department away from his father. As far as I know, they still live out in that house on the lake. It's fallen into disrepair, and he spends the money from his pension on booze."

That sounded about right. I'd never liked Hunter's father. He was a horrible man, mean and ill-tempered. He went out of his way to be gracious to me whenever we'd crossed paths, but I figured that was simply because I was from a prominent town family and he didn't want to risk ticking off Grandpa. I never understood how Hunter turned out to be such a strong individual the way his father was always trying to break him down.

"Well, I hope Hunter is happy," I said, moving to the coffee machine so I could fill the additional filters. When the rush hit, it was best to be able to grab a filter and just slip it inside rather than deal with ripping apart finicky bags.

"I'm sure you do," Grandpa said with a smile, causing me to fix him with a suspicious look.

"What's that supposed to mean?" I was edgy, and only part of it was because of the hangover.

"I didn't mean anything by it." Grandpa turned his back to me, pouring oil on the grill and watching it warm. "Do you want breakfast to help with that hangover before people start arriving?"

Breakfast sounded wonderful. What I wanted even more was an explanation. "What did you mean by that?" I refused to let it go. "If you're suggesting that something is going on between Hunter and me ... well ... that's just ludicrous."

His eyes were full of sympathy when he turned back. "I know nothing is going on with you and Hunter ... yet."

He just had to throw in that last word. "It's not going to happen. We're adults now. We have nothing in common."

"I wouldn't say that. You both like certain things: hikes in the hills, coffee in the morning, taunting Detroit Lions fans."

"The stuff of great romances." I rolled my eyes. "We were kids when we were together."

"And I think you still care about him. That's neither here nor there, though. I'm not going to get involved in your personal life. That's not my way."

I couldn't swallow my snort. "Since when? You've always stuck your nose in everybody's business. If they share blood with you, you tell them how to live their lives."

"Only if they're doing it wrong."

"Oh, so everybody in this family but you is living life wrong, huh?"

"Pretty much." He didn't seem bothered by the assertion. "Do you want to know what your problem is?"

"No." I turned back to the coffee filters. "I don't have a problem. I'm perfectly happy, thrilled even, to be here."

"Yeah, you're full of it. That's not what I'm talking about. The job stuff will work itself out when you're ready. You'll start writing again when you're ready. I'm talking about your other problem."

"I don't have a problem."

"Your problem is that you hide your emotions. You feel the need to bury them. Do you want to know why?"

Ugh. He always asked that question. I hated it. "No. I want to talk about something other than me."

"We're talking about you right now." He was firm enough that I knew he wouldn't let me weasel out of the conversation. "The reason you're so closed off is because your mother was too open. She foisted conversations you weren't comfortable with on you at a young age and you never got over it.

"Like ... do you remember when you got your first period?" he continued. "She announced it to everybody in the family, as if they should throw a parade or something. You were mortified."

I was still mortified sixteen years later. "I really think we should talk about something else."

He barreled forward as if he hadn't heard me. "You got so frustrated she was telling anyone who'd listen that you blurted out the truth. You'd actually started your period six months before then and simply didn't tell anyone because you knew she would be obnoxious about it."

"Can we talk about something other than my first period?"

"Hey, I don't want to talk about it either." He gave me a reproving look. "Trust me. There's no man who wants to talk about his granddaughter's period — unless he's some gross SOB who should be shot anyway. That's not the point."

"What is the point?"

"Your mother being so open made you want to do the exact opposite, so you closed yourself off. That's why you're the way you are."

He sounded so sure of himself that, for a moment, I questioned whether he was right. Then I made a face. "Hunter and I aren't getting together. It won't happen. We're not kids any longer." And, besides, I silently added, he showed exactly zero interest in me the previous day. He was interested in work, nothing more.

"If you say so." Grandpa picked up a spatula. "Where did we land on breakfast?"

"I could eat," I said, earning a grin from him.

"Your usual?"

"You remember my usual?"

"I remember everybody's usual. Hash browns, eggs over medium, whole wheat toast, and sausage links. Sometimes you'll have ham, but you lean toward the links. David prefers French toast doused in a sea of syrup. I expect you to take a plate out to him at the gas station in about an hour, by the way. He's a slow starter when he opens."

"I guess it's good your memory is intact." I flicked my eyes to the front of the restaurant. The front door was still locked, but somebody stood outside. "Do the customers line up before the doors open?"

"No. Why?"

"Because someone is out there." I squinted for a better look. "I think it's Hunter."

Grandpa straightened. "He's here?"

I nodded. "Maybe he has more questions about Roy's death. Speaking of that, do you know who would want to kill him? According to just about everybody who works here, that list is long and sundry."

I waited for Grandpa to answer. When he didn't, I turned back ... and found the spot in front of the grill deserted.

"No way." He'd bolted. He knew Hunter was there to question him, so he took off and left me to handle the situation. "Ugh. Men."

I stomped to the front of the restaurant, struggling with the lock. It had always been tough. When I finally managed to open it, Hunter looked sheepish.

"Sorry I'm here so early," he started.

"It's okay." I locked the door behind him and motioned for him to follow. I had no idea where my grandfather had decided to hide — odds were he was up in my apartment — but I had no intention of leaving Hunter hanging. "Coffee?"

"Is it ready?"

I nodded. "I'm hungover. I spent the night hanging with Alice and we drank way more than was smart. There's definitely coffee."

He smirked at my answer. "Coffee's good." He sat at the counter and waited for me to deliver the cup, appreciatively inhaling the intoxicating aroma before sipping. "Still as good as I remember."

"You don't even come in here for coffee?" I felt bad, as if I'd somehow cut him off from something great. "You know, you don't have to avoid this place. You can come here whenever you want. Just because I wasn't here ... ."

"That's not the only reason," he said hurriedly.

"Okay, well ... you're still welcome."

"I know. It's just weird because it's your family. They're not my family, even though there were times they felt like it. Losing them, on top of losing you ... ." He didn't finish the sentence. He didn't have to.

"I'm sorry."

"About what?" He looked genuinely confused.

I thought about what my grandfather had said. Could he be right? Was I closed off? If so, was it something I could fix? Heck, did I even want to fix it?

"I'm sorry about all of it," I said finally. "I knew that the distance would be the end of us and yet I held on too tight. I couldn't help myself. Then, when you couldn't move down state with me, I told myself it was because you didn't care. I knew that wasn't true."

"It definitely wasn't true." His green eyes clouded over. "I wanted to be with you. I just couldn't. There was no way I could make it work financially."

"And I was too self-involved to see that."

"I wouldn't say you were self-involved."

"No?" I arched a dubious eyebrow. "Most everyone I know says I'm self-involved. There's no reason to lie and spare my feelings."

"Yeah, well ... ." He pursed his lips, and then changed the subject. "Is your grandfather here? I need to question him. He disappeared yesterday afternoon even though he knew I was looking for him."

That was news to me. "You haven't talked to him at all?"

He shook his head and sipped again. "Nope. He took off and when I stopped at his house your grandmother said he wasn't home, but his truck was parked in the garage."

That didn't sound like my grandfather. Usually he tackled a problem immediately — unless it was a minor annoyance and then he foisted the irritation off on us. "I ... um ... ." I glanced over my shoulder, over the swinging doors, and found the spot in front of the grill still empty. "I don't know where he is." That wasn't exactly a lie. Of course, it wasn't the complete truth either.

"Was he here earlier?"

I didn't know what I was supposed to say. Lying to a cop seemed a bad idea. Still, I would've done it if I thought it was necessary. Lying to Hunter was different.

"He was here," Hunter surmised, shaking his head. "Did he leave when I showed up at the door?"

"I'm not sure when he left. All of a sudden, he was just gone."

"Uh-huh." Hunter looked dubious. "He doesn't think that hiding from me will make this go away, does he?"

"I'm not sure what he's thinking. We haven't really talked about the Roy situation. I was slow this morning because of the hangover. I should've opened with that. Maybe then I wouldn't have had to hear the period story for the hundredth time."

Hunter drew his eyebrows together. "The period story? Do I even want to know?"

"Absolutely not."

He laughed at my vehemence, the sound low and warm. "Well, can you send him a message for me? Tell him I'm not going to stop coming around until he answers my questions. Hiding from me won't work."

"I'll tell him."

"Thank you." He finished off his coffee and stood. "I wish he wasn't such a pain in the butt. All he's doing is dragging things out."

"You don't really think he's a suspect, do you?" Suddenly, I was worried at the prospect.

"I'm sure it will be fine." He must've read the fear in my eyes, because he extended a hand and rested it on top of mine. The instant our fingers touched, an electric charge passed through us.

He obviously felt it, too, because he jerked back his hand.

"The air must be dry," I said lamely, hoping to explain away the crackle.

I didn't expect his response. "I have a girlfriend." The words practically tumbled out of his mouth.

"Oh, um ... ." I had no idea what to say.

"I have a girlfriend and it's serious," he stressed, taking a step back from the counter and avoiding eye contact. "I'm sorry."

I worked my jaw. "There's nothing to be sorry about," I said finally. "Nothing happened."

He moved toward the door, his eyes finally latching with mine. "I have a girlfriend," he said for the third time.

"So you've said."

"I just wanted to be clear on that." He pushed on the first door and then became distracted fiddling with the same lock that had tripped me up the first time. "Tell your grandfather I'll be back. Make him stop hiding from me."

"Yeah. I'll get right on that."

FIVE

I was still fuming about Hunter's insistence on volunteering his girlfriend news — three times — when I wandered back into the kitchen and found Grandpa standing before the grill as if he didn't have a care in the world.

"So, eggs and hash browns?"

I glared at him. "Where did you go?"

He was the picture of innocence. "What are you talking about? I've been right here. You took off to check the door. Who was it, by the way?"

I wanted to crawl over the counter and shake him. "Really?"

"I'm always curious when someone knocks on the door fifteen minutes before we open. That right there is a dedicated customer."

I folded my arms over my chest. "It was Hunter."

"Oh, yeah?" Grandpa's expression reflected mild bafflement. I had to hand it to him, he was a master at pretending to think one thing when I knew he was wondering about something else. "Did he want breakfast?"

I shook my head. "Oh, cut the crap." I'd been living in Shadow Hills full time a grand total of three days, yet it felt as if I'd never left. "I know darned well that you took off when you realized it was him. I want to know why."

"I have no idea what you're talking about. I never left this spot."

"I didn't suddenly go blind."

"You were blind drunk last night, so it seems a possibility."

I growled. "That won't work on me. Not even a little. What are you hiding?" Something horrible occurred to me. "Oh, geez. You didn't kill Roy Axe, did you?"

Grandpa's eyebrows practically flew off his forehead. "How can you possibly ask me that? I mean ... really, Stormy. I'm your grandfather. You're supposed to have more faith in me."

He was definitely full of crap. "You're hiding something." I was certain. Unfortunately, I had no idea what that "something" could possibly be. He was my grandfather, but it wasn't as if I'd been present in his life the last few years. I'd been too wrapped up in myself. That made me feel guilty. He was standing there trying to convince me I was an idiot even though I knew better, though, so the sentiment was quickly extinguished by hot rage. "What is it?"

"I'm not hiding anything. And, because of your attitude, you're on your own for breakfast. I hope you're happy." He turned on his heel, heading to the aisle behind the grill. There was nothing back there except the dishwashing rack, but he seemed perfectly content to hide behind the exhaust port that covered the back of the stove area.

"I'm not simply going to forget that you're acting like an idiot," I called out. I was convinced he could hear me. "Hunter isn't an idiot either. He won't stop until he talks to you. He told me to tell you that."

"Oh, is that what's wrong?" I still couldn't see Grandpa, but he'd confirmed he was hiding in the far aisle. "Are you upset because you're going to see him again? I thought you didn't care."

"I don't care." Especially now that he made a point to tell me he had a very serious girlfriend. "Hunter Ryan is nothing but a memory. You need to accept that."

"I'll accept it as soon as you do."

"Whatever." I heaved out a sigh and turned back to the front of the restaurant. There were now three regulars lined up outside the door. "I'm going to open. You'd better prepare yourself."

"I'm always prepared. I'm like a Boy Scout that way. Perhaps you should prepare yourself."

"I've got everything under control."

"I FEEL LIKE I'M DYING," I complained to my Aunt Trina about twenty minutes into the lunch rush. I'd barely made it through the breakfast rush, thinking things would get easier when more wait staff showed up.

I was wrong.

"You're just not used to it." Trina had short hair, the type popular in the seventies. She dyed it an unnatural shade of red. I'd never seen anything like it outside of a crayon box. She was blond like my mother, but I'd never seen a single photo of her without what she referred to as her Starburst of Love. I very much doubted that was a real color, but she insisted it was. "Things will get better."

She took a drag on her cigarette and flicked the butt out the back door. It was illegal to smoke inside an eating establishment in Michigan. Trina flouted that law every chance she got — as long as my grandfather wasn't around to witness the dastardly deed. Right now he was up in my apartment. Again. He'd taken his newspaper. Again. I didn't want to think about what he was doing up there. His absence was enough to embolden Trina, though, who didn't bother stepping outside for her nicotine fix.

"Have I told you how happy we all are to have you back?" she asked, beaming at me. She had a megawatt smile, her greatest asset. Unfortunately, the smile was often the only thing firing on all cylinders. "You're my favorite niece."

"Uh-huh." I didn't believe that for a second. "I bet you say that to Alice all the time, too."

"She's my second favorite."

"I'm going to ask her when I see her."

Trina lowered her voice to a conspiratorial whisper. "She lies. Don't believe anything she tells you."

Brad, who had taken over cooking duty, snorted as he regarded his younger sister. He was the middle child — two sisters older, one sister and a brother younger — and acted as if he'd been overlooked his entire life. As the first boy in the family, I doubted that was true, but my perception meant nothing to him. All he cared about was how he felt.

"If Trina is telling you tall tales, Stormy, you should run away now," he instructed. "She's a bad influence. In fact, I've warned my kids that they can't hang around her." He leaned forward, as if he was going to whisper, and then bellowed the rest of his story. "She smokes pot behind the storage building."

I stared at him for a beat, unsure what I was supposed to say. "Okay?" I managed.

"I don't smoke pot behind the storage building," Trina scoffed. "Why would you say something like that?"

"I've seen the butts."

"Well, you don't know what you're talking about." Trina turned her knowing gaze to me. "I smoke pot in the woods. Only an idiot would smoke

42

out in the open like that. I store the butts close to the building so I can roll another joint out of them when I have enough."

I forced a smile. "How ... awesome."

"How do you even know what a joint butt looks like, Brad?" Trina challenged. "Only someone who knew from personal experience would be able to say with any degree of certainty what was in the ash tray behind the storage building."

Brad's mouth dropped open in outrage. "I don't smoke pot. It's illegal."

"Actually, it's legal in Michigan now," I pointed out. "You can smoke it wherever you want."

"It's not recognized on a federal level," Brad barked. "She's breaking the law."

"It's more fun when I can wind him up before I do it," Trina explained. "Don't ruin my fun."

Working with family was such a joy. "Okay, then." I tugged my shoes back on, ignoring the way my feet screamed. The new Skechers were supposed to help, but I'd had them less than a day before Hunter confiscated them. After what happened while I was wearing them, I no longer wanted a return on my investment. "I'm heading back in."

Trina offered up a haphazard wave. "Have fun."

My cousin Annie was holding down the fort when I rejoined her near the front counter. She was listening as some guy — I had no idea who — regaled her with a deer hunting story that would've bored me to tears in five seconds flat. She, however, kept a polite smile on her face and periodically nodded to let him know she was still listening.

"And then that deer hopped up on two legs and tried to punch me in the face," the man said, solemn. "It was like a movie."

I knew better than to ask but I couldn't stop myself. "Have you seen a lot of deer boxing in movies?"

"Not nearly enough." He kept his gaze on Annie. She was willow thin, had no hips to speak of, and ran five miles a day. Her skin glowed as a result of healthy eating and exercise. She reminded me of one of those athletes they photograph for the front of fitness magazines. I wanted to hate her but she was just too pleasant.

"There's a new table coming in," I said, grabbing menus from the slot at the end of the counter. "I'll take it."

Annie nodded. "Sure. Chet and I are having a nice discussion."

It didn't sound that way, but I was looking for an escape. The two women who took the corner booth on the far side looked like a good option.

"Good afternoon," I greeted them without looking at their faces. "Welcome to Two Broomsticks. My name is Stormy and I'll be your server. Can I start you out with something to drink?"

Neither of the women immediately spoke, and when I shifted my gaze to the one on my left I almost choked on my own tongue as recognition hit me like a fist in the face. "Oh, hi."

"Hello, Stormy." She beamed at me as if we were old friends. "It's been a long time."

"I'll say." I felt like an idiot. Phoebe Green was the worst person who ever lived. Okay, I'll give you Hitler and anyone who appeared on a reality show, but Phoebe was right up there with them.

We'd been sworn enemies in high school. I forgot how the animosity started, but it progressed to endless threats of hair-pulling and one-upmanship. When I was named homecoming queen (mostly because I was dating Hunter and he was voted king thanks to his position on the football team) she ran a smear campaign to make sure there was no repeat performance at the winter formal. She was standing on the stage with Hunter several months later, and they were forced to dance, something she endlessly rubbed in my face in the months that followed. Hunter always told me to ignore her, but it wasn't easy. She spent two years stalking my boyfriend, trying to break us up via any number of horrible acts. She was one of the few people I was happy to put in my rearview mirror when I'd left Shadow Hills.

And now I was waiting on her. Life could be so cruel.

"Phoebe." I felt as if I was drowning in quicksand. The longer I stood there, the smaller I felt. "I didn't know you were still in town."

"Oh, I never left." She gave me what I assumed she thought of as her friendliest fake smile. There was no warmth in her eyes, but there was amusement. She was enjoying herself far too much. "I've always loved this town and what it has to offer. I never wanted to leave. You, on the other hand, couldn't wait to get out — and now you're back."

"Now I'm back." It took everything I had to keep from jabbing my pen in her carotid. Every nerve ending sparked with outrage as I recoiled at the thought of having to wait on her. "Do you guys need anything to drink?"

"Iced teas would be great."

"For both of you?"

"Absolutely."

"Okay. I'll give you a second with the menus. I'll be right back."

I was breathing hard by the time I slipped through the swinging doors. I was so wrapped up in the fact that Phoebe was on my turf that I almost missed Trina as she futzed around with the soda machine.

"The CO2 is out," Trina announced to no one in particular.

"Then change it," Brad shot back.

"You know those tanks are too heavy for me. You have to do it."

"I'm cooking. I'm doing my job. The CO2 is your job. The problem with society is that nobody wants to work."

Trina's eyes fired with indignation. "It's your job."

"I don't think so."

Their yammering was more than I could take. "I'll change the freaking CO2 tank if you go out there and take my table," I offered Trina.

"I don't want to take your table." Trina shook her head. "I'll change the tank."

"But ... ."

"No, no, no." She patted my arm. "You need the money."

I scowled. Obviously my mother had been talking out of turn. Again. We were going to have to have a long discussion at some point. "Fine."

I filled the glasses with iced tea and returned to the booth. I was determined to pretend everything was okay, whether I felt it or not. "Here we go." I delivered the iced teas and yanked out my order pad. "What will it be?"

"I'll have the chef's salad with no cheese or ham, fat-free dressing on the side," Phoebe said.

That sounded like the worst lunch ever. "Great. And you?" I focused on her friend.

"I'll have the same." The woman handed over her menu and I turned to leave, but Phoebe called out to stop me.

"Actually, Stormy, it's good that you're here," she supplied. "I've been trying to set up a meeting with your grandfather and he's always dodging me. Now that you're back, perhaps you can serve as a facilitator of sorts."

I was instantly suspicious. "A facilitator?"

She nodded, that fake smile she'd been practicing in the mirror since she was three plastered in place. "I don't know if you're aware, but I'm head of the DDA now."

I stilled. "The DDA?"

"The Downtown Development Authority."

"I know what it is." My temper was bubbling to the surface.

"Oh, good, that will save us time." Her smile widened. "We're in the middle of a big push to beautify all the businesses. You know, add some flowers, and wash the windows, new coat of paint."

Two Broomsticks Gas & Grill hadn't been painted since before I was born. I could see where this conversation was headed. "You want Grandpa to paint the restaurant. I'll mention it to him." I tried to make my escape again, but Phoebe was having none of it.

"I was talking to Monica Johnson the other day — she's my best friend — and we both think the restaurant would be lovely if he painted it blue. I think the town council would really enjoy that."

I couldn't see my grandfather painting the restaurant any color that would make the town council happy — mostly because he made it his life's mission to fight with it at every possible opportunity — but I managed to keep from snapping that out. "I'll mention the color blue."

"You should really meet Monica. She's relatively new to the area."

"Well ... if I have time." I had no idea who Monica was, but if she was willingly hanging out with Phoebe something must be wrong with her. I had no inclination to find out what that something was.

"You two have a lot in common," Phoebe blathered on.

Would this conversation never end? "How so?"

"You used to date Hunter. Now she does. In fact, they're very happy. Like ... really, really happy."

It was like a punch to the gut. She knew it would be. "How great for them."

"So, do you want to meet her?"

"Sure. We'll set something up." This time there was no stopping me when I turned to retreat to the kitchen. Phoebe called out to get me to stop, but I pretended not to hear her. My heart was pounding by the time I made it into the kitchen and found two salads waiting for me on the counter. "What's this?"

My cheeks were burning and I thought for sure I would have a few minutes to collect myself before having to face Phoebe again.

"Those are the salads they ordered," Brad replied.

"But I didn't even put in their orders."

"They always order the same thing."

"They always ask the same thing, too," Trina offered. "They want Dad to paint the restaurant blue. He said the only way he would do that is if Smurfs take over the world and force him."

I was still trying to wrap my head around the salads. "But I didn't even put in the order."

"They're ready anyway." Brad's smile was tight. "Take them out. If you're not fast enough, she'll come back here to complain and watch us work, and nobody wants that."

"Nobody," Trina echoed.

It was the one time I'd ever seen them agree on anything. Still, I was feeling helpless when I shifted my eyes to the left to gauge an encroaching figure. Grandpa had obviously finished his afternoon trip to my bathroom.

"You know what fun is?" he asked me as I fought to catch my breath.

I watched with unveiled interest as he lifted the turkey from one of the salads and licked it before placing it back on the salad.

"Did you just ... ?"

"I didn't do anything," he said, feigning innocence. "I have no idea what you're talking about."

For some reason, the small act of defiance made me feel better — even if it was a gross violation of food regulations. "Thanks, Grandpa."

"Don't mention it, Dolly."

The nickname made me smile. He'd called me Dolly on and off since I was a kid. I was the first female grandchild. He'd spent more time with me than some of my other female cousins. The boys still reigned supreme, but I was hardly the forgotten grandchild. "I guess I should take this out."

"Definitely," Grandpa agreed. "While you're out there, tell her the only way I'll paint this restaurant blue is if she tells me the exact color of her boyfriend's balls so I can make them match."

My mouth dropped open. "I can't tell her that."

"Fine. I'll tell her when she stops in tomorrow."

His reaction made me laugh. "I'm taking the salads out now."

"When you're finished, you can knock off for the day. You're still getting used to the pace."

That was music to my ears. "Thanks a lot."

"Don't mention it."

SIX

I was still agitated after my shift ended, so I went upstairs to take a long shower. By the time I was cleaned up and dressed, it was midafternoon and I had absolutely nothing to do.

People always say they want to live in a quaint town. The problem with that is they never take into account the realities of doing so. Sure, everybody knows everybody and there's a charming feel to almost every interaction. Even when people hate each other for some perceived slight from twenty years earlier, the insults are more amusing than dangerous.

In Shadow Hills, for example, people carried guns regularly, but almost nobody was ever shot. There was the occasional drunken sign-shooting contest, of course, but those only garnered warnings from the police department. Nobody ever died. In the city, if you saw a gun you ran in the other direction. In Shadow Hills, you greeted the individual carrying the gun with a warm cup of coffee and "oohs" and "aahs" over what a nice piece it was.

On the flip side, half the people in the city couldn't pick their neighbors out of a lineup. In Shadow Hills, neighbors knew every secret — and it wasn't always pretty.

I tried to distract myself with cleaning the apartment. I'd barely messed it up, though, so it took only twenty minutes. I had nothing to unpack because I didn't own anything other than a few changes of clothes and an old castle sculpture that I'd carried since I was a teenager. I had nothing to do but sit around and stare at the walls. I considered running to the hardware store to paint over the dull cream color, but I decided that seemed like too much work.

I couldn't get the situation with Roy out of my mind. Grandpa was acting squirrelly. Heck, he idled at squirrelly. He was acting completely out of sorts. He hid from Hunter and then pretended otherwise, a move he had to know would ultimately backfire. It wasn't as if Hunter would simply give up because he stopped by once and Grandpa wasn't around.

I knew Grandpa was incapable of killing anyone. Probably. He'd threatened more than a few people during the course of his life. The instances before I was born were still related — accompanied by gales of laughter — around the family dinner table. As far as I knew, though, he'd never followed through on a threat.

As for Roy, he was a jerk. That's the one thing everyone could agree on. He was bombastic, sexist, misogynistic, racist, and occasionally ageist. He was lecherous to the point of making any female in his vicinity uncomfortable. He wasn't an overt groper, but he had no problem patting a shoulder or rubbing a back without invitation. And his eyes invaded every personal space imaginable. He made everybody uncomfortable. But was that enough to kill him?

I decided to head down to his real estate office. My mother pointed out the office regularly when I was a kid. She would then curse under her breath. She was no fan of Roy, who apparently enjoyed messing with fellow real estate agents. She'd repeatedly called him "an unethical ass." My mother fancied herself an "Earth first" hippie and lover of all mankind (unless you were her daughter and regularly screwed up), so that was saying something.

I wasn't surprised to find a crowd hanging out in the small park next to Roy's office. I recognized a few of the faces well enough that I could put names to them. I would need a gentle reminder on a few others. Two or three were strangers.

I approached Erin Higgins first. I recognized her from high school. She'd been two years behind.

"Hey, Erin."

She sat on a bench, a tissue clutched in her hand as she dabbed at her red-rimmed eyes. It was obvious she'd been crying, and it made me wonder when news of Roy's death had spread. I'd assumed everyone found out the previous day, because Shadow Hills couldn't keep a secret.

She looked up through teary lashes and took a moment to place me. "Stormy?"

I nodded and forced a tight smile as I sat next to her. "How's it going?"

The look she shot me was incredulous.

"I mean ... other than the obvious." I felt like an idiot, but I forced myself to swing the conversation to a place I could get information. "Obviously this is a very sad state of affairs."

"Oh, you think?" Erin shook her head as she swiped at her smearing eye makeup. "Roy was the best boss ever. He didn't deserve this. He was a nice guy. Well, kind of. Either way, he paid well. Now what am I supposed to do?"

"You worked for Roy?"

"Yeah. I figured that was why you were here, to pay your respects and stuff."

Ah, well, this is where things got sticky. "I'm definitely here to pay my respects. I haven't been able to sleep since I found him yesterday." That wasn't true. I slept just fine under the nurturing hand of whiskey. She didn't need to know that, though.

She jerked up her head. "You found Roy?"

Well, that answered that question. I thought for sure everyone would already know that tidbit.

"They said a waitress at Two Broomsticks found him, but I had no idea it was you."

"It was my first day back on the job." I shot her a rueful smile. "It wasn't a very nice welcome home."

"I'm sure Roy thought that, too."

I studied the street, the people who passed. "Do you know who might've wanted to kill him?"

Erin looked offended by the question. "No. He was a wonderful man."

She was covering, but I couldn't blame her. In her mind, I was probably casting aspersions on her boss. He might be dead, but that didn't mean she wasn't loyal.

"He was an ass," a new voice volunteered from my left, causing me to snap my head in that direction. Sandy Gellar was in her thirties — she'd graduated when I was in middle school — and looked great for her age. In fact, if I didn't know her, I would peg her age at twenty-five.

"Sandy." I flashed a smile. I had fonder memories of her than Erin.

"Stormy." She returned the smile, taking a long moment to look me up and down. "I'm sorry to see you back."

I knew she didn't mean it as an insult, but it bothered me all the same. "Yeah, well ... ."

"You were the talk of the town when you sold that first book. Heck, you were the talk of the town before that, first because you actually got out of here to attend college and then because you dumped Hunter Ryan."

Ugh. Why did everyone have to bring up Hunter? Yes, we were close for a time as teenagers. That was a decade ago. We were both adults and he'd clearly moved on — as he'd told me repeatedly. "I doubt I left him broken-hearted."

"But you did. He moped around here for months. Actually, now that I think about it, it was more like years. But he's over it. He has a girlfriend."

I narrowed my eyes. "Have you been hanging around Phoebe Green?"

She made a disgusted face. "Why would you suggest that? Phoebe is like toe jam."

"What's toe jam?"

"That gross stuff you scrape out from between your toes."

It was an oddly apt comparison. "I'm not here to talk about Hunter. I'm interested in Roy."

"I hear Hunter is investigating Roy's death," Erin noted. "I wonder if he'll interview us." She looked happy at the prospect, but then caught herself. "Not that Hunter hanging around would make up for Roy being dead or anything. It's very sad."

"Nobody is happy about Roy's death," Sandy shot back. "He was our boss. Finding a new job is going to be a pain."

"You worked for him, too?" I couldn't hide my surprise. I didn't under-stand how she could work for a guy like Roy.

"I know what you're thinking." Her smile was benign. "Roy didn't have the best reputation."

That was an understatement. "No, he didn't."

"He was a wimp when someone called him on his actions, though," she explained. "He cornered me near the copy machine one day. I told him that it wasn't going to fly — I'm not going to put up with crap like that — and he immediately backed off."

"Did he try it again?"

"Once. At a Christmas party." She smiled at the memory. "There are about five real estate agents who work out of this office. They all had dates or spouses, and some of the bank people were at the party, too, because we work with them all the time.

"I was a little tipsy — and he was way over the line — so I yelled at him in front of everyone. He was mortified," she continued. "I wasn't sure he would remember the next day, but he must have. He never said an untoward thing to me again."

"Still, he couldn't have been easy to work for."

"He wasn't, especially for anybody new and single." She rummaged in her purse, coming back with a cigarette, and lit it before continuing. "Sometimes I don't think he even realized that what he was saying was rude or derogatory. Like, if a single woman came in he'd always be, like, 'Your husband must be running late.' In his mind, it was a perfectly acceptable thing to say."

"But I get where he was coming from," Erin interjected. "It's almost impossible to buy a house without a second income."

"You don't have to be loyal to him now that he's gone," Sandy argued. "He can't give you that disapproving look that you hated so much."

"He never gave me that look!"

"Oh, please." Sandy rolled her eyes as she blew out a cloud of blue smoke. She clearly had little respect for the young secretary and had no problem making sure the overwrought woman knew it. "He gave all of us that look. It was his way. Well, all the females. He was different with the men."

Now we were getting somewhere. "How was he different?"

"He respected men."

"Oh no he didn't," another man argued, jumping into the conversation without invitation. "He didn't respect anybody but himself."

I took a moment to study the newcomer. I recognized his face — it was older, boasting more lines than almost anybody else milling about next to the real estate office — but I couldn't remember the name.

"Really?" Sandy wasn't buying what the interloper was trying to sell. "I seem to remember you getting bonuses five years in a row even though you sold less than me, Melvin."

Things slid into place. Melvin Montgomery. My mother had briefly worked in an office he ran when I was in middle school. She hated him, said he was a jerk of first-class proportions, and was excited when she made enough money to finally leave that office and start one of her own. How did Melvin end up working for Roy if he was his own boss?

Melvin balked at the statement. "How do you know that?"

"I make it a point to keep tabs on my co-workers," Sandy replied, blowing a long string of smoke into Melvin's face. The more I watched her, the more I wondered if she wasn't a constant problem in the office. I liked her attitude — she had no intention of taking crap from anyone — but she was aggressive. That couldn't go over well with her co-workers. "I know darned well you got five-figure bonuses each year for the past five years. I got nothing, even though I brought a lot more money into the office."

Melvin turned an accusatory glare on Erin. "Did you tell her?"

Erin's already pale face blanched even whiter. "Why would you think that? I'm a secretary ... or was."

"Yeah, but Roy made you do all the grunt work, including delivering bonus checks. You're the only one besides him who knew."

"That's not true." Erin blew a raspberry, something I expected from a teenager, not a working adult. "He never told me anything. He just barked orders while calling me 'honey' and commenting on my skirts."

I arched an eyebrow. "And despite that you think he was a good boss?"

"He paid me well," Erin said stubbornly. "I was socking money away to get my own place so I didn't have to live with my parents. Now that's over."

"You still live with your parents?" I was horrified at the thought, though I was almost at that point when I finally agreed to return home and work in the family restaurant. Thankfully the apartment above the restaurant was part of the deal. Otherwise I might've actually considered living in my car.

"Hey, you don't understand." She jabbed a finger in my direction. "Not all of us had a chance to leave this place and go to college. Most of us had no choice but to stay. That's why nobody understands why you're back. I mean ... you made it. You were out of here. Why would you throw all that away to come back here?"

Now it was my turn to be defensive. "It's not as if I had it easy."

"You were on television." Erin jutted out her lower lip. "We all saw you with those mean women on *The View*. They spent six whole minutes asking you about your book. You didn't need to come back."

Ah, if only that were true. I slid my eyes to Sandy, who watched me speculatively. "It's not that easy," I insisted after a beat. "Everyone thinks I got rich off that book, but I didn't."

"Hey, I'm not casting aspersions." Sandy held up her hands. "I understand why you're back. I understand about the book industry."

"You do?" That was refreshing.

She bobbed her head. "After you got that big book deal I researched it. I've always wanted to write a book."

I had to bite back a sigh. The number of times I'd heard that statement was staggering. The number of people who made that claim without putting in the work to write a book was astronomical. False dreams about how easy writers have it deluded so many people.

"I get that you didn't get rich," she continued. "Then that second book of yours didn't sell at all and they tossed your contract before you could write a third."

This conversation was getting more and more uncomfortable. "Yeah, well ... it wasn't what I thought it would be." There was no sense in lying. No one would believe I was back working at the family restaurant out of the goodness of my heart. On top of that, lying made me feel icky — unless it was for a good cause, like getting my mother off my back. "I didn't have a choice but to come back."

"Nobody doubts that," Sandy reassured me, her eyes drifting to an incredulous Erin. "Well, at least nobody with a brain."

I had to get this conversation back on track. "So, about Roy. Can you guys think of anyone who'd want to hurt him?"

"Hurt him?" Sandy screwed up her face. "There are a lot of people who wanted to hurt him. He was a gross old man who said disgusting things. He was also cutthroat when it came to business."

"Fair enough. What about killing him? Would any of those people want him dead?"

"I'm sure many would. Wishing someone dead and making it happen are vastly different, though."

She wasn't wrong. "Were you aware of any arguments he had recently?"

"I don't think you understand. The man had nothing but arguments," Sandy replied. "I can't think of one person in this town who liked him. Not one."

I pursed my lips. "What about his wife?"

Sandy snorted. "That woman had more reason to hate him than anyone. But she put up with him for, like, forty years or so. Why snap now?"

I didn't have an answer. "Well, thanks for your time." I stood, debating what to do. "Where does everybody hang out these days? Do they go to the coffee shop after hours or anything?"

Sandy's eyes lit with amusement. "Are you asking if there's a hangout for twenty-somethings in this town?"

Was that what I was asking? "Maybe. Is there?"

"Not really. It's the same town you remember. Now that we're adults, there's even less to do — unless you want to start bowling."

I'd rather cut off my own toes with the lid from a tin can. "Thanks again for your time. If you think of anyone who might've wanted to kill Roy, I'll be working at the diner for the foreseeable future. Don't hesitate to stop by."

SEVEN

I returned to the apartment long enough to realize that the town was already making me feel penned in. I lasted a full two hours before I took off again. I needed air.

In the city — any city — there is always somewhere to go. That's what I liked about it. As an only child, I was accustomed to entertaining myself. That didn't mean I liked being alone. In the city I could go to a coffee shop or movie theater and sit with a group of strangers without interacting with them and never feel alone. I didn't have that option in Shadow Hills.

For lack of anything better to do, I put on my hiking boots — they were one of only three pairs of shoes I owned these days — and headed to the river. It was one of my favorite haunts when I was a teenager. Hunter and I spent hours walking the banks. He liked looking for fishing spots and I was perfectly content dangling my feet in the water and listening to him talk for hours about the future.

Most guys of a certain age aren't chatty. Hunter was the opposite. His home was so stifling, his father such a terror, that he was relegated to silent visitor status under his own roof. He loved the energy of my family. None of them were capable of keeping their mouths shut, something he found amusing. He was also amazed that no one came to blows despite the political arguments.

When it was just the two of us, conversations were quieter. We talked about books and movies and our plans for the future. At the time, a niggling voice at the back of my head told me that his dream of becoming a sports-caster was unattainable. I refused to believe that, though. We had dreams and wanted to live them together.

Hunter was a standout athlete, the quarterback of the football team, pitcher on the baseball team, and power forward on the basketball team. He liked playing pickup games in the high school parking lot. He also liked taking walks in the quiet woods that surrounded the town, something we liked to do together.

I had no idea why I decided it was a good idea to make the trek alone today. I could've called Alice to see what she was up to, but I knew walking in the woods wouldn't be on her list. She had a thing about bugs. I wasn't a big fan either, but she absolutely freaked out if a bee buzzed near her face. She wouldn't agree to hang in the woods (let alone go for a five-mile hike) and, after I came up with the idea, that's all I wanted to do.

I entered the trees from the path behind the restaurant. The walking trails that led to the river were long and winding, but I remembered the route I wanted to take.

I'd barely made it a mile when I found the first landmark, a small clearing where Hunter liked to fish. We would spread out a blanket on the bank and I would relax with a book while he amused himself catching rock bass after rock bass and throwing them back. I once asked him why he never kept any. His response confuses me to this day.

"Some things are only meant to be tamed for a little bit, Stormy. Fish are one of them."

I always thought it was a rather bleak philosophy, but I laughed. He seemed to expect it. Now, looking back, I couldn't help but wonder if he was talking about me. It seemed such a deep observation for a teenage boy.

I ran my fingers over the underbrush, which was much thicker than I remembered. Boot prints lined the bank, which seemed to indicate someone was still fishing here. For some reason, that made me feel better. What Hunter and I had was a memory, but nobody had yet completely stolen this place from us.

After a few minutes of silent reminiscence, I selected another path along the river, revisiting some of our other favorite spots. The old tire swing was still there. A closer study told me that the rope had been replaced recently. The footprints scattered along the ground were smaller. That meant this was no longer a teenage hangout, but rather one for smaller kids. That was prob-ably how it should be, but it still made me sad.

The next stop on the nostalgia train was the inlet that opened into a small meadow. I couldn't count the number of picnics Hunter and I had enjoyed there — mostly when he was hiding from his father and his notorious temper. We'd make an entire day of it. Sometimes he'd be sporting bruises on his arms or face, but he'd refuse to answer questions about how he received them. Over time, I learned not to ask. I was gearing up to give the meadow a good once-over when I heard voices and froze.

At first I thought I heard only two voices, but the longer I listened I realized there had to be at least eight or nine people. I ducked my head under a branch, planning to hide in the bushes until I could ascertain who I was dealing with. Unfortunately, in the years since my last visit somebody had cleared out the bushes that used to line the meadow. I found myself completely exposed — and staring at a group of people I knew well.

"Stormy," Hunter said, lifting his eyes to meet mine in surprise. "What are you doing out here?"

It took me a moment to catch my breath. I'd been thinking about him and here he was. Sadly, he wasn't alone. I recognized most of the group surrounding him.

"Just taking a walk," I replied dully, scanning each face in turn. When I landed on one I remembered well, I broke into a wide grin. "Sebastian Donovan! I can't believe you're still in town."

The man in question — he was a man, no longer a boy — stood. He boasted a delighted smile and the same blond hair I remembered from high school. It hadn't darkened one iota. "Stormy?" He started in my direction, his arms already open. He enveloped me in a hug before I could catch my breath. "Welcome home."

For some reason, the words — delivered with equal parts warmth and wonder — caused me to choke up. "Hey." My voice was raspy, earning a side-long stare from Hunter. He hadn't said a word when Sebastian hurriedly crossed over to me. Now he looked sad.

"It's so good to see you." Sebastian had always been the effusive type. That obviously hadn't changed as he slid his arm around my shoulders and urged me toward the circle of people, one of whom was assembling a bonfire. "This is fortuitous. I was just telling Hunter that I thought we should invite you to our little group. He didn't think it was a good idea and I was about to give up on it, but here you are." His grin was infectious and I returned it.

"Yeah, well, Hunter probably didn't want me here because my grandfather is a suspect in a murder," I offered.

"That's not true." Hunter shook his head. "I just wasn't sure you'd want to hang out with us. I'm guessing the charms of the country are lost on you now."

The statement grated. "I can like the country even though I've lived in the city."

"I didn't say otherwise."

"That's exactly what you said."

Sebastian arched an eyebrow and drew me closer to his side, his gaze speculative as he glanced between us. "The country is lovely," he said after a moment. "It's a quiet life and we all love it. I want to hear about your time in the city. I bet that was exciting."

I held Hunter's gaze for a beat longer and then forced a smile for Sebastian. "It's not nearly as exciting as it sounds. Besides, I didn't spend much time in any one city. I think six months was my limit."

"Yes, you were always restless," Sebastian agreed.

"Always," Hunter echoed, sighing as he sat in one of the nylon chairs next to the fire. "She couldn't wait to get out of here she was so restless."

Sebastian ignored the statement and pulled me to a spot on the other side of the circle. "Do you remember everyone?"

It shouldn't have felt like a trick question, and yet it did. "Sure." I smiled at the assembled faces in turn. "Matt, Olivia, Ben, Celia, Finn, and ... ." I trailed off as I furrowed my brow at the final face. "I'm so sorry, but I don't remember you." I felt like a bit of an ass. I'd graduated with only fifty-three people. I should've been able to remember all of them.

"Oh, don't feel bad," Sebastian reassured me. "She's new. She didn't move to Shadow Hills until long after you were gone. In fact, she's only been here about a year now."

That made me feel better. "I'm Stormy. It's nice to meet you." I extended my hand, which she took, but the look she shot Hunter sent my antennae up. If discomfort were a sweater, she'd fill it out fabulously.

"I'm Monica Johnson," she said.

I froze. I recognized the name thanks to Phoebe.

"She's my girlfriend," Hunter volunteered, stretching his long legs out in front of him as he held my gaze through the growing flames.

I swallowed hard. I should've realized this was how my day would go. "It's nice to meet you." My voice was strong and clear, a small relief.

"You too." She said the words but there was no warmth in her eyes. She obviously knew who I was and wasn't happy in the least that I'd invaded what looked to be an intimate affair.

"Sit with me," Sebastian instructed, as if reading my mind. "I want to hear all about your time away."

That sounded like pure torture. "Oh, well ... ."

"I insist." Sebastian's gaze was pointed. He had no intention of letting me escape. "We have drinks and everything. You need to be reintroduced into our little society."

I was caught and I knew it. "That sounds great."

AN HOUR LATER, MOST OF THE DISCOMFORT I'd been feeling upon stumbling across the group had dissipated. Other than Monica, who was determined not to like me, I easily fell into old rhythms with the others. It was almost as if I hadn't left.

Almost.

"I can't believe you're running the funeral home now," I exclaimed, wide-eyed. I was three beers in and starting to feel the effects. After the previous evening with Alice, drinking probably wasn't a good idea. My nerves refused to let me relax without liquid courage at the ready, though.

"It's a good living," Sebastian protested.

"Yeah, but you have to touch dead bodies."

He shrugged. "There are worse things. By the way, I have to dress them, too."

I dissolved into giggles at the thought of him dressing dead bodies. I kept picturing Barbie dolls. It seemed a hilarious notion. "I just ... it's so gross." I looked to Hunter for confirmation. "Don't you think it's gross?"

He shrugged again. He didn't exactly look relaxed, but he obviously wasn't uncomfortable. His girlfriend, on the other hand, clung to his arm as if she expected him to throw himself on the fire in an effort to get closer to me. I did my best to avoid her gaze, even though I recognized that was probably making things worse.

"I'm kind of used to it now," Hunter supplied. "He's been doing it for three years on his own. He apprenticed at the funeral home for three years before that."

I tried to picture Sebastian as an apprentice and shuddered. "Nope. I'm sorry. It's weird. Who wants to date a guy who touches dead bodies all day?" The question was out of my mouth before I thought better about asking it.

Hunter's gaze immediately darkened and he sent me a small, almost imperceptible, shake of the head.

"I'm not really in the dating frame of mind these days," Sebastian said evasively, his eyes going to the fire. "If I ever am in that frame of mind, I would only want someone who accepts me for who I am."

My heart gave a little ping. I'd always suspected that Sebastian was gay. I'd never come right out and asked him, but there were hints when we were growing up. Coming out in a town as small as Shadow Hills was a daunting prospect. It was full of alpha males who would verbally abuse him, maybe worse. I was sure some already suspected.

I swallowed hard, doing my best to backtrack. "I'm not in a dating mood either," I offered, willingly opening myself up to ridicule — and speculation — to save Sebastian from embarrassment. "In fact, I'm thinking of becoming a nun. Do they still have that convent out on Grand Traverse Bay?"

Hunter snorted, choking on his beer as he shook his head. "Oh, geez." He tilted his chin up so he was looking at the stars as he cleared the liquid from his nose. "I forgot you were obsessed with that place when we were younger. You made me drive out there at least once a month to spy on the nuns."

"Hey, we all wanted to spy on the nuns," Matt countered. "I was convinced they were really witches in disguise. I mean ... nuns? Who wants to be a nun?"

"I think it's a noble pursuit," Monica countered, her eyes flashing as she glanced between Hunter and me. It was obvious she didn't like trekking through memories to find a safe topic of conversation. "There's nothing better than being closer to God, right?"

"If you say so." Sebastian made a face and retrieved two beers from the cooler, handing me one before cracking the tab on another. We were going old school and drinking our Bud Light from cans. "I can think of a million other jobs I would rather do."

"Like touching dead bodies for a living?" I asked.

He laughed and elbowed my arm. "You need to get over that if you're going to hang out with me. There's nothing wrong with working in a funeral home. In fact, it's one of the few jobs unlikely to be downsized or shipped overseas. People are always going to die."

"I guess." He had a point. "Maybe I should've gone into the funeral home business. It's probably preferable to where I ended up."

"I don't think you ended up in a bad place," Hunter argued, somber. "It's not where you thought you would be at this point in your life, but it's not as if you're destitute."

"And you were on television," Sebastian enthused. "Who doesn't want to be on television?"

"Yeah, but because of that everybody knows I had to come back here a failure. I'm right back where I was when I was sixteen."

"Which is probably the worst thing in the world to you," Hunter muttered. "Your life sucked back then, right?"

The vitriol in his voice surprised me. "I ... no." I shook my head, unsure how I was supposed to answer. "I look back on those years as the best in my life. It's just ... I thought things would be different." I didn't know what else to say.

Perhaps sensing trouble, Monica cleared her throat, forcing my gaze to her. "Do you want to leave again?" She looked hopeful. "Are you just back long enough to save money, maybe write another book and then head back out on the road?"

I'd been wondering that myself. The more I thought about it, the more I realized that seemed unlikely. "I don't know." I opted for honesty. "I didn't realize how much I missed Shadow Hills until I came back." My eyes lingered on Hunter a moment and then moved back to the stars. "I would like to find some balance, maybe live in both worlds, but that's probably not possible. I think my moment in the sun is over."

"It's only over if you let it be over," Hunter growled. "The Stormy I knew would've chased her dream no matter what. You act as if you've already given up."

"Not given up. I think I'm just coming back to reality."

"You can live your dreams in the real world," he persisted. "It might not be what you always pictured, but it doesn't have to be one thing or the other. You can live multiple lives."

It was a nice thought. "Maybe." I took a long pull on my beer, working overtime to ignore the dark looks Monica cast in my direction. "Right now, I'm just happy to be back with old friends. Everyone needs to tell me what they've been up to. I want to get caught up."

"Oh, I'll start." Sebastian's hand shot in the air. "I've got great gossip."

I arched an amused eyebrow. "About yourself?"

"Is there any better kind?"

EIGHT

I was drunk. Again.

This was becoming a bad habit, and I regretted it the second I stood and realized I wasn't completely steady on my feet.

Sebastian laughed at the way I gripped my chair and immediately reached out to steady me. "Need help?"

I shook my head. "I'm totally fine."

"Uh-huh." He looked dubious. "Where are you going?"

That was a delicate question. "Um ... over there." I pointed toward a stand of trees. "Nature calls." I laughed at my own lame attempt at a joke. "In this case, kind of literally."

"Ah." Sebastian nodded in understanding. "Do you need someone to go with you?"

"I think I can manage." My eyes inadvertently went to Hunter as I straightened. As teenagers, he'd always stood guard when I had to relieve myself after a night of drinking in a field. He looked concerned, but didn't get up to help, for which I was grateful. "I'll be totally fine."

"You have three minutes," Sebastian said. "After that, I'm coming looking for you. Don't wander too far into the woods."

"I'll be fine." His concern was sweet but unnecessary. "I grew up in these woods."

"You haven't been back in years. Be careful. And, seriously, don't wander too far. If you get lost, you'll never hear the end of it from your mother. We'll have to call out search dogs and stuff. You'll be on the news, and it won't be as funny as that time Matt got lost when we were fifteen."

For his part, Matt didn't look thrilled to be reminded of the event. "Oh, man. I still maintain that I knew exactly where I was."

"Which is why you walked around all night trying to find your way back to the road," Sebastian countered.

"Yeah, yeah, yeah."

I smiled to myself as I picked my way through the chairs, doing my best to look sober even though I'd had one too many. Okay, maybe three too many. It was beer, though, and I used to be able to put a six-pack away. Apparently that was no longer the case.

"Maybe she shouldn't go alone," Hunter said as I focused on my destination. If he thought I couldn't hear him, he was wrong. But I didn't respond. I didn't want to give him the satisfaction of admitting the walk in the dark — and what I had to do once I got there — held little appeal.

"She's fine," Sebastian countered. "See. She's walking ... mostly ... straight."

"Someone has to make sure she gets home okay," Matt warned. "If she goes missing, Charlie won't be happy. You know how he feels when his grandkids act out."

"That's her problem," Hunter shot back, causing the hair on the back of my neck to stand on end. He was an abrasive cuss when he wanted to be. "She shouldn't have drunk so much. She's a lightweight. Always has been."

"Yes, but before she had a knight in shining armor to walk her back," Sebastian teased. "Maybe she forgot that little detail."

"That's not my problem."

Thankfully their voices grew muffled the more I walked. Once on the other side of the trees, I looked for a convenient spot to do my business. I picked a tree to lean against and fumbled with the clasp on my jeans. That was another thing about the city. There was no lack of bathrooms. I forgot how undignified it was to have to relieve myself in the middle of a forest.

It took longer than it probably should have to finish, and I was grossed out when I realized there was no toilet paper. When I finally settled myself, I knew that I would have to spend the next hour sobering up before heading home. I remembered the path back to the restaurant well ... as long as there was light to lead me. Unfortunately, the only light illuminating the path was the moon. Full the previous evening, it still offered some minimal comfort.

I was about to stumble out of the bushes when I heard excitable chatter again. These voices were much closer. Monica and Hunter. They'd moved away from the group and were talking in low voices, but not so low that I couldn't make out what they were saying.

"I think we should go." There was a pout to her tone.

"It's still early," Hunter argued. "Let's stay another hour."

"Why?"

"Why not?"

He sounded annoyed and she sounded whiny. It might've been the beer talking, but it didn't sound as if it made for a lasting relationship.

"You know I hate hanging out in the woods like this," she replied with an irksome sniffle. "We do it once a week. I don't understand why you insist on hanging out with these people."

"They're my friends," Hunter replied evenly.

"Things change." Her tone was clipped. "You're a police officer now. You could be running the department in a few years. Do you think police chiefs hang around in the woods drinking with their old high school buddies and telling the same ridiculous stories over and over again?"

"I'm twenty-eight. I won't be chief anytime soon."

"But you could be up for a promotion soon," she persisted. "Do you want to lose out on that because one of your co-workers catches you drinking in the woods?"

"Yeah, there is no advancement in Shadow Hills. You're either chief or an officer. That's it."

"The argument still stands."

I felt guilty listening to what was obviously meant to be a private conversation, but I continued soaking it in.

"It really doesn't," Hunter shot back. "Nobody cares that we're out here. In fact, everybody — and that includes the chief — knows that I come out here once a week. It's not a big deal. Nobody drives. We're all adults and we clean up after ourselves. It's not as if we're breaking the law."

"Yes, but it feels so ... high school."

"Then go." Hunter was never one to hide his feelings. When he was annoyed, he let you know. Obviously Monica wasn't great at picking up on his moods.

"We came together."

"So? You know the way back to the road. Your house is closer than mine. It will take you ten minutes to walk home."

"In the dark? Alone?"

"You're the one not having a good time."

They were silent for a long time. I took the opportunity to peer around the bush separating me from them. It took me a moment to make out their hazy shapes in the darkness. I quickly dropped my head to avoid being seen. They were standing in the dark staring at one another.

"I'm not walking back alone," she said, breaking the silence. The chill from Monica permeated me from feet away. "We came together and we're leaving together."

"I'm not ready to leave." Hunter was obstinate. He was worse when he felt his back was to the wall. "I'm having fun."

"Really?" I couldn't see the eye roll, but it was obvious in Monica's voice. "Maybe you don't want to leave because of *her*."

I pursed my lips. She hadn't used a name, but it didn't take Sherlock Holmes to figure out who "her" was.

"What 'her?'" Hunter asked blankly.

"Oh, don't do that," Monica snapped. "Her. Your ex-girlfriend. The woman you've been staring at all night."

Hunter let out a hollow laugh. "I haven't been staring at her. Don't be ridiculous."

"I'm not blind, Hunter. You haven't been able to take your eyes off her."

"Has it ever occurred to you that she was sitting directly across from me? When I lift my head, she's right there. I would have to strain myself to look away from her. I wasn't staring."

"Why are you so defensive?"

It was a fair question, and I was eager for his answer. Had he really been staring at me? I wouldn't know because I'd been working overtime not to look at him. I didn't want to give his girlfriend — who was even more insecure than warranted — a reason to hate me. It sounded as if she already did, though. Ah, well, it's not as if we were going to be the best of friends. If she thought Phoebe was fun to hang around, we had absolutely nothing in common.

"I'm not being defensive." Hunter lowered his voice. "You're the one acting like a big baby. Stormy and I had a relationship a million years ago. We were teenagers, for crying out loud. There's nothing going on now."

"I would love to believe that."

"Believe it. It's true."

"Except that everyone in this town has a story about you and her," Monica fired back. "It was hard enough to listen to them when she wasn't sitting directly in front of me with her stupid pale hair and those big blue eyes. Everyone, and I do mean everyone, because I've heard it at least thirty times since we started dating, says they were certain you two would end up together.

"Her mother approached me at that festival in Hemlock Cove three weeks ago and said she was crushed to see us together because she always wanted you for her daughter," she continued, making me frown. "You laughed like it was some inside joke and didn't tell her that was never going to happen."

"There was no reason to tell her," Hunter fired back. "She knows Stormy and I didn't work out. She knows why things fell apart. The only one who doesn't seem to understand is you."

"Yeah, I don't think that's true."

"Well, I don't know what to tell you." Hunter sounded less than sympathetic. "These are my friends. I like hanging out with my friends."

"Does that include Stormy? That's a stupid name, by the way. Why would anyone name their kid that?"

"One of the Kardashians named a kid that and you were fine with it. You think the sun rises and sets on what they do. You've made me watch that stupid show a hundred times."

"First, the Kardashians are entrepreneurs," Monica snapped. "They're smart women who have launched so many successful businesses I've lost count."

She was a Kardashians fan. Obviously she was evil.

"Second, what does that have to do with anything?" she continued. "You never sat through more than two episodes no matter how much I begged."

"That's because the show is stupid," Hunter muttered glumly.

"And yet you watch fishing shows."

"I like fishing. I don't like the Kardashians."

"Ugh." Monica let loose a short scream of frustration. "I don't understand why we're standing in the middle of a field fighting. I'm over this ... and I'm leaving. You're walking me home whether you like it or not. That's what a gentleman does."

Hunter muttered something under his breath but didn't offer further resistance. I waited another thirty seconds and then pushed my way through the bushes. I expected to find the spot they'd been standing empty. Instead, I came face to face with my ex ... and he didn't look happy.

"Oh, um, I was just finishing up," I offered lamely, grateful it was too dark for him to see the color climbing my cheeks.

He didn't say anything for what felt like a really long time. I was certain he was going to call me out for eavesdropping. Instead, he merely shook his head and let loose a long sigh. "Are you okay?"

"Compared to what? I didn't pee on my jeans, if that's what you're worried about." I was going for levity. It fell flat.

"I mean are you okay to walk home? You haven't been in these woods for a long time. Sebastian is right. You're likely to get lost if you try finding your way back yourself."

"I'm okay," I reassured him. "Don't worry about me."

He didn't look convinced.

For a moment, he looked so lost that all I wanted to do was comfort him. Then Monica decided to screech from the trail.

"I'm waiting, Hunter!"

I had to press my lips together to keep from laughing at the morose look that crossed his features. "I think your girlfriend wants you," I said finally.

"Yeah, well ... ."

It would've been smart to keep my mouth shut at this juncture, but that had never been my strong suit. "She's lovely, by the way. I hate her."

Instead of being offended, he mustered the first real grin I'd seen since I stumbled across his group. "Thank you. That means a lot."

"Don't mention it."

SEBASTIAN INSISTED ON WALKING ME home. I didn't feel it was necessary and took the lead. He had to correct my course twice, so I was secretly thankful for the assist. I could never admit that out loud, though.

"Tell me about Monica," I instructed when we were about ten minutes from the restaurant. Sebastian had kept up a steady stream of gossip since we'd set out, telling me about everyone we went to high school with, whether I wanted to hear or not. This was my first chance to get the real dirt on Hunter's disagreeable girlfriend.

Sebastian's eyes gleamed with interest under the moonlight. "What do you want to know?"

I shrugged. "Whatever you want to tell me."

He wagged a finger and made a tsking sound with his tongue. "No, no, no. That's not how this works."

"You're not going to gossip about Monica?" I was keenly disappointed. "You've gossiped about everyone else. This is a letdown."

He snorted. "Oh, I have plenty of gossip about her. I just want you to admit why you're really interested."

"I like gossip."

"That's not why."

"It is."

He shook his head and pinned me with a probing look. "Just admit why you're interested and I'll tell you everything you want to know."

I knew what he was asking but there was no way I could admit it. "I already know she hangs out with Phoebe Green," I said. "That means she's basically the Devil. I don't need your dirt. I already have my own."

He laughed, delighted, and slung his arm around my shoulders. "You always were a stubborn little thing," he lamented. "Just for the record, I know why you're curious about her. If you're worried, don't be. It's not as if she and Hunter will last for the long haul. Frankly, I'm surprised they're still together. I thought she was a goner about three weeks ago, but they're surprisingly resilient for a temporary couple."

"Maybe it's true love and they just hit a momentary rough patch."

"It's not true love. As for the rough patch? The whole relationship has been a rough patch as far as I can tell. Hunter has never really been all that into her."

"Then why are they still together?"

His smirk was back. "Do you know what happened three weeks ago?"

I was at a loss. "The town got together and pitched a Taco Bell to the Downtown Development Authority? You have no idea how much I miss Taco Bell. That would be a lifesaver."

He smirked. "We ran into Alice at the bank. We both happened to be there at the same time and got to talking, as we always do. Then your cousin came in and made an announcement that changed the entire conversation."

I had a sinking suspicion I knew what announcement was. "Oh, yeah? It's a nice night, huh?"

His grin only widened. "She told us you were coming back to town, and not just for a visit. All Hunter's bold talk about dumping Monica flew out the window after that. He's been putting up with some outrageous crap from her ever since. I think we both know why."

"She's pretty."

"That's not why." Sebastian let loose a long sigh. "Listen, I'm not going to poke my nose into your business ... ."

"Yes, you are."

He laughed, the sound warm and friendly. "Fine. I will stick my nose into your business. I don't think it'll matter. You two will find your way back to each other. It's written in the stars."

"Oh, geez." I rolled my eyes. "That is the schmaltziest thing I've ever heard."

"And yet it's the truth." He turned serious. "You guys might've been suffering from a severe case of puppy love as kids, but that doesn't mean it wasn't the real deal. I don't think anyone who ever saw you together doubted what you felt for each other."

"We were still kids."

"It doesn't matter. Some things are meant to be. I believe you and Hunter are one of those things."

My heart skipped, and then steadied. "It's sweet that you're still a romantic, but Hunter has been cold. He made sure I knew about his girlfriend earlier this afternoon. He isn't interested in me."

"You keep telling yourself that."

"I will because it's the truth."

"I've got twenty bucks that says you're wrong."

"It's a bet."

"I'm going to win."

"No, I'm going to win."

"Honey, you can't even find your way home from the woods. You're so lost you don't know up from down right now. That's all going to smooth out now that you're home ... and Hunter is going to be part of it. Mark my words. I'm totally going to win."

I was too tired to argue. "I guess we'll just have to wait and see."

NINE

My dreams were dark.

I couldn't see anything, and yet I could hear voices.

There was laughter ... and whispers ... and something akin to cackling. The voices weren't altogether unfriendly, but they were disturbing all the same.

I heard talk of wine, a solstice celebration — and there was something about inappropriate leggings. It made no sense.

It wasn't exactly a nightmare. It wasn't exactly comfortable either.

The good part was that I knew it was a dream. The bad part was that I was having trouble forcing myself to wake up.

When I did manage to wrench open an eye, I found the most peculiar sight. There was nothing but white surrounding me.

"What the ... ?" Instinctively, I stuck out my hands, expecting to push the sheets off my head. Instead of colliding with fabric, though, my hands hit something hard.

I panicked and began to squirm, shoving with all my might against the hard surface directly above my face ... and pushing myself down. That shouldn't have been possible because I went to sleep in my bed. There should be no down, and yet there was.

It took tremendous effort, but I managed to push off hard enough to flip over. What I found defied explanation. I was floating a good three feet over my bed and the hard surface I'd woken to was the ceiling.

My eyes widened so far I thought they might pop out of my head. I struggled to find my voice, but the terror flowing through me was too much. I couldn't manage even a squeak to prove I hadn't developed laryngitis during the night. I don't know who I would have called for. It was early. If I screamed, the only people who might hear me were in the restaurant below — and how would I explain it to them?

I tried swimming back to the bed. No joke. It was a modified doggy paddle of sorts. Unfortunately, I couldn't aim and found myself swimming all over the bedroom.

"What is happening?" When I finally found my voice, it was to ask the most inane question imaginable — and still there was nobody there to answer.

Through sheer force of will, I managed to swim back to the spot above my bed and aimed my attention at the mattress. I wanted a soft landing if I fell, and that's what happened when I heard a voice. It was deep, gravelly, and full of annoyance.

A shot of terror coursed through me as I jerked my head, and that was when I finally landed with a thump, bouncing on the bed with enough force that the headboard rattled against the wall.

"What are you doing?" Grandpa poked his head inside my bedroom without knocking.

I was so glad to be on solid ground that I didn't bother admonishing him. "I ... what?" I stammered as I blew my hair out of my eyes. I could only imagine how I looked.

"Are you hungover again?" His eyes were speculative as they looked me over.

"Of course not." That seemed like the right answer, though it wasn't really true. I was most definitely hungover. My throbbing head was proof of that. The weird dream — and it had to be a dream, because there was no other explanation — took precedence over everything else. "Why would you ask that?"

"You look like you're hungover."

I made a face and combed my fingers through my hair. "How would you know?"

"Please." He rolled his eyes. "I've raised five children and ... however many grandchildren."

I seized onto the only part of the statement that was likely to derail him. "You don't know how many grandchildren you have?"

"Too many." He pursed his lips. "Were you out with Hunter?"

I wanted to scream. "Why would you ask that?"

"Because you look ... different. You have a glow about you."

That's because I dreamt of floating over my bed and decided to do the dog paddle until I woke up. Relating that to him would probably only make me look worse.

"If you must know, I was with Sebastian Donovan last night. He walked me home."

Grandpa continued to stare.

"Aren't you going to give me grief for being out late with a man?" I challenged. "Where's all the 'Did you do something dirty' talk now?"

He shook his head. "You can hang out with that man as late as you want. Nobody will give you grief about it."

I frowned. "And why is that?"

"You know."

I waited, expecting him to say something derogatory. When he didn't, I looked at him in a new light. "Well, thank you for not saying anything nasty."

"Why would I say something nasty?"

"You're not known for holding your tongue on certain subjects."

"Probably not," he agreed. "That boy, though ... he's been through enough. He's harmless, and he's always been a good customer. I think it's good that you're hanging around with him. It's better than being alone."

Grandfather could always take me by surprise, no matter how old I was. "Well ... great. I think we'll be spending a lot of time together, so that will be good."

"Uh-huh." Grandpa shook his head and moved to the door. "Get up. You're running late for work."

That couldn't be right. I glanced at the clock on the nightstand, cringing when I realized he was right. "I'm sorry," I mumbled. "I can be ready for work in fifteen minutes."

"You should've been ready for work fifteen minutes ago," he pointed out.

"I overslept." In the annals of lame excuses, that was right at the top.

"You might not oversleep if you went to bed at a reasonable hour — and stopped drinking when you have to work the next day. I know you're going through a lot and have yet to come to grips with the way your life trajectory has changed, but you have to get it together. I'm willing to help you, but you have to be willing to help yourself."

I narrowed my eyes. "I've got it. There's no need to be a pain."

"Then don't be late for work again. That's the one thing I can't stand."

I already knew that. Oddly enough, he was lax on most rules. He was a stickler about washing our hands after using the restroom and showing up on time, but other than that he was pretty easygoing.

"I'm sorry." I meant it. "It won't happen again. I just … it was a weird night."

Grandpa arched an eyebrow. "Hunter?"

I couldn't swallow the growl that escaped. "Will you stop asking that? He's not the be all and end all of my world."

"If you say so." Grandpa was blasé as he moved through the door. "You have twenty minutes."

"I'll be there."

"Then you have to take breakfast to David. He's running the gas station today."

I frowned. "You know I hate the gas station. We agreed when I came to work for you that I wasn't doing shifts in the gas station."

"We did agree on that." He nodded perfunctorily, but I didn't like the gleam in his eyes. "We also agreed you would be on time. Your punishment for being late on your third day is to keep your cousin fed all day while he does the job you hate."

Ugh. Family. This is how it always went. "Fine." I threw my hands in the air. "I'll wait on David hand and foot today. I guess it's better than listening to Uncle Brad's conspiracy theories."

"Oh, you'll be doing that, too." Grandpa's smile spread so wide it threatened to swallow the bottom half of his face. "He watched a new documentary last night about how alien abductions and global warming were conceived by the same cabal to discredit certain politicians and he's ready and raring to go. He called me before I went to bed last night to tell me. Do you know what I told him?"

I didn't want to know. "I'm sure it was lovely."

"I told him that you believed in alien abductions. He's looking forward to a lively day of debate."

I narrowed my eyes until they were nothing more than slits. "I hate you sometimes."

"That's what grandfathers are for. Now get moving. If you're late, I'll make you wash windshields during your breaks."

I pushed myself out of bed and raced to the bathroom. "Fifteen minutes. Time me."

THE MORNING SHIFT WAS ESPECIALLY brutal. It seemed every Shadow Hills denizen decided today was the day to have breakfast at the

diner. Between waiting tables and running trays of food out to David —
who lorded it over me that I was his servant for the day every time we were
face to face — I was exhausted by the time the midmorning lull came
around.

"Have some coffee," Grandpa suggested as I leaned against the counter and
watched him eat his second breakfast. He was like a hobbit. He had eight
meals a day.

I frowned as I stared at the concoction on his plate. "Is that quiche?"

"Of course not. Like I eat quiche."

"It looks like quiche."

"It's eggs, onions, and tomatoes all mixed together."

"Like an omelet?"

"If it was an omelet, I would've said it was an omelet."

And I thought I was the crabby one today. "Fine. It's not an omelet." I held
up my hands in mock surrender. "What's wrong with you?"

"Nothing is wrong," he snapped. "Why do you assume something is
wrong?"

Something was definitely wrong. His mood had shifted about thirty
minutes earlier when Brad showed up to take over cooking duties. I wasn't
sure why, but I had a feeling it couldn't possibly be innocent. Nothing the
man did turned out to be innocent.

"*Sorree.*" I took a step back and looked to the door as it opened, grinning
when I realized it was Sebastian. "I think I'll focus on the customers instead so
there won't be any more invasive questions."

"That would be great." Grandpa's tone was dry as he focused on his
breakfast.

Rather than take a seat in the cafe, Sebastian planted himself next to
Grandpa and gave his plate some serious side eye. "Is that quiche?"

Grandpa growled as I slashed my hand in front of my throat as a form of
warning. Sebastian only grinned in response. He had no fear of my
grandfather.

"Do you want something?" I asked Sebastian as I poured some coffee.

"Can I still have breakfast?" he asked hopefully.

"It's after eleven," Grandpa noted. "We only serve breakfast until eleven."

"Yeah, but I really want breakfast." Sebastian used his wheedling voice,
which always made me laugh.

"You can have breakfast," I offered. "Brad is cooking. He'll do what I say as
long as I listen to his alien nonsense." Now that I thought about it, I wasn't
sure making Sebastian happy was worth it. "Or you could just have lunch."

"I'll have egg whites and an English muffin," Sebastian countered, causing me to frown.

"Egg whites and an English muffin? That's, like, the lamest breakfast ever."

"On that we agree," Grandpa muttered. "That's not real food. This is real food." He gestured toward the hodgepodge of ingredients on his plate.

"That looks like a really weird quiche," Sebastian said. "I've never been a fan of quiche."

"It's not quiche! We don't eat quiche in Shadow Hills."

"Does the Downtown Development Authority know about that rule?" Sebastian teased. "I think they're going to have issues if you try to exert that sort of force over the town. They're only happy if they're the ones instituting arbitrary rules."

"Make him stop," Grandpa groaned. "I'm trying to eat breakfast in peace, for crying out loud."

I considered making Sebastian move — or at least making the attempt — but it was more fun to watch Grandpa squirm. "I'll put your order in." I offered him a serene smile before slipping through the swinging doors, pulling up short when I realized Brad had my cousin Lana trapped by the refrigerator, explaining how aliens were a mass hoax on the population perpetuated by fear-mongering Democrats. Ray guns, however, were apparently really in the works thanks to the Republicans.

"Order," I called out, tacking the slip onto the wheel before sliding back through the doors. The last thing I wanted was to listen to Brad spout more nonsense.

Sebastian was still talking to Grandpa. "I'm just saying that pre-paying for your funeral is the new thing. Everybody is doing it."

Grandpa made an exaggerated face. "Why would I possibly want to think about death before it's necessary? What kind of a crazy person does that?"

"The type who wants to save his family the exorbitant costs of a funeral."

Grandpa's frown grew more pronounced. "So, basically you're saying you gouge people when they're at a weak moment and if I was any kind of father I would save my children from that by purchasing your most expensive casket right now."

Sebastian's grin never wavered. "I would never recommend our most expensive casket. It's garish. White with a red velvet interior. Only Elvis would like that casket. The rest is mostly true, though. Don't you want to save your loved ones the added stress of trying to ascertain what sort of accommodations you would want for your final resting place? You could pick everything out yourself and be happy for all eternity."

"How will I be happy if I'm dead?"

"Maybe happy wasn't the right word. You'll be comfortable."

"Yeah, I don't think I'll care about that," Grandpa said. "Besides, the funeral business is a scam. Throw me in a fire when I'm gone and be done with me. That's my philosophy."

I had to bite the inside of my cheek to keep from laughing at Sebastian's horrified expression.

"How is it comfortable to be thrown in a fire?" he asked.

"Again, I don't care about any of that. Besides, there's nothing after death. When you're dead, you're dead."

"But ... don't you want to be reunited with your loved ones in the afterlife?"

Grandpa's expression was incredulous. "You've met my so-called loved ones. Would you want to spend eternity with them? Of course not. I want some peace and quiet, and I'm certain I'll get it only when I'm dead."

"But ... ."

"No." Grandpa shook his head, firm. "All this funeral stuff is nonsense. You'll never convince me otherwise. When you're dead, you're dead."

"You really are crabby this afternoon," I noted when Sebastian ceased talking. I took the opportunity to top off their coffee mugs. "You were in a good mood when you woke me up this morning."

"I wasn't in a good mood," Grandpa shot back. "You were late. I'm never in a good mood when someone is late."

"You were having a good time razzing me," I countered.

"That's always fun, but that doesn't mean I was in a good mood." Grandpa jutted out his chin and stared at the television over the counter. "Can't you guys go someplace else and stop bugging me? I'm watching the news."

When I flicked my eyes to the television, I found he was watching *The View*. "I thought you hated this show."

"Of course I hate it. They're loud-mouthed broads who should shut their holes. I like watching them bicker."

"Fair enough." I turned my attention to Sebastian. "Do you want to move to a table?"

He cast one more fond look at Grandpa and then nodded. "Sure. Your grandfather is having a bad morning. It probably has something to do with Hunter, who is already on the move and heading in this direction."

Grandpa's only reaction was a slight widening of the eyes. Otherwise, he remained perfectly still. I knew him well enough to know that he was bothered by the news.

"Is that why you're so crabby?" I asked, refusing to let it go. "Are you going to pull another disappearing act right before Hunter shows up?"

"I have no idea what you're talking about." Grandpa was haughty now. "If Officer Ryan wants to discuss anything, he knows where to find me."

"He tried to question you twice and you disappeared both times," I persisted. "That's not like you — unless you have something to hide."

Grandpa practically blew up, something I'd witnessed only when someone ordered poached eggs or he dropped his glasses in the grease trap. "I'm not hiding anything. Why won't you let it go?" He hopped to his feet and pinned me with a dark look. "I didn't do anything. The quicker you get that through your head, the better."

He stomped toward the swinging doors, leaving me to press my lips together and exchange a worried glance with Sebastian. The gregarious funeral home operator looked as worried as I felt. He obviously had no idea the size of the can of worms he would be opening when he decided to tease Grandpa about Hunter.

"And one more thing," Grandpa said as he was perched between the doors. "This one might be fun to share a drink with, maybe even hang out with from time to time, but he'll ruin your dating life if you expect to get back with Hunter."

Now it was my turn to be defensive. "Stop saying that! I don't want to get back with Hunter. You're just trying to irritate me."

"Apparently it runs in the family." There was some extra flounce in Grandpa's step as he disappeared into the kitchen.

"He's totally going to hide, isn't he?" Sebastian said after a beat.

"Yup." I bobbed my head. "He's been doing it for days. I can't figure out why."

"Maybe he killed Roy."

"He didn't."

"Maybe you're in denial about it."

"I'm not."

"Really? You're in denial about Hunter. He's right about that."

I didn't bother to hide my glare. "I'll check on your breakfast."

Sebastian sipped his coffee and grinned. "Apparently you get your denial tendencies and your penchant to hide when a conversation gets tough from your grandfather."

"Ha, ha, ha."

"I'm serious."

What really terrified me was the possibility that he was right.

77

TEN

S ebastian hung out until I finished my shift and then followed me up to my apartment. His expression was dubious as he glanced around.

"Are you a minimalist? If so, we can't be friends."

I laughed at his reaction. "I don't know that I would say I'm a minimalist. It's more that I own nothing, so I can't decorate."

"I don't know. Who doesn't like a painting of a bear catching a fish?" He moved to the lone piece of art on the wall, a piece that was painted by my great-grandmother when she opened the restaurant. The birch bark frame made it all the more tacky in my book, but he seemed intrigued. "Do you know who painted this?"

"I think it was my great-grandmother."

"Really?" Sebastian looked intrigued. "Is she still alive?"

"Yeah. She lives in Florida. She still comes up once a year to visit the family."

"She's the one who gave the restaurant the name, right?"

I laughed and nodded. "Yeah. I think my grandfather would've changed it long ago if he could. She made keeping the name a point of contention when she sold it to him, so he's stuck. He thinks Archer's Fine Dining has a certain ring to it."

Sebastian chortled. "I don't know. I like the Two Broomsticks thing. Besides, living so close to Hemlock Cove, I think the name is a bonus these days."

"Yeah," I agreed, sliding into the bedroom. I gave the bed a long look, as if I expected to be swept into the air again, and then shook my head. "I'm going to change really quick and then we can head downtown for coffee."

"That sounds good to me." His voice told me he was drifting through the apartment. "I have to be back at the funeral home at two o'clock."

"Oh, yeah? Do the caskets get unruly if you're not there to supervise them?" I laughed at my own lame joke.

"Vera Axe is coming in to make arrangements for Roy."

I froze, my shirt halfway over my head. "Vera is going through you for Roy's arrangements?"

"You sound surprised." Sebastian's voice was closer this time, but I didn't rush to shut my bedroom door. I wasn't concerned about him seeing me in my bra. "I am the premiere funeral director in Shadow Hills."

"You're the only funeral director in Shadow Hills."

"My statement stands."

I chuckled as I slipped into a T-shirt and a pair of well-worn capris. By the time I returned to the living room, Sebastian had made himself comfortable on the couch. His gaze was speculative as I moved to join him.

"What?" I was feeling self-conscious. I still couldn't shake the dream — or the fear that almost caused my heart to pound out of my chest as I tried to rouse myself from it. The panic I'd felt when flying over the bed had been real. I knew what happened had only been a vivid hallucination thanks to my beer-soaked mind. That didn't change the fact that I felt off my game because of it.

"I was just thinking." Sebastian eyed my hair. "Have you ever considered layers?"

The question caught me off guard. "Yeah. I had layers when I was doing press for the book. I hated them. It took me two years to grow them out."

"Is that why your second book didn't sell as well? Were you fixated on your bad layers?"

I let loose a sigh. "I don't want to talk about the book."

"Which one?"

"Either one."

"Does talking about it make you sad? Do you feel as if you've missed out on something important? Is it worse to be close to living your dream and then lose it?"

The tidal wave of questions caused my stomach to tighten. "Sebastian ... ."

He didn't allow me to unload on him. "I want to know what you're thinking."

"I'm thinking I could use some real coffee," I said pointedly. "I don't mind the stuff in the diner, but I'm a Starbucks girl, and the closest thing we have in town just so happens to be right next door to your funeral home."

"Yes, that was a stroke of luck." Sebastian stood, resting his hands on my shoulders as he stared soulfully into my eyes. "You haven't lost everything until you believe it. Have a little faith in yourself, Stormy. I think the best things in life are still in front of you."

He was so serious I could do nothing but stare ... and then laugh. "Have you been reading motivational books again?"

He balked. "I did that one time."

"You did it every winter when we were in high school. You always got depressed around February and needed a pick-me-up."

"That's ... completely true but not relevant to this conversation," he challenged. "I'm serious. I know you're struggling. Anyone who has ever met you can see it. You had high self-esteem as a teenager, one of the reasons I gravitated toward you. There was never time to feel sorry for yourself in Stormy's world."

The words made me smile. "I don't really remember that. I felt sorry for myself a lot back then."

"When?"

"I don't know. I just remember feeling sorry for myself."

"I believe you didn't start feeling sorry for yourself until after you said goodbye to Hunter."

"Ugh. Here we go." I rolled my eyes. "Why must every conversation come back to him? I don't understand."

Sebastian snorted. "You understand. You just don't want to acknowledge it because you have that whole girl power thing going for you."

"And what's wrong with girl power?"

"Absolutely nothing. I'm all for girl power. Trust me, I always fancied myself the pink Power Ranger for a reason. That doesn't mean you can't have a man in your life and still be all about the girl power."

What he said made sense, but I didn't want to deal with Hunter. "He has a girlfriend. I'm trying to ... fix my life. I don't think either one of us is looking to each other for anything other than the occasional, 'Hello, how is it going?' I'm sorry if that disappoints you."

"Oh, it disappoints me on a level you can't possibly fathom. I don't believe it. You do, though. Well, at least right now. When things change, I'll be here for you. Now, let's get coffee."

I wasn't in the mood to argue further. "We definitely need coffee if we're going to keep this up for the next few hours."

"I told you I have to go to work."

"I'm going with you."

He paused at the door, surprise etched across his handsome face. "Why?"

"I have a few questions for Roy's widow."

His smile turned into a frown. "That's a really bad idea."

"Are you banning me from the funeral home?"

"No, but ... I don't want you scaring away my customers."

"I have no intention of scaring away your customers," I reassured him. "I just want to feel her out. She might know who was angry enough at Roy to kill him."

"I hate to break it to you, honey, but she was probably angry enough to kill him. Can you imagine being married to the guy?"

"I promise to be on my best behavior. She won't even know what I'm doing."

"Okay, but if I feel you're stepping over a line I'm going to lock you in the cooler with our newest guests."

The thought gave me the shivers. "I swear I won't do anything to embarrass you."

"Then we'll give it a shot. I'm kind of curious about what she has to say, too."

VERA AXE LOOKED OLDER than I remembered and shorter. Her shoulders were sloped and she had the appearance of a woman who had been through eight wars as she shuffled into the funeral home.

"How are you feeling, Mrs. Axe?" Sebastian immediately moved to her side. He'd changed into a staid black suit that set off his broad shoulders, the picture of concern as he helped her to one of his ridiculously cute settees.

"I've been better," she replied dryly, her eyes momentarily landing on me. "Do you have another customer? We had an appointment."

"That's Stormy Morgan." Sebastian's response was smooth. "She just moved back to town. She's interested in joining my team here after she goes through training, so I'm allowing her to serve as an apprentice. If that bothers you, she can wait in the other room."

I frowned. I didn't like the idea of anyone believing I wanted to apprentice in the funeral home business. That was creepy on a level that made my skin crawl.

"I guess that's okay." She eyed me speculatively for a moment. "You're Charlie's granddaughter, right?"

"One of them," I confirmed, nodding. "Actually, I'm his favorite grand-daughter."

"Is that saying much?" Vera's expression was sour. "Everyone knows Charlie favors his grandsons. If you don't have testicles in his world, you're a non-entity."

Sebastian's eyes lit with an amusement he quickly dampened. "I guess that's why he's always been fond of me."

"If you say so." Vera let loose a sigh, her eyes going to the casket display at the far end of the room. "Are those my choices?"

"Those are the most common models," Sebastian reassured her. "We have a whole catalog of other caskets if you're interested. I can have them here in less than twenty-four hours if you find something you like."

"And what if I just want to throw him in a pine box and have him cremated?"

The question obviously caught Sebastian off guard. "Oh, well ... um ... ."

"That's how my grandfather wants to be put to rest," I offered. "It's not a terrible idea. Caskets are really expensive."

Sebastian shot me a dirty look over Vera's shoulder. "They're also beauti-ful, and a fine final resting place. I mean ... who doesn't like the idea of a comfortable casket?"

I raised my hand but he ignored me.

"If you prefer cremation, I understand," Sebastian continued. "Many fami-lies are choosing cremation these days. There's worry of overcrowding in cemeteries ... and concern for the environmental footprint."

"Oh, that's not why I want him cremated," Vera countered. "I don't care about any of that. I'll be dead long before global warming becomes a concern and I don't really care if it's a hardship for the next generation because they're all jerks."

I pressed my lips firmly together and averted my gaze. I just knew if Sebastian and I made eye contact,we would both start laughing.

"All right," Sebastian said, choosing his words carefully. "You don't have to justify your reasons for wanting cremation."

"It's not a justification. He was a jackass, an Axehole really. Oh, yeah. I've heard the variations on that name for years. They were warranted.

"Listen, Roy was a jerk. I knew it better than anybody else," she contin-ued. "You don't have to pretend with me. I'm only bothering with a proper burial because people in town will think I'm cheap if I don't. If it were up to me, I'd throw him out in the middle of the street and let people spit on him."

"I'm sure he had some good qualities," I hedged, desperately looking for something to latch onto.

"Sure he did." She flashed a smile more grimace than grin in my direction. "He was great when it came to doing yard work."

That wasn't what I was looking for, but it was better than nothing. "Well, that's something, right?"

"Absolutely. He kept the hedges trimmed because he liked peeping in Marla Stinski's windows. She doesn't like wearing clothes inside her house — heck, she probably doesn't like wearing them outside either, but she knows she'll get ticketed if she's not careful. Roy realized that if he didn't keep the hedges maintained he wouldn't be able to see her in the buff."

My mouth dropped open.

Vera kept on as if she didn't have an audience hanging on her every word. "He also kept the branches on the large maple tree at the back fence trimmed properly. That's because the Stevenson girl likes to lie out in her bikini. We have one of those privacy fences, so he had to get on a ladder to look at her. He trimmed so many branches last year the tree looks naked from the waist down."

"Oh, well ... how old is the Stevenson girl now?" I tried to do the math in my head.

"Sixteen," Sebastian answered grimly.

That sounded about right. She'd barely been walking when I'd left for college. "Well, maybe he considered himself an artist," I offered brightly.

Vera's lips curled into a sneer. "What does that have to do with anything?"

"Artists study the human form in a clinical manner."

"Yeah, that wasn't it. Roy couldn't draw a stick figure unless the stick was in his pants. He did enjoy adding penises to photos in the newspaper. He thought it was funny, even if the photos were of an accident scene or a murder victim. He would leave the newspapers behind in restaurants so other customers could enjoy his artwork."

I chewed my bottom lip. It sounded as if Roy was an even bigger jerk than I remembered. "Still, you married him," I pressed. "There must've been something about him you liked."

"When Roy and I met, I was looking for a way out of my father's house. He was a strict disciplinarian and believed the only way a daughter could leave the nest is if she was married. At the time, I thought Roy was the answer to my problems."

"See." I forced a smile I didn't really feel. "He was good for something."

"Yes, he was a true joy," she drawled, rolling her eyes. "If I knew then what

I know now I would've stayed with my father. He might've been a real killjoy, the sort of guy who never laughs and doesn't think others should either, but at least he didn't get his rocks off staring at underage girls."

Helpless, I looked to Sebastian to take over the conversation. He looked just as lost.

"So ... the most inexpensive box we can find and cremation?" All the excitement he'd been feeling earlier in the day deflated, leaving his shoulders hunched. "Do you want a tombstone or shall we just stick a little sign in the ground and be done with it?"

"Oh, I want a tombstone." Vera flashed her teeth. "Do you think I can put 'beloved philanderer' on it without turning the town against me?"

"Um ... ." Sebastian looked uncertain.

"Are you sure he cheated on you?" I asked, knowing it was probably the worst way to turn the conversation. I couldn't help myself. "I mean ... just because he liked looking at other women doesn't mean he acted on his impulses."

"Oh, honey, you're sweet." Vera shot me a pitying look. "Do you know how many women have contacted me over the years to tell me my husband was cheating on me?"

"That doesn't necessarily mean it was true."

"Two of them claimed to be pregnant with Roy's babies."

"There are ways to prove that."

"He paid them off."

I was done trying to find a single good thing about Roy. It was a wasted effort from the start. "I'm really sorry." I meant it. "He sounds like an absolutely horrible man."

"He was. I still have a responsibility, and I mean to see it through."

"Then we'll help you." Sebastian grabbed his notepad and headed toward the couch. "You know, there's this really garish tombstone they've been trying to get rid of. Someone somewhere thought it was a good idea to make one in a puke green color. You can get them for a song now that they're discontinuing the line."

Vera brightened considerably. "That sounds great. He would hate that."

"I think I know a few more things he would hate. There's a spot in the cemetery where the squirrels hang out and crap all through the summer. It smells terrible. Those spots are inexpensive."

"Sign me up."

This wasn't how I planned to gather information, but it was better than nothing.

ELEVEN

T wo hours with Vera was my limit. The joy she took in picking out the things she knew Roy would hate made me sad. Sebastian got into the spirit of the endeavor, but even he looked wiped out when she finally left.

"Did you at least make a profit?" I asked as I stretched out on the settee. It was surprisingly comfortable for such a small piece of furniture.

He nodded and flopped in the chair next to me. "I made a fairly decent profit. The markup on this stuff is astronomical."

"I bet. It's one of the few businesses that can get away with almost anything and nobody will call them on it."

"You make me sound like a con artist."

"Not you personally," I reassured him. "It's just the thought of profiting off death. It seems somehow wrong."

"Some people could say that about food," he pointed out. "Food is necessary for life, but it's not a luxury. Your family makes a living off the backs of those who are starving."

"No, my family makes a living off the backs of those who are too lazy to cook for themselves," I countered. "Nobody is forcing them into the restaurant."

"Nobody is forcing them into the funeral home either."

I rolled so I could meet his gaze. "I wasn't getting a dig in at you. I was just commenting on the circle of life."

"Oh?" He looked amused. "Are you feeling philosophical this afternoon?"

It was a fair question. "I'm feeling ... something." I pushed myself to a sitting position, mostly because I was afraid the hangover would finally catch up with me if I remained prone, and the last thing I wanted to do was catch a catnap in a funeral home. "What do you know about Roy?"

"I think we just heard an earful."

"Yes, but that was from Vera's perspective. She did give me a few things to think about. She focused on his sexual appetite, which was apparently disgusting. Other people hated him for any number of reasons. Not everything had to do with his wandering eye."

"Ah." Sebastian nodded in understanding. "You want to know what sort of dirt I've heard about Roy."

"Pretty much. I'd heard stories about him before I left. I never paid much attention to them. The only thing I remember is that it was a running joke not to get near his hands. I guess, in hindsight, that wasn't much of a joke."

"He had a horrible reputation when it came to women ... and apparently teenagers. I never really heard about the teenagers. I might've said something if I'd had."

"You and me both. What are some of the other stories you've heard?"

"Well, I heard he borrowed Frank Farmington's snowblower but never returned it."

"I doubt that's worth killing over."

"I'd agree, but they had a big blowup over it."

"Really?" I smiled to encourage him. "What sort of blowup? Were punches thrown?"

Sebastian chuckled, obviously tickled by my enthusiasm. "The thing with Roy is that he wasn't the physical sort. He was a blowhard and would say the dumbest crap imaginable, but nobody ever worried he'd back it up."

"Give me a for instance."

"For instance, his fight with Frank. Apparently they'd been going at each other for some time, Roy denying he'd ever borrowed Frank's snowblower and Frank calling him a big, fat liar."

"Did something happen to the snowblower in question?"

"I believe Roy broke it, because that plays into the story. Anyway, there was a festival downtown — it was an offshoot of the Hemlock Cove summer festival last year — and Frank approached Roy during the carnival. Actually, if I remember correctly, Frank stalked Roy through the festival because Roy kept hopping on rides to avoid him."

"Did Roy really think that hopping on a five-minute rollercoaster ride was going to dissuade Frank?"

Sebastian held out his hands and shrugged. "I've never been able to fathom the things Roy did. Delaying the inevitable only irritated Frank. He was foaming-at-the-mouth mad when he finally caught up to him."

I tried to picture the scene in my head, smiling. "So, what happened? Don't leave me in suspense."

"Patience, grasshopper. I'm getting to it." He flicked his fingers at me and grinned. "So, picture it, Roy thinks he's shaken Frank and is back to being a blowhard as he exits those flying swings that everybody pretty much hates."

I frowned. "I didn't know those were still a thing."

"Only at really depressing festivals, which is what we have here, because Hemlock Cove has a lock on all the good carnival companies. Anyway, Roy decides to hang out between the swings and the flea market, calling out to anybody he sees and making a general nuisance of himself. That's when Frank finally cuts him off from any avenue of escape and approaches him."

"You tell a story like my grandmother," I complained. "It goes on and on, and there's no buildup of suspense."

"I'm an excellent storyteller ... and I'm getting there. Roy is talking nonsense, as he usually does, when Frank appears behind him and asks about his snowblower. Roy looks like he wants to run, but there's nowhere to go."

"You definitely remind me of my grandmother."

"Shut it," he warned, his eyes flashing even as his lips curved. "So, Frank starts yelling about how Roy is a dirty thief. He mentions how Roy has borrowed power tools from every guy in a ten-block radius but never returned them. He theorizes Roy is making money by selling these tools."

"Is that possible?"

"I'm telling my story."

"Okay, Grandma, keep going."

He flicked my ear and smirked. "Roy swears up and down he returned the snowblower. He feigns ignorance as to what happened to it. Frank tells him he's full of crap and mentions how much he hates him. Blah, blah, blah.

"They go back and forth for a good twenty minutes, to the point someone called Hunter to break it up," he continued. "Frank explains why he's upset and Roy denies even borrowing the snowblower at this point. To ensure a ceasefire, Hunter suggests he go to Roy's house with him to search his garage.

"Roy balks and has an absolute meltdown. He claims he never borrowed Frank's snowblower and demands Hunter get a search warrant if he wants to enter his garage. The whole thing has garnered the attention of almost everybody now and there's a whole bunch of people watching the show.

"Roy's other neighbors, the ones who claim they loaned him tools as well, start chiming in, saying they would like to look inside Roy's garage," he continued. "At this point, Roy is pretty much melting down. He's calling anyone within earshot names and then does a complete one-eighty when Hunter suggests he's going to try to get a warrant."

"What does he do?" I asked. "Roy, I mean."

"He starts writing checks for the power tools. He writes one for anybody there, anybody who ever loaned him anything."

"Are the checks good?"

"Aha. Smart girl." Sebastian snapped his fingers and grinned. "The checks are not good. They all bounce. Turns out that Roy switched over his bank account before anyone could cash the checks."

That sounded demented — and interesting. "Did Hunter go back with a warrant?"

"He did. And when he went inside Roy's garage he found it completely empty. Except for a broken snowblower."

"Then why was Roy so worried?"

"I should emphasize the fact that the garage smelled like bleach and looked as if someone had recently cleaned it."

"So Roy was hiding something in his garage," I mused. "Could it have been the power tools? Was he demented enough to throw everything away rather than give it back?"

Sebastian pursed his lips and shrugged. "Your guess is as good as mine. There are a number of hunches regarding what Roy had in his garage. Some people claim he was cooking meth."

That made me smile. "I seriously doubt that. You could smell it."

"That's what I said, but you know how people are. Others say he was running an illegal gambling hall in his garage."

"Do you believe that?"

"Not really. For people to gamble there, they would have to visit the house — and nobody would be caught dead visiting Roy's house without a gun pressed to their head."

"Okay. What does that leave?"

"I don't know, but if you find out I'll be happy to spread the gossip for you."

I SPENT ANOTHER HOUR BANDYING ideas around about Roy's garage. There were so many possibilities and ridiculous rumors. I had a good time listening to them all — and contributing a few of my own. My favorite was that Roy was an underworld pimp running a brothel out of his garage. That one made me laugh out loud.

By the time I'd left, I was feeling markedly better. The hangover was gone and all I had to decide was what I wanted to do with the rest of my afternoon. I was halfway down the sidewalk in front of the funeral home when something caught my attention out of the corner of my eye. When I swiveled and stared at the cemetery at the edge of the property, I didn't see anything. Still, I couldn't shake the notion that someone was watching me.

On a whim, I started in that direction. I could cut through the cemetery — even though I'd never been particularly fond of the property — and get to the restaurant from that direction.

Because it was small, Shadow Hills had just the one cemetery. I took my time, my eyes bouncing from tombstone to tombstone. I searched for the source of the movement I was positive I'd seen when leaving Sebastian's funeral home, but I saw nobody. I was just about to write the whole thing off to my imagination — which seemed to be throwing party after party these days — when my eyes landed on a familiar marker.

William Archer. My grandfather's father. His mother was still alive — and on her third husband — but his father had died when I was fairly young. I had only one memory of him, and it wasn't exactly illuminating. He'd been sitting at the formal dining table in my grandparents' house, playing chess with Brad, and talking about some ridiculous political conspiracy theory that involved ranking members of the first family being aliens.

I smiled at the memory. Perhaps that's where Brad got it. He was especially close with my great-grandfather. It was possible he'd inherited that part of his personality. Lord knows I'd picked up a few unsavory tendencies from my grandfather.

I bent over long enough to clear away a few weeds, jerking up my head when a shadow passed over me. I scanned the nearby graves, frowning when I found no one near me before returning to my task.

The shadow appeared again.

"Okay, who is here?" I hopped to my feet and planted my hands on my hips. I was positive someone was messing with me. "Sebastian, is that you?" I shook my head, disgust rolling through me. "It's not funny. You know this place has always freaked me out."

He didn't immediately show himself. I was convinced it was him — until I remembered I'd seen the movement ten seconds after I'd left the funeral home. There was no way he could've made it to the cemetery that quickly.

Even if he was in a playful mood, he wouldn't go out of his way to frighten me.

"I'm serious," I shouted as my heartbeat ratcheted up. I could feel someone watching me. No matter where I looked, though, I couldn't find a source for my agitation. "This is not funny."

No one responded. No one was there. That only served to weird me out further.

"Screw this," I muttered, picking up my pace and scurrying toward the far end of the cemetery. I wanted out of there. In fact, I couldn't move fast enough to escape the fear rushing through me. I kept glancing over my shoulder to see if anyone was giving chase. That would've been a welcome development. The more distance I traveled without seeing anyone, the more unsettled I felt.

I was three-quarters of the way across the cemetery when the sky opened up. It had been sunny only an hour before. Now it was overcast and pouring.

"Great," I growled as I put my head down. I would be soaked by the time I got back to the restaurant.

I didn't regain my composure until I hit the sidewalk on the other side of the cemetery. My heart was still pounding. Now I just had to walk a mile in the rain to get home.

A truck pulled to a stop next to me. I didn't bother looking up. I knew better than to get inside a vehicle with a stranger. I was better off walking in the deluge.

"Stormy, what are you doing?"

I recognized Hunter's voice and jerked up my chin, my eyes going wide when I found him sitting in the cab of his truck, an exasperated look on his face. If that wasn't bad enough, he wasn't alone. Monica was with him — and she didn't look happy.

"I was at Sebastian's place," I offered. "It didn't start raining until I was already heading back."

"And you're just going to walk home in this?" He looked exasperated.

"I don't have much of a choice. I'm already wet."

He let loose a low growl. "Get in the truck."

One glance at Monica told me that was the exact opposite of what she wanted. "I'm good."

"Get in the truck," he repeated.

"Um ... really, it's fine. I'm already wet. It's not cold out. It's just rain. I'll survive."

As if on cue, a low rumble of thunder filled the air and a flash of lighting illuminated the sky.

"Get in the truck," Hunter ordered, his tone no-nonsense.

"You heard her, Hunter," Monica argued. "She's fine walking. It's not that far."

"A big thunderstorm is coming," Hunter shot back. "She's not walking back to the restaurant in it. That's, like, a mile. She could be struck by lightning."

Monica wasn't about to back down. "Do you know the odds of that?"

Hunter held her gaze for a long moment and then focused on me. "Get in the truck, Stormy. If I have to wrestle you in the entire town will be talking. Do you want that?"

Part of me did because I knew it would agitate Monica. The other part, though, recognized it would be bad for all of us if the Shadow Hills rumor mill kicked into overdrive.

I scuffed my foot against the pavement as I trudged to the backseat door. "I really would be fine."

"Get in the truck!" He was beside himself.

I was soaked when I hopped in, water dripping from my drenched hair. I hadn't bothered with makeup this morning, a small favor because any mascara or eyeliner would be spreading down my cheeks.

"Put your seatbelt on," Hunter ordered.

I did as I was told. Now that I was in his truck, I wanted this ride to be over as quickly as possible.

For her part, Monica looked as if she was about to go nuclear. Still, she plastered a smile on her face. It was more horror movie than romantic comedy. "So ... you were hanging out with Sebastian?" she prodded as Hunter pulled back into traffic.

I nodded. "Yeah. I sat in on his meeting with Vera Axe. She picked out the things she thought Roy would hate the most for his funeral."

"I'm not surprised," Hunter said, his eyes on the road in front of him. The rain was coming down so hard he had to reduce his speed. "They didn't have the best of marriages."

"No," I agreed. "The way Sebastian made it sound, Roy didn't have a single friend in town. Is that true?"

"I don't think it's much of an exaggeration. Roy had one of those personalities that everybody hated. He couldn't seem to adjust his attitude and make friends."

I swiped at the water on my forehead. "Did you manage to track down Grandpa?"

Hunter scowled. "No. He conveniently disappeared right before I showed up. Your uncle Brad seemed confused when he went looking for him."

No surprise there. "Did you tell Brad you were going to visit Grandpa?"

"I called the gas station to see who was working. Brad was there. Why?"

I heaved out a sigh. "Next time you might want to show up unannounced and go through the back door."

"Why?"

"I think that might be the only way you're going to get your man."

"I'll take it under consideration. Thanks for the tip."

"No problem."

We lapsed into uncomfortable silence. Monica broke it as we pulled into the restaurant parking lot. "Have you considered going on Tinder to look for a date?" she asked, fixing me with a pointed look. "A girl like you would be very popular. Not now, with your hair looking like this, but otherwise."

I had no idea what to say. I decided to steal a line from Hunter and make my escape. "I'll take it under advisement. Thanks for the ride. I really appreciate it."

TWELVE

I thought the ride was going to be the worst part of my day. But that happened when Hunter moved to exit the vehicle with me.

"What are you doing?" Monica asked, her tone accusatory.

"Walking Stormy inside," he replied blandly. "I'll be right back."

"But ... ."

He ignored her and focused his gaze on me. "Come on."

I felt like an idiot climbing out of the truck. I knew I should probably say something to Monica. "So ... um ... it was nice seeing you again." I offered her a bright smile that was all false light and delight.

She glared at me. "You should really take better care of yourself so others aren't forced to do it."

I pursed my lips. "I would've been fine walking," I said at the moment a bolt of lightning split the sky. The thunder followed so quickly I jolted. "Totally fine."

"Come on, Stormy," Hunter barked, making me realize he was as uncomfortable with this interlude as me.

"Right." I slammed the door shut and dragged my feet to the front of the truck, where he was waiting as the rain pelted down. "You really didn't have to pick me up. It's my own fault for not realizing a storm was coming."

"It would be helpful if you watched a weather report," he agreed, moving toward the door. He smiled as he held it open for me. "You always did like walking in the rain, though."

A burst of warmth washed over me. I knew what memory he was tugging on. It involved him, me, linked hands and huge mud puddles. We were filthy and flirty by the time we were finished. "This was a little more than a rainstorm. I really appreciate the ride."

"It's okay."

"I don't think Monica believes it's okay."

"She's just ... ."

"Unhappy with life?" I suggested when he didn't finish. I expected him to argue, but he simply nodded.

"That's one way of looking at it." He followed me inside, our bodies brushing against one another when I had to pull up short to avoid a customer checking out at the register. One of my cousins was handling the task and the look she shot me was priceless.

"What happened to you?" she exclaimed. "Did you already tick off Hunter so much that he tried to drown you in a puddle?"

"I'm saving that for next week," Hunter quipped, his eyes steady as they scanned the restaurant. "Is your grandfather here?"

That's when it hit me. "You didn't pick me up out of the goodness of your heart. You just wanted a reason to look for Grandpa." I hadn't meant to say it out loud — really, what was the point? — but the look Hunter pinned me with made me wish I'd kept my big, fat mouth shut.

"I picked you up because it wasn't safe for you to be walking in the storm," he shot back.

"Yeah, but you walked me inside for Grandpa."

"Does it matter?" He furrowed his brow. "Is there a reason I shouldn't take advantage of the situation?"

The question, reasonable on the surface, grated. "Whatever." I shook my hair, internally smirking when some of the water hit him directly in the face. "I'm going upstairs to get cleaned up ... unless you need something else, that is."

"Can you check the back for your grandfather for me?"

He had a pair on him. I couldn't believe he'd asked given my current state. "Sure. No problem." I stomped toward the kitchen, throwing open the swinging door and poking my head. "Is Grandpa here? The fuzz is looking for him."

From behind the grill, Brad lifted his chin. "He took off for his afternoon constitutional about forty minutes ago."

I frowned. That probably meant he was up contaminating my bathroom.

Hunter didn't need to know that. "Thanks." I turned back to my ex and held out my hands. "Sorry. He appears to be absent."

"Where does he take his afternoon constitutional?" Hunter challenged. Apparently he still had super hearing or something. I would have thought the exhaust fan and the other noises in the kitchen would've drowned out Brad's response.

"All manner of places," I replied. "Wherever he can take a newspaper and disappear for an hour — he really should eat more fiber — that's where you'll find him."

Hunter didn't look amused. "Does he go home?"

"Sometimes."

"And other times?"

"You'll really have to ask him. This is one aspect of my grandfather's life I want no part in."

He held my gaze for a measured moment and then shook his head. "Just tell him I'm looking for him."

"I believe that's the standard message I convey to him these days," I said dryly. "Is there anything else?"

For a moment, I thought he was going to say something important. The expression that crossed his face was enough to tug on my heartstrings. Ultimately, though, he shook his head. "Watch the rain, Stormy," he said as he moved toward the door. "You need to take care of yourself."

He echoed the sentiment his girlfriend had tossed in my direction only minutes before. "I can take care of myself, Hunter. You don't have to worry yourself acting as my protector. Not anymore."

"You always could take care of yourself. That doesn't mean you always have to." He turned back, his eyes lit with an emotion I couldn't quite identify. "That's always been your problem. It doesn't always have to be you against the world."

I was taken aback by his vehemence, and when I risked a glance at my cousin, I found her eyes wide as she watched with rapt attention. "It feels like it is me against the world," I said. "Always."

"Well, you need to get over it. Just ... get over yourself. People want to help. Let them." He looked beyond frustrated as he swung back toward the exit. "Tell your grandfather I'm looking for him," he said to my cousin. "I won't give up until we have a long conversation."

"Okay." My cousin was solemn as she nodded.

. . .

ANNOYED WHEN I HIT MY apartment, the feeling grew exponentially when I heard noise in the hallway. I knew who it was without looking.

"You know, I'm going to have the locks changed so you can't hide up here whenever the mood strikes," I announced as I stalked toward my bedroom. "You can't just wander in here whenever you want. This is private property."

Grandpa was blasé as he emerged from the bathroom, newspaper clutched in hand. "It is private property. My private property. I own it."

"Yeah, but I'm ... leasing it."

"Really?" He hiked an eyebrow. "I don't remember signing a lease. Maybe I'm growing forgetful in my old age. I thought we just agreed you would pay me a couple hundred bucks a month until you were back on your feet, and then we'd figure something out going forward."

He sounded reasonable, which I absolutely hated. "Whatever." I charged into my bedroom, shutting the door so I could change my clothes. I expected him to be gone when I emerged, but I wasn't that lucky. Instead, I found him sitting on my couch staring at the painting his mother had finished. "Why are you still here?"

"You looked like you needed to talk," he replied, his gaze drifting to me. "What's wrong with you?"

Oh, there were so many ways I could answer that question. "What makes you think anything is wrong?"

"Because you're a mouthy pain in the behind. I have a lot of grandchildren. I also had four teenagers in the house at one time. I know about being mouthy. You're taking it to a personal level."

I flopped onto the couch next to him. "You really have no idea how many grandchildren you have, do you?"

"You guys multiply like rabbits."

"You could do the math and commit the number to memory so you're not always grasping."

"What fun is that?"

He was right. I was in a foul mood, but it had nothing to do with him. "I got caught in the rain. Hunter picked me up and drove me back here."

"That hardly sounds like the end of the world."

"His girlfriend was with him."

"Ah." Grandpa nodded knowingly. "I take it you two aren't going to be fast friends."

"We're not going to be slow friends either. She's ... mean." It was a stupid word. I was an adult, for crying out loud. Only middle-schoolers used that word to describe a nemesis. If I'd used the word I really wanted to throw out there, Grandpa might try to wrestle me down and wash my mouth out with soap.

"Mean, huh?" He chuckled, amused by my obvious discomfort. "Dolly, do you know what your problem is?"

One of these days I was going to shove that question right back down his throat and make him choke. "I'm pretty sure it's Monica ... and Hunter ... and the fact that I own five pairs of pants and now one of them won't dry out for days."

"I've already told you that you can use the washer and dryer at our house."

"That's not the point."

"No, the point is that you feel like sitting around and pouting. I can't help you there." He stood with a grunt. He was a big guy. Eight meals a day had done him no favors. "When you're in the mood to talk like an adult, you know where I am."

"I'm not pouting." I was sixty-five percent sure that was true. "I'm just ... taking stock of my life."

"Well, try doing it with a better attitude. If you keep up like this, you'll be bitter. I have two bitter sisters. I know what you'll find at the end of that road, and it isn't pretty."

"I'll take it under advisement."

He smirked. "You do that." He hesitated at the door that led downstairs. "Hunter's gone, right?"

I narrowed my eyes, suspicious. "How long do you think you're going to be able to hide from him?"

"I'm not hiding. That's a ridiculous statement."

He was never going to own up to his actions. Not on this one. I was too tired to press him, though. "He's gone. Trust me. His girlfriend isn't the type to sit in the parking lot and stake it out. You can escape."

"I'm not escaping. I just ... don't like cops."

That was news to me. "You should probably take advantage of this window and run."

"It's the end of my shift. I'm going home. It has nothing to do with Hunter."

I didn't believe him. "Have a good rest of your day."

"You too. Don't be late for work tomorrow."

"I won't." I'd learned my lesson. I had no intention of leaving my apartment tonight. "I'll see you tomorrow."

"I'll be the one with the coffee."

. . .

97

I SPENT THE REST OF THE AFTERNOON reading and lazing about. In the city, I always felt as if I couldn't find enough hours in the day to get everything done. Here, back home, I had time to just sit and think. Self-reflection was allowed, though it wasn't how I wanted to spend my time.

I moved my pity party to the balcony. The restaurant had closed two hours earlier and it was eerily silent as I stared at the trees behind the storage building. The darkness allowed me to think about the events of the past few days ... and it wasn't a pleasant reverie.

My biggest issue was the dream this morning. No matter how I tried to shake it, there was a worry in the back of my mind that it had really happened. It was ridiculous, of course. I hadn't been floating over my bed. I most certainly hadn't been swimming through the air like the world's most uncoordinated fairy. It *had* to be a dream.

A very realistic dream.

Whispers of magical powers weren't uncommon in this area. Given the trick Hemlock Cove had managed to pull off — seriously, their rebranding efforts had the town thriving when others in the area were dying — it was a common topic of conversation. My great-grandmother decided on the name for the restaurant. There were numerous stories as to why she chose the name, some so wild there was no way they could be true.

My great-grandfather was a milquetoast. I would never come out and say that to my grandfather, but all the stories painted him as a bland man who sat back and let his wife have her way. My great-grandmother, on the other hand, was a spitfire. She did what she wanted, when she wanted, and didn't care if society at the time believed men should be in charge. She was in charge, and no one could tell her otherwise.

She'd named the restaurant long before Hemlock Cove turned to a witch theme to keep commerce humming. In fact, she'd left the area long before the rebranding talk even started. When she returned to town every summer — I made a mental note to check when her visit would happen this year — she always headed to Hemlock Cove for a day or two. She still had friends there, and even rented a room in a bed and breakfast where one of those friends resided.

I still didn't understand the name. Two Broomsticks. It was witchy, which was a great benefit given the overflow of tourists flocking to Hemlock Cove, but it seemed out of place for the years before witches were a thing. I'd asked my grandfather about it a time or two, but he always shook his head and turned dark when I brought up the topic.

"Ask your great-grandmother." That's all he would bark. This year, when she finally showed up for her visit and upended our lives, I would ask her. I honestly cared enough to hear the answer.

I was just about ready to call it a night and turn in early — after the past two nights, a full ten hours of sleep sounded heavenly — but a hint of movement near the storage building caught my attention.

My first reaction was fear as my heart lodged in my throat. After a few seconds of watching, though, I realized that whatever was down there was too small to be a threat. Even if it was a rat, it was hardly something to fear.

The creature finally darted out into the alley under the streetlight, allowing me to get a gander. My heart pinched for a different reason this time. It was a kitten. A very tiny kitten.

I put my hands on the balcony railing and leaned over, looking for an adult cat. I knew there were a bunch of cats that hung out in the woods behind the storage building. They liked to forage the dumpster. Some of them were quite fat because they lived the high life here. Of course, some of them died horrible deaths because they were feral and had to survive winters.

I watched the kitten play a full five minutes before I made up my mind. It seemed happy chasing bugs in the darkness, but I wouldn't be able to live with myself if I didn't at least try to do something. The alley behind the restaurant was busy and those big delivery trucks wouldn't stop for a small animal.

I used the external steps to approach the kitten. I expected him to take off in the opposite direction when he saw me. He'd probably scatter for the woods the second he noticed me. Instead, he merely stared, as if daring me to approach.

"Hey, buddy." I flashed a smile even though it was a wasted effort. It's not as if the kitten could read facial expressions. "What are you doing out here?"

The kitten batted at my hand when I reached out to scoop him up. It wasn't much of a fight. When I grabbed him on the second attempt, he shot me a dirty look — until I started scratching behind his ears. Then, suddenly, he was all cuddles and purrs.

Crap. Most feral cats — even tiny kittens — hated humans. This one seemed to crave human contact.

"Do you belong to someone?" I stared into the kitten's eyes. His fur was matted, but he looked relatively healthy, other than being a bit thin. I knew I couldn't leave him out here. I would have to hold onto him for the night and then take him to the animal shelter the following day. At least then he would have a chance at a home.

"Well, I have some tuna upstairs," I said uncertainly. "How about some food and a place to sleep for the night? I'll help you move along the chain tomorrow."

The kitten licked my chin, melting my resolve a bit. "I'm not keeping you," I warned, deadly serious. "My grandfather will never let me have a cat above the restaurant."

A noise over my left shoulder caused me to jerk, clutching the kitten closer to my chest. When I peered in that direction, I found nothing — and yet I felt something. There were eyes on me, and they didn't feel like they were of the feline variety. In fact, I was positive it wasn't an animal watching me. The pricking on my skin made me feel something bad was about to happen.

"We'll keep talking about this upstairs," I reassured the kitten, scurrying toward the steps that led to the balcony. I didn't know why I was suddenly so fearful, but every fiber in my being was screaming for me to find safety.

I tripped twice going up the stairs but managed to keep hold of the bundle of fur pressed against my chest. Once inside, I locked the sliding glass door and shoved the sawed-off broom handle that was always propped against the wall into the track so nobody could pull it open if the lock failed.

I stood there a good ten minutes, watching the darkness.

I didn't see anything.

I didn't hear anything.

I felt something, though, and it was evil.

THIRTEEN

The kitten slept on my head. My dreams were convoluted, more darkness and whispering voices — many so snarky that they made me laugh, even though it felt invasive, as if I was listening to other people's private conversations — but I woke well-rested.

Then I remembered the feeling from the previous day.

The kitten padded out into the kitchen after me. He appeared ready for more tuna. I fed him and drank my first cup of coffee in front of the sliding glass doors. In the bright light of day, there was nothing amiss. I still couldn't completely shake the remnants of fear that seemed to want to cling to me like lint.

I didn't have a litter box. I told myself that it was a waste of money because I had no intention of keeping the kitten. I dragged one of the rectangular flower boxes from the balcony into the kitchen. There were no flowers — apparently I was expected to provide those myself if I wanted floral decorations on the balcony — but there was dirt.

"You're to do your business in here," I explained to the kitten as he studied the box with disdain. "Don't go anywhere else. My grandfather will not be happy ... and he eats kittens for his third breakfast." I laughed at my own stupid joke, but the kitten didn't seem impressed. "I'll take you to the shelter when I'm done with my shift."

As if understanding, the kitten yawned and walked away from the flower box. I followed him and watched as he climbed into the bed, nestling among the pillows. He was already half asleep.

"You're not staying," I warned him. "I can't have a cat. Cats live forever and I don't plan on being here more than a few months. A year at most." Even as I said the words, they seemed improbable. There was no way I would be able to build my bank account in a few months. I was here for at least a year, maybe longer if I couldn't get my act together.

"You're definitely not staying," I repeated as I headed into the bathroom. "Even if I wanted to keep you — which I don't — my grandfather wouldn't stand for it. He hates cats."

"I DON'T HATE CATS," GRANDPA ARGUED when I told him about my feline guest. He was prepping the kitchen for the breakfast rush when I descended the steps. I was ten minutes early this time, so he didn't give me grief. I told him the story of the kitten to fill the silence.

"Yes, you do."

"No, I don't. Why would you think I hate cats?"

"Because ... well ... because you've never had one."

"I've never had a horse either, but I don't hate horses," he pointed out. "I have no problem with cats, other than they're sneaky. I just prefer dogs."

"Are you saying I can keep him?" The thought hadn't even crossed my mind other than in a far-off reality where I liked the idea of having something to devote my attention to.

"Why not?" Grandpa had his practical face on. "Cats are easy compared to dogs. You don't have to walk them. Feed them. Clean their litter boxes. That's it. Cats are easy."

"I guess." I remained unconvinced. "I don't know that I want a cat, though."

"Why?" Grandpa's gaze was piercing. "Are you saying you can't take care of a cat? If so, you definitely shouldn't have one. There's nothing worse than a person who takes on the responsibility of an animal and then refuses to follow through. If you think you can take care of the cat, what's the problem?"

I didn't immediately answer. I couldn't. There was nothing I could say that wouldn't make me look bad or launch a debate I had no intention of getting into.

"Ah." Grandpa bobbed his head after watching me futz with the coffee filters for a few moments. "You don't want a cat because you expect to pick up and move again the second you manage to write a book someone wants to buy."

That was insulting — mostly because it was true. "I just don't know where I see myself landing," I argued. "I mean ... can you see me spending the rest of my life here?"

He shrugged. "Why not?"

"Because ... ." I didn't want to insult Shadow Hills. He was loyal to the town and didn't like when others weren't. Still, he couldn't possibly overlook the town's deficiencies.

"Because you want to live in the city," he surmised. "You might as well come out and say it."

"I *might* want to live in the city," I confirmed. There was no sense in lying. He knew me too well.

"Why?"

"I like the city."

"Do you?" He looked dubious. "As far as I can tell, you've spent the last six years of your life living in ten cities. Ever since you left college, it's been city after city. Have you loved any of them?"

"I loved New Orleans." That was true. I'd found true inspiration there. I'd also found humidity headaches because I was there in summer and so many annoying tourists that I lived in a perpetual state of annoyance.

"Can't you visit New Orleans?"

"I ... ."

When I didn't finish my response, he barreled forward. "It seems to me that you can live almost anywhere if you get this book thing off the ground again. Why do you have to live in a city?"

I swallowed hard. "I guess I don't. It's just ... I can't stay here."

"Why?" He held up his hand before I could answer. "Let me guess. You can't be close to Hunter."

I wanted to strangle him. "Not every decision I make is because of Hunter," I shot back. "You need to stop saying that."

"Why?"

"Because it's not true."

He folded his arms over his chest and pinned me with a pointed look. "Why really?"

"Because it bugs me," I hissed, letting my temper get a foothold. "You have no idea how much I hate hearing his name ... and so relentlessly from practically everyone I come in contact with."

"Then do something about it."

"Like what?"

"Like tell him how you feel."

"And how do I feel?"

"You know how you feel."

Honestly, I didn't. My heart and mind were mired in an endless tug of war where Hunter was concerned. I was over this conversation, though. "You're right. I do know how I feel. I'm annoyed that people keep bringing up my high school boyfriend as if he's somehow relevant in my current life."

Instead of being impressed with my straightforward argument, Grandpa snorted. "Please. You still have feelings for him. You might've buried those feelings, but he's always been at the back of your mind. Have you ever considered that you self-sabotaged as a way to get back here — to him — and that's why your second book didn't sell?"

That was the biggest load of horse-pucky I'd ever heard. "That is not what happened. I was dating another guy when I was writing the book."

"Oh, really? What was his name?"

"Tim ... or Tom. It was one of those."

"That's what I thought." Grandpa looked smug. "You don't have to wedge yourself into one life, Stormy. You can make your own life ... and Hunter can be part of it. If you give him the chance, that is."

"He has a girlfriend."

"He has a shield."

"I don't know what that means."

"She's a shield," Grandpa repeated. "That's how he wields her, anyway. He doesn't care about her. Oh, don't get me wrong, I'm sure he doesn't want anything bad to happen to her, but he's not emotionally invested in that relationship. He only keeps her around because she makes a convenient obstacle for you."

I worked my jaw. He wasn't the first person to suggest something similar. "I don't know that I want to stay here for the rest of my life. I mean ... it's tiny. There's not even a Starbucks."

"And I'm happy for that," Grandpa fired back. "You don't have to spend the rest of your life here. You can have a life that involves travel ... and Hunter ... and cities ... and those trails by the river that you love walking so much. You can design your own way."

He was making far too much sense for me today. "I need to wipe down the tables in the front," I muttered, increasing the distance between us. "By the way, when can I start working later shifts? I'm not a morning person. I think I would be better handling lunch and dinner hours."

Grandpa rolled his eyes. "Fine. Run away from the conversation. That's what you always do."

"I'm not running. I'm genuinely curious."

"You can start working later shifts when you're off probation."

"And when will that be?"

"When you stop showing up late for work."

"I was on time today."

"And when you stop running from questions."

He was nothing if not persistent. "I think I have answered all your questions."

"As long as you think that, you'll be lost. You need to get it together, kid. You're not a teenager any longer. You're an adult, and everything you want is here. You just have to see it."

I hated it when he sounded reasonable. "I'm going to check the front."

I heard his sigh from behind me. "Stormy, the world isn't against you. You only think it is."

"It doesn't feel that way."

"Then you need to change your way of thinking. There's a whole world out there just waiting for you to take control. Do it. Embrace who you're supposed to be."

He made it sound so easy. "Maybe I don't know who I'm supposed to be."

"You do. You're just afraid to admit it."

THE MORNING RUSH WAS A BLUR. WE WERE especially busy thanks to an influx of tourists from Hemlock Cove. Apparently there'd been an incident the night before. The women who took over most of the cafe section couldn't stop talking about it.

"There were lights over the trees," one of them enthused. "One of the witches set them on fire ... and there was a wedding ... and I think there was some weird bird attack. It was amazing."

I smiled as she recounted her adventure. "Can I get you anything else?"

"We're good for now."

When I turned back to the coffee counter, I was surprised to find Hunter perched on a stool. He was positioned in the spot I'd left Grandpa in only twenty minutes before.

"Hey." I automatically poured him a mug of coffee without asking. Much like me, he needed caffeine poured directly into his veins until noon to make it through the rest of the day. "Do you want something to eat or are you just here stalking my grandfather again?"

Hunter's smile was rueful. "I'm a great multi-tasker."

"You always were," I agreed, handing him a menu.

"Can I still get breakfast?" he asked, gripping the laminated page without glancing at it.

I shifted my eyes to the clock. "It's after eleven."

"I know, but ... ." He looked like a puppy begging for food. "Breakfast is the most important meal of the day," he reminded me.

I glanced over the swinging doors to see who had taken over grill duty. David was there, so I nodded. "Yeah. You can have breakfast. Don't tell Grandpa I bent the rules for you."

Hunter's grin was warm and wide. "Thank you."

"French toast?" I already knew the answer. It was his favorite.

"Do you have that cinnamon bread I love so much?"

"Of course."

"Then give me a double helping."

My eyebrows hiked. "Hungry?"

"Let's just say I think it's going to be a long day."

"Monica or my grandfather?" The snarky question was out of my mouth before I thought better about asking it.

He didn't appear insulted on his girlfriend's behalf. "Yeah, um, I'm sorry about her."

I wasn't expecting such a genuine response. "It's fine." I averted my gaze.

"It's not fine." He was firm. "She was rude to you. It's not fair. She shouldn't be making you feel guilty for accepting a ride in the middle of a storm."

He seemed to be in an open and giving mood today, which made me want to grill him about Monica. That would likely spoil the truce we were enjoying, so I managed to curtail my baser urges. "It honestly is fine." I flashed a genuine smile before taking his order into the kitchen. "This is for Hunter," I told David pointedly.

David glanced at the ticket and nodded. "I won't tell Grandpa."

"I'm not afraid of him," I shot back.

David snorted. "Right. None of us are afraid of him."

Rather than comment further, I left him and took the pot of coffee around the restaurant, topping off cups. When I returned to the cafe section, I found the corner table had been snagged by a familiar face.

"Vera," I noted as I returned the pot to the warmer and inclined my head in that direction.

Hunter lifted his chin and stared. "She's been out quite a bit since Roy died."

It was a statement, not a question. "Do you suspect her?"

"The wife is always a suspect."

"That wasn't really an answer."

"No," he agreed, rubbing his chin as he watched my cousin Annie approach Vera. "It doesn't look like she's alone today."

My eyes shifted to the man walking through the door. He was distinguished, dressed in a relatively expensive suit, and he made a beeline for Vera. He didn't greet anyone else in the restaurant, which was practically unheard of in town where everyone pretty much knew everyone else. I didn't recognize him. "Who is he?"

"Barry Buttons," Hunter replied with a grimace, distaste evident.

"I need more information than that," I prodded.

Hunter slowly dragged his eyes back to me. "You don't remember Barry? He was your basketball coach when you were in seventh grade."

The fact that he remembered that seemed a small miracle. Now that he brought it up, though, I did remember the man. "He was, like, the world's worst coach. He was barely there."

"He only did it because his daughter was on the team and he was going through a divorce," Hunter explained. "He wanted to look like an involved parent, and that was the only way he could think to do it."

"Stephanie Buttons is his daughter."

"She is. She doesn't live here any longer. She moved to Traverse City about two years after we graduated. Last I heard, she was married and had three kids. Her brother is still around. He's as much a loser as the father. Stephanie is the only decent one in that family."

I pursed my lips. "I remember her being nice."

"She was. Him, though ... ." Hunter made a tsking sound and shook his head. "He's the worst of the worst."

I racked my brain trying to remember tidbits about Barry. "He's an attorney."

"He is."

"Why would Vera need an attorney?" My mind was racing now. "You don't think that she's worried she'll be arrested?" I knew I was grasping, but the unsettling feeling from the night before had stuck with me through the morning. I couldn't help wondering if it would disappear once Shadow Hills' one and only murderer was behind bars. If that was Vera, so be it.

"He's not that sort of attorney," Hunter replied, stroking his chin, thoughtful.

I watched him, enjoying the intense look on his face. He was always the sort who enjoyed gnawing on a problem until there was nothing left but masticated bones ... and a solution.

"What kind of attorney is he?" I asked when it became apparent that he wasn't going to expand on the earlier statement.

"He's a divorce attorney."

That was enough to knock me back a step. "Wait ... why would Vera need a divorce attorney? Her husband is dead."

"That is a very interesting question."

I was silent for a moment, myriad possibilities flooding my mind. "Do you think she was considering divorcing Roy before he was killed?"

"If she was, she conveniently left that out during our initial interview."

"So what does that mean?"

"I don't know." Slowly, he let his eyes drift back to me. "It's interesting, though."

"I guess." I didn't know what response he was expecting. "Are you going over there?"

"For now I'm just going to watch. We'll see how things progress."

FOURTEEN

"They're arguing about money," I announced when I came back to Hunter for the fifth time. He'd long since finished his breakfast, but we'd turned our spying into a game of sorts. He couldn't approach Vera and her attorney. But I could continue topping off their coffee and they barely paid me any attention.

"What kind of money?" he asked.

"American money. How should I know?"

The look he shot me was withering. "You are ... so much work." He flicked me between the eyebrows, causing me to glare. It was something he did to irritate me when we were teenagers. "What are they arguing about in regard to money?"

I should've known that's what he was asking. I was having too good a time to cut it short. "They're talking about selling the house and how much she can get for it."

Hunter turned pensive. "She wants to sell her house?"

"That's what it sounds like. He's telling her it's a mistake because she won't get very much for it and she has bills to pay."

"Did he say what bills?"

"No, and I didn't ask. Why is that important?"

"I don't know that it is important." He rubbed his strong chin. "It doesn't make sense for Vera to move from this area. Her house is paid for. The cost of living is low. She'll inherit everything from Roy's estate."

"Unless there is no estate."

"How can he not have an estate? He's been working his entire adult life. He should've been socking money away all that time."

"Not everybody starts planning for their retirement when they're sixteen," I teased, remembering back to the things he told me about the shoebox of money he was hiding in his basement when we were teenagers.

"Hey, I want to make sure my golden years are spent on sunny beaches."

"So you're surrounded by girls in bikinis?"

"So ... I can rest." He took on a far-off expression for a moment and then shook his head. "I'm curious about why Vera would make the decision to pack up and move out of the blue. This is her home."

"Yeah, but we don't know what was going on between her and Roy," I pointed out. "Maybe she never wanted to stay here. Maybe he made the decision to stay. It's possible she's always wanted to live somewhere else."

"Like you."

It was a pointed statement, and it made me feel uncomfortable. "Like me," I conceded. "I always thought that I wanted to live in the city. Don't get me wrong, the city appeals to me on a certain level, but the older I get, the more I realize that there's more to picking a place to settle down than being able to go to a midnight movie screening."

His smiled. "That was one of your big complaints back in the day. You wanted to be able to see blockbusters at a place that had more than one screen. Was it everything you hoped for?"

I shrugged. "Sometimes. I guess I wish I had someone to go to the movies with. I don't dislike seeing a movie alone, but we used to dissect the movies we saw together. I would do it from a narrative perspective and you would make fun of the action scenes. It's not as much fun when you don't have someone to talk with after."

His gaze was serious. "Are you staying?"

The way his demeanor shifted told me he hadn't meant to blurt out the question. It was right there, though, and I couldn't ignore it.

"I don't know. I didn't think so when I first came back, but ... I'm starting to wonder."

"About what?" His full attention was on me now. He didn't as much as glance in Vera's direction.

"About everything. The other day, when I was walking along the river, I forgot how much I missed it. I didn't let myself think about things like that when I was away, because ... I don't know ... it made me sad.

"I mean, there I was, doing what I was supposed to be doing but nothing felt right," I continued. "I want to write books. That hasn't changed. I'm starting to think the life I convinced myself I needed wasn't the one I really needed. I spent all of my teen years dying to get out of this place."

"And now?"

"Now I can't seem to remember why."

"Yeah." Sadness permeated his taut features.

"My grandfather suggested that I've been trying to force myself to live a certain way because that's what I thought I wanted and it would be a disappointment if I turned out to be wrong. You know how I feel about being wrong."

He smirked. "And what do you think?"

"I think ... I think ... ." I wasn't sure how to respond.

"You don't have to tell me," he said finally. "It's none of my business."

"It's not that. I just ... don't know. I think that I keep freaking myself out over ridiculous stuff and can't seem to stop myself. Last night I rescued a kitten from the alley and I was certain there was someone watching me, even though I'm pretty sure I would've seen someone if they were really there. I spent a half hour sitting in the dark by the sliding glass doors, convinced someone was out there."

He frowned. "If you were afraid, why didn't you call me?"

That was a ridiculous suggestion. "Um ... I'm pretty sure your girlfriend would have a fit if I started calling in the middle of the night."

"She wasn't with me." He placed his hand on mine. "If you're afraid, call for help. You don't have to do everything alone. I don't understand why you can't see that."

The second his hand touched mine a jolt of energy coursed through me. He felt it, too. I could tell by the way his mouth twitched. This time he didn't remove his hand.

"I imagined it," I reassured him, my mind immediately going to the other part of the conversation. Why wasn't he with Monica? They were obviously dating, and had been for at least several months. Were they not spending nights together?

"I don't care." Hunter was firm. "If you're afraid, call."

"Call you?"

"Yes." He answered without hesitation. "I'm a police officer. It's my job to keep the population safe."

That wasn't the answer I wanted, but it made sense. "Well ... ." Slowly, I withdrew my hand. Being in close proximity to him caused me to lose my head. He cleared his throat, perhaps feeling the same way, and turned back to Vera. "I wish I knew what was going on with them."

"Is there a way to find out?"

He shrugged. "Not that I can think of. I could go over there, but it's not as if they're going to volunteer information to a cop."

I tugged on my ear, considering. "What about Barry's son? He was, like, a year older than us."

Hunter's expression turned dark. "Bobby."

"Bobby Buttons." I laughed at the name.

"Are you seven?" He was giving me a hard time, but I liked the way his lips curved.

"It's a stupid name," I protested.

"It is a stupid name, and he's an annoying guy."

"Meaning?"

"Meaning that he still lives in high school. He still pretends who was popular back then matters. He still wears his letterman's jacket."

"You were a popular guy," I reminded him.

"Yes, but I don't still wear my letterman's jacket."

"That's because you don't have it."

"I ... ." He trailed off. "I forgot. You had it when we broke up."

"And you never got it back. I'm sorry."

He shrugged. "It's not like it's the end of the world. Once you're out of high school, a letterman's jacket is pretty useless."

"Yeah, but it was yours."

"I don't care." He flashed a smile that didn't make it all the way to his eyes. "Of all the things I lost that day, the letterman's jacket ranks dead last on the list of things that matter."

My heart constricted. "I ... ."

He barreled forward before I could say something stupid, which was for the best. "As for Bobby, he still hangs around at the high school, playing basketball in the afternoons."

"Seriously?" My eyebrows migrated north. "Who does he play with?"

"Other guys who can't let go of high school. Why do you care about Bobby?"

"I'm just thinking that Bobby might be able to shed some light on his father's relationship with Vera. If I remember correctly, Barry never could keep his mouth shut. If anybody knows the intricate details of their relationship, it's likely to be Bobby, because his dad told him."

"Maybe." Hunter turned thoughtful. "It's something to consider."

He flicked his eyes to the clock on the wall and straightened. "Geez. I didn't realize it was so late. I need to get going."

"Hot date?"

"Work. What about you?"

"I definitely don't have a hot date. Other than Sebastian, I've been spending all my time with my grandfather."

"Who keeps avoiding me. I can't figure out how he's dodging me."

I had a few ideas ... and I was related to all of them. "I'll tell him you stopped by again."

"For all the good that it will do."

I SHOWERED AND CHANGED CLOTHES after my shift. The kitten was passed out on my bed and I told myself I didn't want to wake him just to take him to the shelter. I figured that could wait, as long as I got some food to last through the night. Part of me knew I was playing a risky game by keeping him longer than necessary. The other part wasn't ready to say goodbye.

Hunter's tidbit about Bobby playing basketball at the high school had me heading there. It seemed odd that grown men — we're talking men pushing thirty — would still be hanging out at the school. Pickup games were a thing when we were seventeen and there was nothing to do. Now, though, it seemed sad.

Sure enough, when I turned the corner that led to the high school I found six men on the court sans shirts. They looked to be going at each other hard, all elbows and picks. I slowed my pace as I headed toward them, squinting to make out faces. Only one of them seemed even remotely familiar as I strolled up.

"Heads up!" a male voice yelled, causing me to instinctively cover my face and slide to the right. The ball that had been careening toward my head flew harmlessly to the side.

The sweaty man who raced over to collect the ball was the only one that I recognized. He offered up a lopsided grin as he regarded me.

"Stormy Morgan. You look exactly the same."

I wasn't sure if that was meant as a compliment. "Tristan Carter. You look ... great." That seemed to be the expected response, especially since he was standing in such a way that all his muscles were on full display. While he'd never been my favorite person in the world, I had to admit that his body was a masterpiece. He looked to spend long hours in the gym. It was working for him.

"Of course I do." Tristan winked before throwing the ball back to the other men. "I'll sit out the rest of this game. Be back for the next one."

There was some grumbling behind my back — I could just imagine what the other players were thinking — but I kept my full attention on Tristan. His hair was the same glossy black that I remembered and he had one of those chins that looked strong in profile but was weak straight on. His smile was exactly the same, and I could only imagine how many women he'd talked out of their panties since high school on the strength of that smile alone. Heck, the number was high even before we'd graduated.

"I heard you were back in town." Tristan used his forearm to wipe the sweat from his brow and took a long swig of water from the bottle he had stored next to the pile of shirts at the side of the court. "I didn't think it was possible ... but here you are."

"Here I am." I kept my smile in place even though being around him made my skin crawl. There was always something about him that I disliked. He had "date rapist" practically stamped on his forehead. At least that was my assumption as a teenager. As an adult, it still felt like the right call. "How are things for you?" I wanted to ask him about Bobby, but if I blurted out the question he might turn suspicious.

"Things are great." Tristan beamed. "I'm working for my father now."

Tristan's father owned the local resort, one of the few places people could find steady employment in the area. There were no factory jobs to speak of — they'd dried up decades ago — and other than a few garages, pickings were slim.

"Oh, yeah?" I feigned interest. "What do you do for him?"

"What don't I do?" His smile never faltered. "I do everything. My father wants to retire. He's making sure I'm capable of running every aspect of the business before handing it over to me."

"Wow. When do you think that will happen?"

"I don't know. Soon."

He essentially was admitting that he was trapped at the whim of his father. From what I knew of the man, he would keel over at his desk before handing the reins over to Tristan. Just like when we were in high school, Tristan was all about perception. He wanted people to think he was a big guy when he was really a small guy trying to walk around in his daddy's shoes.

"Well, it sounds like you're leading a very interesting life." I flicked my eyes to the other players. They were laughing and leering. It was obvious they thought Tristan was putting the moves on me, which I had no doubt he was about to attempt. "So ... I'm actually looking for someone." I changed tactics quickly. There was no sense prolonging the conversation. "Bobby Buttons. I heard he plays with you guys."

Tristan drew his eyebrows together. "Bobby? Why are you looking for him?"

"I just wanted to catch up with him."

"I don't remember you hanging out with him in high school."

"I don't really want to hang out with him. I just ... have something I want to ask him."

Tristan wrinkled his nose, dubious. "I don't know what to tell you. He's not here today. I think he had some work to do at his father's office."

"I didn't know he worked for his father, too. There must be something in the water."

"You work for your grandfather. That's what people are saying."

"I am back working for my grandfather," I agreed. "I was including myself in the statement."

His smile was back. For a few seconds, it appeared as if he was getting defensive. Now his world-famous charm was back on display. "Yes, I guess we're all where we're supposed to be. You got out for a bit. You were a big deal, on television and everything."

How I wished people would stop bringing up the television interview. It wasn't a fond memory, even though I thought it was a big deal at the time. Now it was something of an embarrassment, especially given the fact that my second book had barely been on the shelves for a month before it was relegated to the bargain bins. "And yet I'm back," I noted. "I guess all things happen for a reason."

"Maybe the reason is so we could hang out," he suggested.

That sounded like something that was never going to happen. "Never say never," I said. "About Bobby ... ."

"Forget about Bobby." Tristan's tone was forceful. "He always shows up when you least expect it ... or want it, for that matter. I'm sure he'll be at the bonfire tonight."

"What bonfire?"

"The one down by the river. The one we have every weekend."

I was taken aback. I thought for certain that Hunter's small group was the only one still hanging in that area. Apparently I was mistaken and I wasn't sure what I was supposed to make of it. "Are you talking about the old party spot?" I had to be sure.

He nodded. "We still hang out there every Friday."

That was so sad, but it benefitted me. "Then I guess I'll see you at the bonfire party tonight." I would be trying to hide from him, but he didn't need to know that.

"Or we could go together," he suggested slyly.

Oh, well, now he'd put me on the spot. If I said no, he'd take it as an insult. If I said yes, I'd want to die.

"I promised Alice I would hang out with her tonight," I lied smoothly. "She said she had plans for a party. I didn't realize it was a bonfire party. We'll be there together."

"Your cousin Alice?" Tristan made a face. "That's kind of one body too many for what I had in mind."

That's exactly what I was afraid of. "I can't dump her at the last second. It's rude. I'm sure we'll see you there."

I couldn't get away from the courts fast enough. Apparently some things never change, and Tristan was one of them. If anyone needed to embrace personal growth, he did. For now, I was free of him.

The night ahead was another story.

FIFTEEN

Alice was less than thrilled when I told her my plans for the night. "I don't want to drink in a field." She was incensed. "We're not in high school."

She had a point. That didn't mean I was going to allow her to wiggle out of this. "We ended up sitting on the floor drinking the other night. How is that any different?"

"Because we were inside — and there were no bugs."

"You need to get over the bugs."

"They're going to inherit the Earth when the zombie apocalypse comes."

Her response made me laugh. "I think that's cockroaches."

"Which are bugs."

I turned back to the mirror and touched up my mascara. This time I wanted to be prepared for a party. "You have to go with me. I told Tristan Carter that you were coming, and you know what a tool he is. If you're not there, he'll hit on me."

"So what?" Alice's brown eyes were fierce. She was having none of my crap this evening, which meant I was ultimately going to have to order her to accompany me. As older cousin, I had power. "He's hot. He's probably selfish in bed, but what does it matter?"

I was mortified. "I'm not sleeping with him."

"Why not?" Alice was blasé. "If anyone needs a good roll in the hay, it's you. Since you don't plan to stay, you might as well go for a guy who you hate. It just makes sense."

I thought about Hunter, about the discussion we'd had about my future. Then I saw Grandpa's smug face and felt conflicted. "I'm not dating Tristan." I was firm on that.

"Then why do you want to go to the bonfire? Is it because Hunter will be there?"

I'd had no confirmation that Hunter would be there. I made a face. "I'm going because Bobby Buttons is supposed to be there."

The look on Alice's face was comical. "You can't be serious."

"I need to talk to him."

"Bobby Buttons is definitely bad in bed," she argued.

I narrowed my eyes, suspicious. "How do you know?"

"Not *that* way." She looked disgusted. "I've heard from other people. He tries to be the world's fastest sprinter in a sport that requires technique. You do not want to be with him."

"I don't," I agreed. "I want to pump him for information. He's Barry Buttons' son, and Barry had his head bent together with Vera Axe in the restaurant today. They were talking a long time, about money."

Alice's expression reflected puzzlement. "Why do you care?"

"Because Roy died in the alley behind my apartment. I want to know who killed him."

"And this has nothing to do with Hunter?"

I jabbed my mascara tube in her direction. "I don't want to hear his name come out of your mouth one more time. Do you understand?"

Rather than quaking in fear, she rolled her eyes. "Please. You're still in love with Hunter. Everybody knows it."

"I am not!" My cheeks burned.

"You always have been." Alice clucked sympathetically and patted my arm. "It's okay. I've always known. That's the reason he and I never hooked up, even though he wanted to." She waggled her eyebrows suggestively. Alice, as a child, had an unfortunate habit of developing a crush on whatever guy I happened to be dating. She was much too young for most of them.

I glared at her. "Hunter wouldn't have dated you."

"Because he knew it would mean you would never date him again. There were times he was so broken-hearted I'm pretty sure he would've risked it."

That's not what I wanted to hear. "He wouldn't have dated you." That was one thing I knew with absolute certainty. "But this isn't about Hunter."

"No?" Alice cocked her head. "Are you sure that you're not chasing information because you want to help Hunter with his case?"

"That's absurd. Hunter doesn't need my help. I'm doing this to clear Grandpa." Even as the words left my mouth I realized how ridiculous they sounded.

"Grandpa didn't kill Roy." Alice stated it as fact. "He's too lazy. The only way he would kill Roy is if Roy somehow tripped over his lap while Grandpa was taking his afternoon constitution and newspapers were razors."

She had a point. "Then why is Grandpa hiding from Hunter?"

"He hates the police. Who doesn't?"

"I don't."

"You like just one police officer. Think about the rest you've ever met. They're all jerks. Remember Rod Ventimiglia?"

I frowned at mention of the name. "I remember. He looked like he should be doing porn in the seventies."

Alice snorted and took the mascara from me. "That's the guy. He was selling drugs out of the back of his cruiser and was caught, like, five times before they arrested him. He makes cops look bad."

"Hunter's not bad."

She sent me a knowing smirk. "He's not."

"I don't have feelings for him," I stressed.

"If you say so." She didn't look convinced. "I'm not in the mood to drink in a field. Why can't we drink here? We had fun the other night. We just won't use the Ouija board this time."

I'd forgotten about the Ouija board. "Yeah, speaking of that ... ." I searched for the right words to express the unease that had been creeping over me the last few days. "Has anything weird happened to you since we played with that board?"

Alice was fixated on her reflection. "Like what?"

Like waking up floating over your bed ... or intense feelings of being watched. "Like anything."

Slowly she slid her eyes to me. "No. Should something weird have happened?"

I got the distinct impression she was playing coy. "I guess not." Now wasn't the time to pick a fight. I needed her to be my wing woman at the party. "You're going to the bonfire. I need backup to make sure Tristan stays away."

Alice sighed. "Fine. If there are any hot guys we don't know, I have dibs."

"Fair enough. You can have all the hot guys."

"Except Hunter, right? He would totally go for me if you weren't an obstacle."

I gritted my teeth. "Just get ready. I want to be out there early." Something occurred to me. "Do we need to take beer with us?"

"They usually have a keg."

I was flabbergasted. "We really are still stuck in high school, huh?"

"You have no idea. Just wait until the thirty-year-old men start streaking because they think it's cool."

I hoped she was exaggerating. Like, really, really hoped.

THE CLEARING WAS ALREADY PACKED WITH people. I tried to count heads but lost the thread around forty.

"This can't be right." I clutched my hoodie tighter and studied the faces. "What are all these people doing out here?"

Alice looked amused at my surprise. "There's nothing to do in Shadow Hills. We really need a movie theater or something. It's basically this or bowling, and we're too young to own our own bowling shoes."

I had news for her. I was never going to be old enough to own my own bowling shoes. "I guess we should find a place to sit."

"Yeah, I'm not standing all night."

Alice called out greetings as we cut through the crowd. Several people waved at me, said they couldn't wait to catch up later, and then went right back to talking to other people. I didn't recognize most of them. The fact that they remembered me was daunting.

"Should I know who these people are?" I asked as we claimed two nylon chairs on the side of the bonfire out of the line of smoke.

"You did go to school with them," she said as she flopped into the chair, stretching out her legs in front of her. "Oh, hey, these things have handy-dandy cup holders." Alice perked up. "We need drinks to put in them."

I nodded. "You get them. I'll keep my eyes opened for Bobby."

She hopped up and took off in the direction of the keg, leaving me to study the crowd. Her seat didn't remain empty long, because Tristan — who I hadn't initially seen — slid into it within seconds of her leaving.

"Hello." He shot me a flirtatious smile as I tried to hide my dismay. "I see you came after all."

"I said I was coming." I kept my tone light as I looked anywhere but at his face. "Alice is with me."

"She is? That's weird. I didn't see her." He kicked back and crossed his ankles, pinning me with a blinding smile. Seriously, if this whole "working for his father" thing didn't pan out he could have a future in Colgate commercials. "Tell me everything about your life for the past ten years."

If I had a drink, I would've choked. That was such a ridiculous request. "Um ... I graduated from high school, went to college, wrote two books, and now I'm back here."

"I know that. I want to know the nitty-gritty. I've always found you fascinating."

That was news to me. "I'm not all that interesting."

"I beg to differ. You've always been fascinating. Isn't that right, Hunter?"

I froze when I realized someone else had joined the party. Very slowly, deliberately, I glanced over my shoulder and found Hunter with Monica glued to his side. I forced myself to swallow because my mouth had gone suddenly dry. "Hey."

"Hello." Hunter's tone was cool. I didn't miss the icy glare he lobbed in Tristan's direction. "I didn't realize you two were spending time together."

"We're not," I offered hurriedly. "I'm here with Alice."

"But she's trading up in the world and hanging out with me," Tristan said pointedly. "We had a charming interlude this afternoon at the basketball courts."

Hunter's eyes narrowed. "The basketball courts?" I could practically see the gears of his mind working.

"I stopped by looking for Bobby Buttons," I explained. I didn't owe him any justification for my actions, yet I couldn't seem to shut my mouth. "I ran into Tristan."

"It was fate." Tristan's grin was wide. Unfortunately, the smile had very little to do with me. I realized that almost immediately, because his attention was fixated on Hunter. This was all about him.

"Oh." I exhaled heavily, realization dawning. "I get it now."

"What do you get?" Tristan asked, jerking his eyes to me. He looked ready to throw down, which I found interesting ... and mildly distressing. Monica also seemed to sense trouble. She'd begun tugging on Hunter's arm in an effort to snag his attention.

"I get that ... Alice has my beer." I was on my feet as fast as I could manage and swooped toward Alice. She seemed surprised by my excited approach. "Thanks so much." I sucked from the cup, trying not to make a face at the taste of the beer. "Is this Milwaukee's Best?"

Hunter smirked. "We're classy. What can I say?"

"It's terrible, but beggars can't be choosers," Alice said, taking the seat I'd just vacated without asking. "What are we talking about?"

"Stormy was going to tell us what she got. She said 'I get it now,' but didn't say what it was that she got," Tristan prodded.

"Like anyone cares," Monica muttered, staring into the distance.

Hunter slid her a dark look but said nothing. I was looking for an escape. I caught sight of Bobby.

"I see someone I need to talk to." I flashed a smile at Monica while steadfastly ignoring Tristan. "It was great seeing you again, Monica. You look really lovely." With that, I spun on my heel and took off in the opposite direction, leaving Alice to clean up my mess. I knew she would complain about it when next we crossed paths, but I didn't care. Getting away from Tristan was the most important thing on my immediate to-do list. I could only hope he would find someone else to focus on in my absence.

Bobby was tipsy when I caught up to him.

"Hey."

He jolted at the sound of my voice, almost tipping over with a clumsy turn. "Um ... hi. Do I know you?"

It wasn't the greeting I expected, but it was an opening. "Stormy Morgan. We went to high school together. You were a year ahead of me."

"Oh, right." Bobby nodded, as if he recognized me, but the vacant expression in his eyes told me that I was just one of many faces he couldn't put a name to this evening.

"You should probably sit down." I grabbed Bobby's arm and led him to a fallen tree, pushing his shoulders so that he sat. "I wonder if they bring water out here." I was talking more to myself than him, but he answered.

"Water?" He made a face. "Who wants water?"

"I think you should have some water."

"I think I need some beer." He made to stand but fell backward with a grunt as he hit the ground.

This wasn't how I saw the evening going.

"What were you thinking?" Alice hissed as she appeared out of nowhere, making me jump.

I looked over her shoulder to make sure Tristan hadn't followed. Thankfully, she was alone. "I'm not sure what you mean," I lied easily.

"Oh, don't even." She narrowed her eyes to dangerous slits. "You know exactly what you did."

"I'm sure you're mistaken." I moved around to the other side of the tree and stood over Bobby, who had given up trying to right himself. He remained stretched out on the ground, his legs still propped up on the tree, staring at the darkening sky.

"Sunsets are really pretty," he noted, a small smile playing at the corners of his mouth. "You're really pretty, too, Sally."

"Stormy," I corrected, pinching the bridge of my nose.

"Is he already drunk?" Alice asked, moving to my side. She seemed to have forgotten she was angry at me in the wake of Bobby's graceful showing.

"Apparently so, but I don't see how that's possible. The party barely started twenty minutes ago."

"Yeah, but he doesn't have the best reputation." Alice hunkered down and pressed her finger to the spot between Bobby's eyebrows, laughing at the way his eyes crossed as he tried to see what she was doing. "This is fun."

That was so not the word I would use to describe what was happening. "We need to sober him up if we expect to get information out of him." I would never talk about someone directly in front of them — that's just bad manners — but it was obvious Bobby wouldn't remember anything we'd said. He was five quiet minutes away from passing out.

"I thought we wanted him drunk so he would talk," Alice argued.

"There's drunk and there's drunk." I inclined my head to where Bobby was moving his hands as if making snow angels. "We need him moderately drunk, not doing ... whatever it is he's doing."

"I'm making grass angels," Bobby announced, grinning.

His response was enough to make Alice laugh. "I see what you mean. I'll see if I can round up some water."

"And I'll see if I can get him in a sitting position." I grabbed Bobby under his armpits and tugged, easing up when something occurred to me. "Did Hunter say anything after I left you guys?"

Alice was already five feet away but she stopped and turned, the impish dimple in her cheek coming out to play. "How much is it worth to you?"

I scowled. "A real friend would tell me without the blackmail."

"Hey, you made me come out here against my will. Now you're making me sober up that idiot. I deserve something for all this effort."

She had a point. "I'll take all the morning shifts next week." Sure, Grandpa had already told me I was stuck with the earliest shifts until I passed probation, but she didn't need to know that.

"Sold." She grinned happily. "I hate working morning shifts."

That made two of us. Resigned to my fate, I blew out a sigh and turned my focus back to Bobby. "You'd better be worth all this effort."

"We should make dirt angels, too. Or ... wait ... how do mud angels sound?"

Like a nightmare in the making. That's exactly how they sounded.

SIXTEEN

S obering up Bobby so we could pump him for information wasn't easy. Finally, under threat of banning him from beer for life (he was drunk enough to believe we had that power), he agreed to drink his water and talk. He rambled from subject to subject.

"Were you this hot in high school?" His eyes roamed my body in a way that made me uncomfortable.

"I was really hot in high school," Alice announced. She'd never suffered from low self-esteem, something I greatly admired about her.

Bobby barely flicked his eyes to her before turning back to me. "I was talking to Stormy."

"Oh, so now you remember my name." I flashed a smile I didn't really feel. "That's ... convenient."

"It just came to me." Bobby's expression was glazed and I knew he was probably in that strange limbo where he thought he was perfectly coherent but would spiral fast. It was time to take advantage of that.

"I don't really remember you from high school," I started, debating how I wanted to approach the situation.

"That's because you were in your own little world with Hunter Ryan." Bobby made a face. "God, I hated that guy. Every girl in the school was in love with him because he was supposedly some great athlete. He only had eyes for you."

My heart gave a little jump. "We spent a lot of time together." Why did people constantly feel the need to bring up a high school relationship? It was unnecessary ... and stupid ... and it made my heart hurt. "That's what teenagers do. They fall hard and then move on."

Except you haven't moved on, a small voice whispered. I was brutal when I shoved it back. "We're here to talk about you, Bobby." I forced myself to be upbeat. "How is your life?"

"It's stupid." Bobby stared at his grubby fingernails. "I mow lawns for a living."

He looked so morose I momentarily felt sorry for him. "You're a landscaper?"

"No. I mow lawns." Bobby leaned back and stared at the sky, as if he was searching for something specific. "I still live with my father and everything. My girlfriend keeps breaking up with me because she says I'm going nowhere. My father agrees. He's really disappointed in me. He wanted me to become a lawyer, too."

"Did you have trouble passing the bar?" I asked.

"I never got that far. I couldn't pass the regular classes to even make it into law school." He leaned against the log and let loose a wistful sigh. "Whatever, right? It doesn't matter."

It obviously mattered to him. I decided to direct him toward a different subject. "Is it hard living with your father?"

Bobby's expression darkened. "He's a pompous ass."

"I bet. I saw him in the restaurant earlier today."

"What restaurant?" Bobby was distracted by the moon.

"Two Broomsticks. I work there."

"Oh, right. The family restaurant." Bobby's eyes were still full of drunken lust when they landed on me. "You didn't live up to your potential either. We should totally hang out together. We can be screw-ups together."

"That's a lovely offer." I wrinkled my nose. "I'm not quite ready to admit defeat yet."

"Yeah. I can see that. You're pretty ... and you don't live with your father." Bobby scowled. "He's such a jerk. He won't stop yelling at me to get a proper job and get out of his house. I warned him that I would sue to stay if he wasn't careful. I saw a guy who did that on television. His parents wanted to kick him out, but he took them to court."

I'd seen that story, too. I was fairly certain the individual in question had lost ... and rightfully so. "So ... your father was at the restaurant with Vera Axe." Bobby needed to be led directly to the topic. "I thought it was weird, because he's a divorce attorney and Vera is a widow."

Bobby blinked several times in rapid succession and I thought for sure he would go off on another tangent. Instead, he actually managed to focus. "That's because Vera was trying to divorce Roy before his death. It had been going on for, like, three years. It wasn't a big deal."

I begged to differ. "I'm not sure I understand. Why was Vera trying to divorce Roy?"

"You've met him. I think the better question is: Why did Vera marry Roy in the first place?"

"If Vera wanted to divorce Roy three years ago, why were they still married?"

"She wasn't going to get nearly as much money as she thought she would," Bobby replied, picking at a stray thread on his jeans. "That's the problem for a lot of women. They watch television and assume they're going to get piles of money in a divorce. They think it's true for everybody ... even if that person has zero money."

I pictured Roy's office. "I thought Roy was doing relatively well. Are local real estate prices down?"

"It depends on the real estate," Bobby replied blandly. "Businesses are being snapped up. People have offered your grandfather a ton of money for that restaurant."

That was news to me. "They have?"

"They want to take advantage of what Hemlock Cove is doing. They're getting stronger every year because of that witch thing. Your grandfather's restaurant even has a witch name already established to take advantage of. I always wondered about that name."

"That makes two of us," I said dryly, hunkering down so I was on an even level with Bobby. It was obvious he wasn't going to last much longer before passing out. I had to get my answers now. "Are you saying Vera didn't file for divorce because she wasn't going to get any money out of the deal?" That seemed a terrible reason to stay with a jackass like Roy Axe.

"It wasn't just that." Bobby started plucking at the grass. "She was angry when she found out he'd been throwing money around on another woman and assumed it was because he was cheating."

Jackpot! "Who was he cheating with?"

Bobby shrugged. "Some woman who worked in his office. He had to pay her off because she left under suspicious circumstances and everyone assumed it was because of some affair. I don't know what those circumstances were, so don't ask. Because I know you're going to ask. I just heard my father talking and knew Vera was pissed because all the money Roy had put away for their retirement was going to another woman."

I exchanged a weighted look with Alice. "Do you know who he's talking about?"

She shook her head. "Roy's had a bunch of women in and out of that office over the years. I always assumed it was because he was a pervert."

"It probably is because he's a pervert. We need to find out which woman he was paying off."

"Because you think she might've killed off Roy?"

"She might at least have some insight for us. Roy might've been worth more dead than alive to Vera. Maybe she killed him off because of this."

Alice's gaze brightened. "I hadn't considered that. I'll ask around and see if I can figure out who it was."

I nodded and stood, casting a look back at Bobby, who had passed out. "Should we just leave him here?"

"He'll be fine." Alice offered up a haphazard wave. "From what I've heard, this is a regular occurrence. He'll sleep it off for a bit and then go home."

"Yeah, but ... he's sleeping with his head against a tree."

"So? Maybe he'll wake up with a sore back and rethink his decisions. If not, it's still not our fault. He decided to get drunk before it even turned dark."

She had a point. "Speaking of drinking ... ." I cast my eyes back to the growing crowd. "Do you want to stay? I know you weren't keen on it before and I have my information now." My eyes scanned for Hunter. I let out a breath when I realized he was still present. Monica was with him, but there was always a chance I might get to talk with him when she was distracted.

"We can stay," Alice said, pursing her lips. "There's no sense running back now."

I was instantly suspicious. "You want to see if you can land Tristan, don't you?"

She was suddenly the picture of innocence. "I have no interest in dating him."

"That's not what I said. You just want to see if you can land him."

Her expression turned mischievous. "I *might* want to land him," she conceded after a beat. "He seems interested in you, though."

What she wasn't saying was that she wanted to land him specifically because his interest was directed at me. It was a game to her. It always had been. I didn't care. If she could distract him for the rest of the night, I'd be more than happy to declare her winner of this particular battle.

"Let's get another beer," I suggested. "It's not as bad as I remember."

"Oh, it's awful. But it doesn't matter. You'll drink anything as long as you can stare at Hunter."

I shot her a dirty look. "I don't care about Hunter. You need to let that go."

She didn't bother to hide her eye roll. "If you say so."

HANGING OUT WITH EVERYONE after we'd gathered the information turned out to be a good idea. I saw so many faces that I'd forgotten about in the years since I'd left Shadow Hills that I had a great time catching up. I was having so much fun that I almost forgot I wanted to pay special attention to the way Hunter and Monica interacted — just in case there was a vibe they might be trying to hide. And then I ran into Hunter by the keg.

"Hey." My cheeks were flushed from laughing when I bumped into him, my empty cup clutched in hand. "Are you having fun?"

He looked me up and down a moment and then nodded. "Sure. I'm here at least once a month. I don't think it's quite as novel for me."

"I've seen so many people."

"I've noticed. You've been a social butterfly."

"Cassandra Dean is over there. She married Byron Presley and they have five kids already. Five kids and she's twenty-eight." I was still doing the math. "She says she's gone three years without a cocktail because she's been pregnant so much. I can't imagine that."

Hunter cracked a smile. "That does seem like cruel and unusual punishment, huh?"

"The thought of kids freaks me out." I had no idea why I admitted it. I was a little tipsy, which wouldn't end up going over well with Grandpa. I was going to have to start limiting my alcohol intake now that I was in a place where the only fun people had was getting together in a field to drink. That could get dangerous fast if I wasn't careful.

"You don't want kids?" Hunter's eyes were probing as he scanned my face.

I shrugged, unsure how I actually felt about the question. "Shouldn't I be able to take care of myself before I become responsible for another human being? I mean ... I'm living in the apartment above the restaurant. I can't even afford the full rent right now."

Hunter's eyes flooded with sympathy. "You'll get back on your feet."

I often wondered if that were true. "I hope so. I'm not sure how much more of this I can take."

"What do you mean?"

"All of ... this." I gestured toward the crowd. The sun had set two hours before and it was dark except for the fire and several lanterns. "Guess what everyone wanted to know when they came up to me."

"Why you were back," Hunter answered. "You can't fault them for that, Stormy. When you left, it was a big deal because almost nobody gets out of here. Then you were on television, for crying out loud, and to everyone stuck in this town that meant you were famous."

I scowled. "I wish people would stop bringing that up. It's the worst thing that ever happened to me."

My response elicited a genuine smile. It was still heart-shatteringly charming, and I hadn't seen nearly enough of it since I'd been back. "I liked the interview."

"You watched it?" I was surprised. That would've been four years after we'd broken up. It couldn't have been easy for him.

"Like I would've missed that." He winked and I felt a small jolt of energy rush through me. "Everyone in town was talking about it. Your grandfather put up a sign above the coffee counter alerting everyone."

"He did?" Tears pricked the back of my eyes. "I can't believe he did that."

"Yeah, well, he did. He was so proud. He told everyone who entered the restaurant that they had to buy your book. He even offered deals for people who showed him a copy of your book."

"I didn't know."

"That's because you never came back during that time." His tone turned accusatory. "It was as if you forgot about everyone in Shadow Hills."

"It wasn't that," I countered quickly. "It was just ... everyone wanted a piece of me during that time. Everyone thought I had something to give. I had to travel all over the United States and sign books at libraries. I was on the road every single day that year. I didn't even have an apartment."

"You didn't?" He looked flabbergasted. "But where was all your stuff?"

"I don't have any stuff," I said. "I have ... nothing. Everything I own can fit in a suitcase."

"That doesn't seem right."

I shrugged. "It is what it is."

"It makes me sad."

He wasn't the only one. "I let things get out of control back then. I don't know why, but I thought it was what I was supposed to want and I went with it. And when it came time to write my second book, I did what I thought I was supposed to do. I figured that would guarantee success. But it didn't.

"When I failed, I found out pretty quickly that none of those people who were so quick to befriend me when I was on *The View* wanted to hang around," I continued. "Before I realized it, I was alone and trying to find inspiration and ... it was over. It was already over at that point, but I didn't see it."

Hunter shook his head. "It's not over. You loved writing more than anybody I knew. You'd absolutely lose yourself in the worlds you created. Don't you remember telling me about those places? You had joy in the process. You'll find that again. You're just going through a bad spot."

"I don't even know if I want it." The words were out before I thought better of them. I wasn't sure if I meant them or was simply feeling sorry for myself.

"What?" Hunter was shocked. "Of course you want it."

Did I? "I'm starting to realize that I gave up everything to get one thing that I thought I wanted. I don't know that it was worth it. Giving up everything, I mean. I feel so empty most of the time."

I didn't know I was crying until Hunter used his thumb to wipe the tear from my cheek. "You listen here," he said in a stern voice, leaning close enough so that only I could hear. "I always knew you would do great things. That hasn't changed. You might not have gotten everything you thought you would the first go-around, but you have plenty of chances to try again.

"Life isn't one strike and you're out, Stormy," he continued. "You have infinite chances to get what you want. You just have to decide what it is that you really want."

He was so earnest. I was just about to tell him that, thank him for bolstering my spirits, when Tristan rounded the nearby tree. I saw him out of the corner of my eye and cringed when his eyes lit up. "Oh, geez."

Hunter followed my gaze and frowned. "I didn't realize he was still here. I thought he'd left."

"We're not that lucky."

"There you are." Tristan swooped in and positioned himself directly between Hunter and me, boxing out my ex-boyfriend and trapping me. "I thought you forgot about me."

"I've been catching up with people," I said. "I could never forget about you."

"Of course not. I'm memorable."

Hunter rolled his eyes behind Tristan's back. "Most douches are," he muttered, forcing me to press my lips together to keep from laughing. "It's just not for the reason you want to believe."

Tristan's gaze darkened. "Do you have something you want to say, Hunter?"

Hunter managed to blank his face, but it looked as if it took monumental effort. "I'm good. Thanks."

"Then you should probably get back to your girlfriend," Tristan said pointedly. "Last time I checked, she was on the other side of the clearing looking for you. She couldn't figure out where you went."

"She's a smart girl," Hunter shot back. "She'll eventually find me."

"I think she already has." Tristan's expression was smug as he inclined his head toward a spot behind me.

When I turned, my heart plummeted to my stomach at the look on Monica's face. She was furious ... and I really couldn't blame her. I wouldn't be happy to find my boyfriend hanging out with his ex. Etiquette demanded she call him on deserting her to hang out with me, and it looked as if she was about to do just that.

"There you are." She stomped over, her eyebrows knitting together when she caught sight of me. "What's going on?"

"Nothing is going on," Hunter replied smoothly. "Everybody was just talking."

"Well, actually Stormy and Hunter were talking when I found them," Tristan countered. "They had their heads together and looked to be having a very serious conversation."

I frowned. Tristan always did enjoy stirring the pot. "It was innocent. We were just talking."

The plea fell on deaf ears. Monica's face contorted into something straight out of a horror movie. "Is that so?" The look she pinned Hunter with sent shivers down my spine. He was probably quaking in his hiking boots, though he looked perfectly calm in the face of her fury. "Do you want to explain yourself?"

"Not really." He was calm as he gathered my cup and started toward the keg. "Stormy and I were talking. That's it."

"He was stroking her cheek," Tristan snapped. "Don't bother denying it, *officer*. I saw everything. You had your thumb on her cheek."

He must've been watching us longer than we realized. "My eyes have been burning from the bonfire smoke," I lied. "He just wiped away a tear." That wasn't entirely untrue.

"I knew this was going to happen," Monica snapped, her eyes flashing with mayhem. "I just knew it. I warned you that she would try to suck you in, Hunter. She's obviously still attracted to you. She's a user. She doesn't really want you. She's just bored. Are you really going to let her destroy our relationship because you're still harboring a crush on her after all these years?"

Despite my best efforts, my temper flashed. "Hey!"

Monica swiveled so fast she almost knocked me over with her flying hair.

"It's the truth," she hissed. "I'm not an idiot. I knew from the moment I saw you that you were after my man. Well, guess what? You can't have him.

"I know everyone in this town talks about the Hunter and Stormy mystique as if you guys were something special, but you were teenagers," she continued. "It was puppy love. He and I have the real thing. No matter how you try to ruin it, you'll never be equal to me. I'm an adult, and I didn't have to come running home to live with my grandfather because I couldn't control my own life."

My temper flared, anger I didn't know I possessed taking root. My hands clenched into fists at my sides and I was certain I would lose control and pummel her face. Instead, something wrenched free from inside of me and pushed through my chest in an explosion of energy.

I couldn't explain it. Heck, I couldn't even see it. I could only feel it, and apparently I wasn't the only one.

At the exact moment my anger grew teeth and attacked, Monica cried out, her hands immediately going to her forehead.

"What was that?" she screeched.

"What was what?" Hunter snapped. He looked angry. His disappointment was aimed directly at Monica. "What are you complaining about now?"

"My eyebrows! They're ... on fire."

Hunter rolled his eyes and nudged away her hands, his eyes widening when he saw what used to be her eyebrows. She was right. The perfect arches were definitely burning. In fact, they'd burned completely off. The only hair left were the scraggly remnants of what had once been magnificently mani-cured half circles.

"How did that happen?" He looked dumbfounded.

That was nothing compared to what I felt. He didn't realize it — and I certainly couldn't say it — but I had a sneaking suspicion I was responsible.

SEVENTEEN

C onfusion reigned for several minutes as Hunter wiped the singed hair
from Monica's face. By the time he finished, there was nothing left
other than a stray hair. She looked ... well, she looked ridiculous, which
would've made me happy under different circumstances. I was convinced I'd
somehow caused it, though, so I was mired in a tidal wave of panic.

"What does it look like?" Monica asked, her lower lip trembling.

"It looks fine," Hunter lied quickly.

Tristan burst out laughing. "It looks stupid. How did you even manage
that?"

I was distinctly uncomfortable with the question and tried to maintain a
calm veneer — complete with a quizzical expression right out of a Lifetime
movie. I feared someone would figure out I was the source of whatever had
happened.

"I didn't do anything," Monica snapped. "I was just standing here. I want to
see."

"It's fine," Hunter repeated, although I got the distinct impression he was
trying to refrain from laughing. "It gives your face ... character."

Monica's glare only deepened. "Give me a mirror."

"I don't have a mirror."

Her eyes moved to me. "Give me your mirror."

It took me a moment to recover my voice. "I don't have a mirror either.
Sorry."

"You did this," she hissed, causing my heart to flutter. "You did this to me."

I opened my mouth to protest, but I wasn't sure I could deliver the denial with any form of plausibility. Thankfully, Hunter swooped in to save me from having to argue on my own behalf.

"How did she do it?" he challenged, calm. "She was standing a good three feet away. She never touched you."

"Oh, she did it." Monica refused to back down, her fingers going to the spots where her eyebrows used to be. "You saw the way she was looking at me."

"And how was that?" Hunter squared his shoulders and shook his head. "You were attacking her, and needlessly. She hasn't done anything to you. Going after her the way you did, it just reinforces your insecurity. You need to get over it."

Monica growled. "Are you blaming this on me?"

"No, but ... you didn't need to yell at her. We were just talking. We've known each other a long time. There's nothing going on between us."

"I think there's only one way to prove that," Tristan interjected. "Stormy should go out with me and then everybody will be happy. And you can put all those ugly rumors to rest about the status of your long-dead relationship." The smile he sent me was blinding — and stomach-churning.

"I think I should go." I refused to dignify Tristan's half-hearted date offer with an answer that was likely to make things worse — if that was even possible.

"You can't leave until you fix this," Monica insisted, gesturing toward her brow.

"How am I supposed to fix that?" I was at a loss. "I'm not a cosmetologist."

"And she didn't cause the problem," Hunter insisted.

"Then how did it happen?" Monica demanded.

"Were you by the fire?" Hunter, ever practical, immediately went to what he thought was a rational answer. "Maybe a spark landed in your eyebrows and didn't ignite until you came over here."

"That is the stupidest thing I've ever heard," Monica shot back.

"No stupider than you insisting that Stormy somehow did it," Hunter argued. "She didn't touch you. She's not some magical being from another planet. You've been drinking. You probably did it to yourself and don't realize it."

"I didn't do it to myself!"

I was over the conversation. Completely and totally over it. "I really have to go." I edged away from the group, desperately searching for Alice so we could make our escape. "It was great catching up. I'll see you later."

ALICE MAY HAVE GIVEN UP ON TRYING to snag Tristan for the evening — apparently he was making it impossible for her to corner him and turn on the charm — but she wasn't ready to leave.

"I'm not done yet."

"You're done." I was insistent as I dragged her away, ignoring her whining until we were at least a quarter of a mile away from the party. It was only then that she stopped fighting my efforts.

"First you make me go to a party I don't want to go to and then you drag me away before I'm ready to leave," she groused, scuffing her shoe against the ground as she glared. "When do we get to do something I want to do?"

"When you come up with a good idea," I muttered, my mind busy as I contemplated what had happened. The initial surprise had given way to panic. I had no doubt I was the reason Monica no longer had eyebrows. How, though? Was it even possible? It didn't feel possible.

"What's up with you?" Alice asked after a few minutes. She was watching me with keen eyes. "Did something happen with Hunter?"

"Of course not." The answer was automatic. "Stop assuming something will happen with Hunter. We're just ... friends." Even saying the word felt wrong. There was no denying the way my body reacted whenever we were near each other. There was a spark there, something that hadn't been smothered by our time apart. For all I knew, it was the sort of spark that would never die, which was frustrating on several levels.

"I saw you talking to him," Alice persisted. "It looked like a deep conversation."

"We were catching up on old times."

"Oh, it was definitely more than that. He was staring at you as if you were the only woman in the world."

"He was not."

"He was. You just can't see it because you're too close to the situation. He was there with another woman and all he cared about was you. If I were Monica, I'd dump him ... and fast. He's going to make her look like a fool before it's all said and done."

Given Monica's reaction this evening, I had a feeling she already felt like a fool. "Do you remember what happened with the Ouija board the other night?" I asked, opting to change the subject.

Alice's forehead wrinkled. "I remember. We were drunk and asking it stupid questions, like if Hunter and I would've been married by now if you hadn't stolen him from me."

I shot her a sidelong look. "We didn't ask that."

"You were drunk. You don't remember."

"I would remember that."

"If you say so." She rolled her eyes and focused on the uneven path. "Why are you asking about the Ouija board?"

"Because ... ." Could I tell her? Would she think I was crazy? More importantly, would she rat me out to the rest of the family and have me locked up for believing something so ludicrous?

"You might as well tell me," Alice offered, as if reading my mind. "Even if I make fun of you — and that is a distinct possibility — it's not as if you have anyone else to talk to. I'm your best bet."

Sadly, that was true. She was pretty much the only one I could talk to. "Weird things have been happening to me," I blurted out, the tension I'd been carrying in my chest immediately lessening. "I mean ... like, *really* weird things."

"I need more information."

"Well, for starters, I woke up floating over my bed the other day." I launched into the tale, leaving nothing out. Alice guffawed so loudly when I got to the part about trying to swim through the air I thought she would fall over. A dirty look from me had her righting herself quickly. "It's not funny."

"It's not funny," she agreed, wiping at the corners of her eyes. She was a masterful liar under normal circumstances, but she wasn't even trying this evening. "You have to admit that picturing you trying to swim to your bed is humorous."

"That's just a different word for funny!" I exploded.

Alice looked around as if expecting people to come out of the trees and join us. "Calm down," she chided. "There's no sense getting worked up."

"How can you say that? I was floating over my bed."

"Or you were dreaming."

I hesitated. "I thought that was the case, but it's not the only weird thing that's happened. There have been other things."

"Like?"

"Like last night when I went down to get the kitten."

"The kitten you're not keeping even though you bought a bunch of tuna to feed it?"

I ignored the question. "When I went down there, things were perfectly calm and fine. After a few minutes, though, I was convinced someone was watching me."

"That happens to me all the time," Alice countered. "We can freak ourselves out easier than others can. Don't you remember when we were kids and we'd walk through the cornfields out on the highway? You told me about *Children of the Corn* and we were terrified for a full week. You knew it was a stupid story, but you were still frightened."

"I was, like, thirteen."

"That doesn't change the fact that we can scare ourselves without meaning to," Alice argued. "Think about it. You were down there with a kitten, realized you were completely alone, and if someone wanted to hurt you, you were vulnerable. That little pebble you inserted into your brain turned into a big boulder and you freaked out."

It sounded so reasonable. "I also think I burned Monica's eyebrows off her face."

This time the look Alice shot me was incredulous. "Um ... what?"

I told her about the altercation at the keg, leaving nothing out. When I finished, she focused on a random detail.

"What's the deal with Tristan?" she complained. "I basically did a dirty dance in front of him and put these on display, but nothing." She grabbed her ample bosom and gave it a squeeze. "Nobody can say no to these."

"Is that really important?" I challenged, frustration getting the better of me. "Tristan is essentially what happens when you step in dog crap and it dries over a five-day period. You're never truly getting rid of that stain after that. We're talking about me here."

"We *are* talking about you," Alice agreed. "We're talking about you and Hunter. What were you saying to one another that got Monica so riled up that she'd attack you that way? I've never really cared for her — she's a witch with a B, if you want to know the truth — but she's usually smart enough not to attack her enemies so openly. You must be deranging her.

"I have to say that I did see it coming," she continued. "I knew she wasn't long for Hunter's world the second I heard you were coming back. I thought he would put up more than a token fight, though — you know, really dig his heels in — but it's as if he's already ceded the battle."

I stared at her for a long time. "We're not talking about Hunter," I snapped, the frustration I'd been trying to tamp down for almost an hour returning with a vengeance. "We're talking about the fact that I think I burned Monica's eyebrows off."

Alice snorted. "There's no way you did that."

"I think I did. It's all a blur, but I swear I felt something rip free from inside of me."

"It's probably all that pent-up lust you've been hiding away for Hunter. I bet if you guys ever hit the sheets — and we all know it's going to happen, because it's been, like, five days and you guys can't stay away from each other — that you'll scorch the world it'll be so intense. Okay, maybe not the first time. You'll both be awkward and stiff the first time, but after that, I bet it'll be really good. You should jump on that and then tell me all about it so I can live vicariously through you."

I wanted to choke her. "I'm serious," I gritted out, my hands clenching and unclenching at my sides. "I know I did that to Monica. You can deny it all you want, but it's true. I burned her eyebrows off."

"But ... how?" Alice's expression was blank. "How could you have possibly done it unless ... ." She trailed off, uncertain.

I waited for her to continue. When she didn't, I almost screamed to drag her back to the conversation. "Unless what?"

"Well, there is this one thing." She chewed her bottom lip, and for the first time since I'd started talking about the weird things that had been happening to me, she looked concerned.

"I'll kill you if you don't spill," I threatened.

"I heard Grandma talking once," Alice explained. "She was arguing with Grandpa. I didn't think much of it. They always argue. She was mad because he made a huge mess in the kitchen and didn't clean it up.

"Anyway, she was yelling and said to him, 'I'm not your mother. It's not as if I can magically clean the kitchen,'" she continued. "I thought it was a weird thing to say, but Grandpa started yelling back that he didn't want someone who could magically clean the kitchen, that he didn't like witches, and that's why he married her instead of the woman his mother wanted him to marry."

"Witch?"

Alice nodded. "That's the word she used."

I ran my tongue over my teeth as I considered the possibilities. "Do you think she was accusing Great-Grandma of being a witch?"

Alice shrugged. "I don't know. It sounded that way to me — especially now looking back. What are the odds, though? I think we would know if there were witches in our family."

My knowledge of Great-Grandma was scant. She'd moved from the area when I was still a small child, leaving the restaurant in Grandpa's capable hands. Still, the name Two Broomsticks had always seemed weird, yet nobody ever talked about why the name stuck. The only thing I knew is that Great-

Grandma entrusted the restaurant to Grandpa with the caveat that nobody ever change the name.

I swallowed hard. "She's due for a visit in about a month, right?"

Alice nodded "Yeah. I don't think you can just wander up to her and ask if you're a witch, though. That might come out wrong — especially if you're still hiding from your mother. She's going crazy because you refuse to visit, by the way. She's spending all her time complaining to my mother."

I wasn't surprised. Her mother, my mother, and our Aunt Trina were a terrifying trio. They fought constantly, and then made up and fought with everybody else in town.

"Why do you think I'm avoiding her?" I said, turning my attention back to the pathway. "She's being a pain and I like to get her really good and angry before having to see her. That usually cuts down on the invasive questions as she spends half the get-together reminding herself that she's angry with me."

"Well, at least you've thought it through." Alice went back to annoyingly scuffing her feet. "What are you going to do in the meantime?"

"About what? And, if you ask me about Hunter again, I'm going to tackle you into the river and drown you right here. There's nothing to be done about Hunter. We're just friends."

She looked dubious, but she didn't press the matter. "I was talking about the witch thing. Are you really going to wait until Great-Grandma gets here? That's a long time, especially if you really are burning off people's eyebrows."

She had a point. "I don't know what to do. I have to think."

"You could always ask our grandmother. She's never been shy when it comes to complaining about Great-Grandma."

That was true. "I have tomorrow off. I'll decide then."

Alice was quiet for a few moments, something I appreciated, and then she pushed things to an uncomfortable place. "What's the over-under for when Hunter dumps Monica and officially asks you out? I say it happens in less than a week. I wouldn't have said that before I saw you together, but it's definitely coming."

"I will kill you," I warned.

"Promises, promises."

EIGHTEEN

I didn't wake with a hangover — at least from alcohol — but my head was fuzzy when I finally crawled out of bed the next morning. The kitten opened one eye, gave me a long look, and then rolled over and went back to sleep. His opinion on how I was spending my time was obvious.

I was still half asleep when I trudged to the kitchen to make coffee. It would've been faster — and probably better — if I'd just gone down to the restaurant and filled a mug there, but that would've meant changing out of my pajamas, far too much work. I was still waiting for the Keurig to finish heating up when Grandpa strolled into my apartment, a newspaper tucked under his arm. He pulled up short when he saw me.

"We have to talk about your drinking habits, kid."

I stared at him for a long moment. "We have to talk about your knocking habits."

"Technically this is my apartment."

"But I live here. What would you have done if I'd been naked?"

He shrugged. He was no stranger to nudity now that I thought about it. In fact, if he was reading the newspaper at home, he refused to wear pants — no matter who wandered into the house. "Laughed while you ran screaming into the bedroom probably."

I heaved out a sigh and turned back to the Keurig. "Try not to be in there all day." The conversation Alice and I had shared on the walk back from the party last night bubbled up. "I need to shower in the next half hour or so."

"Big date?" Grandpa didn't seem to be in a hurry to get to the bathroom, which didn't bode well for the schedule I was setting in my mind.

"If you say the name Hunter, I'll wrestle you down and beat you with that newspaper."

He chuckled. "Right. Good luck with that." His gaze was speculative as he looked me up and down. "What did you do last night?"

"I drank in a field." I saw no reason to lie. "Apparently everyone I went to high school with still hangs out in the same field on weekends."

"There's not much to do in this town," Grandpa conceded, moving the newspaper to his other hand. "Do you want to tell me what's bothering you?"

Did I? Would he think I was crazy if I told him about burning Monica's eyebrows off her face? What was I thinking? He would jump straight on the crazy train and call the men in white coats to fit me for a straitjacket before I was even caffeinated. "Nothing. Why does something have to be bothering me?"

"You have one of those faces that expresses everything. You get that from me. You can't hide what you're feeling, and right now you're feeling stressed."

He was good at reading people, I had to give him that. "Maybe I'm stressed because my grandfather walks into my apartment without knocking — and uses up all my toilet paper."

"No, that's not it."

I narrowed my eyes. "That could be it. You don't know everything about me."

"I know that you're internalizing something. You always were the worrying sort. I remember when you were a kid and there was a chickenpox outbreak at school. You were convinced you were going to get it and die."

"I did get it."

"You didn't die. You were sick for three days, ate ice cream for every meal, and watched utter nonsense on television."

"*Lost* was not nonsense."

"It was an island with giant polar bears. It doesn't get more nonsensical than that."

"They were from a research project."

He rolled his eyes. "The point is, you're a worrier. You always have been. You get that from your grandmother."

I blew on my coffee to cool it before taking a sip. When I risked a glance in his direction again, I was uncomfortable with the level of scrutiny he was applying. "Speaking of Grandma, I thought I would visit with her today. She doesn't have anything planned, does she?"

Grandpa arched an eyebrow. "You're going to see your grandmother?"

"What? That's allowed."

"You haven't visited her since you came back to town. Why are you going there today?"

"Maybe because I haven't visited her yet. She's stopped by the restaurant a few times. We've talked." I was feeling defensive, though his comment wasn't entirely unearned. I'd spent the better part of my time in Shadow Hills avoiding as many members of my family as I could. "I thought it would be nice to catch up."

"It would be nice," Grandpa agreed. "She's having coffee with her friends this morning. It's a regular date."

"In the restaurant?" I didn't want to ask my questions in front of an audience. That wouldn't work.

"She doesn't like coming here for coffee. She jumps from house to house with her pack of beauty-parlor complainers. Today they're at Charlotte's house. She'll be home by noon."

That was a timetable I could work with. "Then I guess you can spend as much time in the bathroom as you want." I figured I would live to regret the offer, but it wasn't as if I could control him. "I'll be out here watching television while you're ... getting caught up on the local news."

"Fair enough." He turned in the direction of the bathroom and stilled. "If there was something really wrong, you'd tell me, right?"

The question caught me off guard. "There's nothing wrong."

"You keep saying that, but you're acting out of sorts."

"I'm not. This is how I act."

"Like a loon?"

"Yeah. I'm a loon. I get it from my grandfather."

"On your dad's side maybe. I'm the smartest man you know."

"If you say so." I grabbed the remote and pointed it at the flat screen. "If that's all ... ."

"I guess." He grumbled as the kitten padded out of the bedroom and stopped in the middle of the room. The ball of fluff seemed confused by our guest. "Are you keeping this thing?"

"I'm going to take him to the shelter."

"It's been about a week."

I made a face. "It hasn't even been two days."

"That's like a week." He glanced at the flower box the kitten was using. "You need to at least get him a proper litter box. That box will be gross before you know it."

"Well, the faster you do your business, the faster I can shower and make a run to the store. He needs regular food, too. He can't have tuna for every meal."

"So you're going to buy a litter box and cat food for a kitten you're not going to keep."

"It's the weekend. The shelter isn't open weekends."

"Yes it is."

"I don't feel like taking him there today." I was feeling cross. "Why do you even care? You said I could keep him."

"You can. He doesn't seem destructive, and I think it's good for you to have a friend who doesn't go by the name Jim, Johnny, or José."

It took me a moment to grasp what he was insinuating. "It's been a rough few days. I'm just getting back in the swing of things. I have no intention of drinking every night, if that's what you're worried about."

"I'm worried that you have a tendency to cover your real feelings until things build to the point you blow."

"What feelings am I covering up?"

"I'm going to say Hunter."

I glared at him. "I don't want to hear his name come out of your mouth again."

"Well, you're doomed to disappointment if you think you can tell me what to say. Nobody is capable of controlling me."

"I guess we have that in common."

"Not as much as you might like to believe. I have no problem expressing my feelings, good or bad, and I don't spend my time hiding. You're an adult now. You need to learn to deal with this stuff."

That was easy for him to say. "I am dealing with it."

"No, you're not. You're avoiding it. That's what you do. Why do you think you spent years traveling even though you knew you were in trouble with the books?"

"Because I like to see things."

"No, because you didn't want to admit you needed help. That's your biggest problem. You insist on doing everything yourself. You need to get over that."

I bit back a nasty retort and turned on the television. "I'll take it under advisement." It was as close as I could come to a dismissal without risking him kicking me out of the apartment.

"No, you're going to keep avoiding for as long as you can. That's the wrong move, Stormy, but you won't understand that until it comes back and bites you ... so have at it."

"I think I know how to live my own life."

"If that were true, you would've figured this out five years ago."

He had a point. There was nothing to say. My life was a mess and nobody knew it better than Grandpa.

I WAITED UNTIL ALMOST ONE TO VISIT my grandmother. I wanted to make sure none of her friends were around. I let myself into her house without knocking — that's the way it works in the Archer family — and searched through the kitchen and living room for her. I found her on the patio flipping through a magazine in the shade.

"Hey, Grandma." I greeted her with a bright smile as I walked through the sliding glass door. The pool — bigger than most — looked pristine and clear, and I made a mental note to come back when I could swim some laps. It was time to get into a fitness routine now that I no longer had a gym membership. Shadow Hills didn't even have a gym.

"Hello, Stormy." She seemed taken aback to see me, but dutifully closed her magazine and gave me her full attention. "This is a nice surprise. What brings you to my neck of the woods?"

How could I broach the subject without looking like a crazy person? "I just wanted to see you." I sank into the chair next to her, making sure my smile was firmly in place. "I've been busy getting settled and haven't had much time to visit with everyone. You were first on my list."

She didn't look convinced. "Have you seen your mother?"

Of course she would ask that. My grandmother was tiny — like, four-foot-eleven — but she had a fiery disposition when she wanted something. I had no doubt my mother had been bitterly complaining about the way I'd been dodging her. My grandmother was predisposed to take my mother's side. "Not yet."

"Is she next on your list?"

"Not today. I have errands to run and stuff. You're the only one on my list today."

"I see." Grandma sipped her coffee and narrowed her eyes. She had a helmet of blond hair that she curled and sprayed into submission every morning. I couldn't remember ever seeing a hair out of place on her head. "How are things at the restaurant?"

That was a question I could handle without too much struggle. "They're okay. Getting used to morning shifts is a bit of a chore, but Grandpa says he'll give me more choice once I'm off probation."

"I can't believe he put you on probation. It's not as if you don't know what you're doing. You spent your teenage years in that restaurant. The skill didn't simply fall out of your head."

"It's been an adjustment," I hedged. "I forgot how fast-paced things can get. I'm okay working with a safety net right now."

"At least you have a good attitude about it."

She was the only one in the family who thought so. "Yeah, well, Uncle Brad is still a trip. Can't you guys take his computer away from him or something? He reads and watches some ridiculous stuff on the internet."

"It had better not be porn."

I almost choked. "I was talking about the political nonsense he spouts."

"Oh, that." She waved her hand. "He likes to think he's informed. He has anxiety, so he thinks if he knows everything he'll be able to head off any disaster that comes his way. What he doesn't realize is that nobody would want him to help deal with a serious situation because he can't get his head on straight. He's horrible in a crisis."

"He's definitely not on the zombie apocalypse team," I agreed, speaking before I thought better of it. "I just mean, you know, if there's a zombie apocalypse, he probably wouldn't make my team." It was a lame explanation, but her eyes twinkled.

"I know what a zombie apocalypse team is. I already have mine selected."

"You do?" I was dumbfounded. "Who's on it?"

"None of your business. You didn't make the cut."

Part of me thought I should be offended, but I had other things to worry about. "So ... I have a question for you."

"I figured you weren't here for a friendly visit. You're not nearly bored enough for that yet. What's your question?"

"It's about Great-Grandma."

Her eyebrows twitched upward. "My mother? I don't ever remember you even mentioning my mother."

"Not your mother. Grandpa's mother."

She made a face. "What do you want to know about *that* woman?"

Her tone told me this was going to be a short conversation. Still, I had to know. It would eat me alive if I didn't ask, and waiting until Great-Grandma's annual visit seemed a dangerous proposition. "Alice mentioned something odd to me."

"Oh, well, if this is a conversation about Alice perhaps I should add some bourbon to my coffee."

The response made me smile. "It's not about Alice. It's about me. She said something and I figured maybe you could confirm it for me."

"About your great-grandmother?"

"Yeah."

"Okay. Lay it on me."

"Here's the thing ... um ... it may sound weird. Actually, it's going to sound totally weird. I don't know a way around that, though. It's one of those questions I need answered, and I think you might be the only one who can answer it. Well, Grandpa probably could, but he's likely to have me thrown in the nuthouse after I ask it. There's less of a chance that will happen with you."

"Spit it out, Stormy," she ordered. "My stories have already started and I want to catch the tail end. There aren't many soaps left, but I like to stick to my routine."

I'd forgotten about her stories. She got me into watching *General Hospital* when I was young. It was a habit I maintained all the way through college. It only fell by the wayside when I started traveling.

"Okay, here's the thing ... ." I took a long, bracing breath. "It's come to my attention that Great-Grandma might've been a witch." I felt absolutely absurd saying the words.

Grandma blinked and sipped her coffee. When she spoke, it was with a calm that I admired. "She is a witch."

"Not the sort of witch who should probably have a B at the beginning of the word, but an actual witch. You know, with magic?"

Grandma nodded. "That's the sort of witch I'm talking about. Why is this coming up now?"

I was floored. "I ... you ... ."

Grandma made a big show of looking at her phone to check the time. "Witches exist, Stormy. Your grandmother isn't exactly powerful, but apparently it runs in her family."

"But ... how is that possible? Wouldn't we all know if we were witches?"

"I'm not a witch. Your mother isn't one. Your great-grandmother claims it skips generations. In fact, on her side of the family, I think there are only three or four witches left to propagate the gene pool. I'm perfectly fine with that, by the way."

I had no idea how I was supposed to respond. "But ... ."

"Is there a reason you're asking about this now?" She seemed puzzled. "Is this for a book? I don't want this showing up in a book."

"Alice and I found an Ouija board in the apartment," I replied dully. "We got drunk and played with it."

"Oh." Grandma's face split with a wide smile. "That's how this all came up? I have to admit, I was a little worried there. If it's just curiosity, it's not a big deal. Yes, there are witches on your grandfather's side of the family. They're few and far between, and the trait seems to have missed our branch of the family completely."

She puffed out her chest, as if proud of what she was going to say next. "I think my genes saved us all. You should thank me."

There wasn't a way out of it, so I merely nodded. "Thank you. You have no idea how happy I am that you saved us."

"Now, if there's nothing else, it's time for my stories. You should stay for a swim. You look as if you need to relieve some stress."

Oh, she had no idea. Witches were apparently real ... and I knew for certain now that I'd burned Monica's eyebrows off the previous evening.

NINETEEN

I was still flustered when I left Grandma to her stories. I needed to think, and I couldn't do that at the restaurant. On a whim, I headed out to a familiar hiking trail that I visited frequently with Hunter when I was a teenager. The trails were well marked and I could wander without getting lost. I still remembered the area relatively well ... and not just because it was seared into my brain as the first spot where Hunter and I had made out.

I parked in the lot overlooking the Jordan River Valley and trudged to the trail. There were no other cars in the parking lot. There were different spots to park along the highway and join the trail. I'd learned that a time or two as a randy teenager when Hunter and I would visit the spot to hang out in private.

Even in the middle of summer, the view was breathtaking. It was better in the fall, when the colors were changing, but that would happen soon enough. I wanted to enjoy the mild weather when I could. The leaves wouldn't turn for another three months. I was fine with that. There was plenty to look at before the weather made its inevitable turn.

The first place I stopped was one of the slow-moving creeks that trickled into the river. I remembered it exactly, and other than a few bushes here and there, the spot was the same. It made me yearn for the past, which wasn't all that surprising given everything that had happened since I'd returned. It was normal to wish for a simpler time ... and that's what I desperately wanted now.

I remembered spending afternoons here after school in the fall. Hunter would wait for me to get out of my last class and then drive to the lot, where we would stare at the vibrant shades of red, orange, and yellow while holding hands and plotting out our future. I never once questioned why Hunter would want to come out here rather than hang out in his warm home. There was no real warmth in his home — it was all a façade — and he needed space to grow. He'd always wanted me in that space ... and I was happy to oblige.

This place became a sanctuary of sorts, which was amusing given the name: Deadman's Hill. There was history that went with it, but I couldn't remember it. We spent hours laughing about the possibility of it being haunted while walking the trails. Now, given everything I'd discovered, it didn't seem nearly as funny.

"This just bites." I rubbed my forehead as I stared at the water. The goal was to clear my head and find some peace. Instead, I was dwelling on what my grandmother had told me, even though she hadn't exactly provided the answers I needed. She seemed so appalled at the thought of anyone following in Great-Grandma's footsteps that I'd covered to the best of my ability. Not only was I fearful, I was embarrassed. What would this ultimately mean for me?

The creek, of course, could provide no answers, so I dusted off my hands on the seat of my pants, determined to move on to another location. I almost jumped out of my skin when I found Hunter watching me from about twenty feet away. He had a stick in his hand, and a surprised look on his face.

"What are you doing here?" we both blurted simultaneously.

He laughed before I did, alleviating some of the tension. Then I laughed because the situation was too strange not to embrace. Besides, if I didn't laugh, I might start crying. That would freak him out ... and probably me, too. And, if I started crying, there was a legitimate possibility I would never stop.

"I didn't mean to frighten you," he said when he'd recovered. "I was just surprised when I saw you. I thought ... well ... it was like going back in time for a bit."

I understood, because it almost seemed kismet when I turned to find him standing there, as if nothing had changed and we were still the same dreamy kids who planned a life they could never share. "It's okay." I flashed a shy smile. "You just took me by surprise. This is Deadman's Hill, after all. I thought maybe the dead man was finally coming for me."

He laughed, as I'd intended. "You should write a book about this place," he said. "You should make it a paranormal mystery thriller. Those things sell like hot cakes."

"I don't know if I'm good enough to plot a mystery. I've never tried. I focused on women's fiction because that way I wouldn't have to deal with a dead body. Now the only thing that's dead is my career."

Hunter's eyes flashed with annoyance. "I really wish you wouldn't say things like that."

"Even if they're the truth?"

"It's not the truth, Stormy." He was firm. "Things haven't gone the way you thought they would. That doesn't make you a failure. It doesn't mean you can't get back everything that you had."

I told myself that he didn't mean for there to be a double meaning to his words, but a small ember of hope ignited all the same. "I just feel a little lost right now," I admitted. "I hate feeling sorry for myself, but that's what I'm feeling these days. I don't know how to explain it."

"It's okay to feel sorry for yourself," he reassured me. "The key is not to let those sorrowful feelings take over your life. I did that and wasted years being a cranky mope."

"You felt sorry for yourself for years?" I couldn't picture that.

He pinned me with a solemn look. "I had a broken heart. It wasn't as easy as I thought it would be to get over."

The statement was more pointed than I expected. "Oh, I ... ."

"I'm sorry." He held up his hands. "That was a horrible thing to say. You're not to blame for what happened to me."

"What did happen to you?" I was legitimately curious. "I mean ... you're stronger than I remember." I realized the observation could've been construed as insulting after I'd already said it. "You were always strong, of course, but you're stronger now. It feels almost miraculous to witness."

He smirked and shook his head, pointing toward the trail. "Let's walk. If we're going to talk about serious stuff, I need something to look at besides you if I want to keep from being embarrassed."

"Fair enough." I was happy for the walk. "You don't have to tell me anything you don't want to. It's not as if you owe me anything."

"No, but I feel like I owe myself this chance to unload some things that have been bothering me over the years."

I swallowed hard. "Are you going to yell? I'm not saying I haven't earned your ire, but I'm not sure I'm up to being yelled at today. Do you think it could wait a week or two? Just until I'm feeling stronger."

He looked amused. "What makes you think I'm going to yell?"

I shrugged. "You used to need to vent. When things got you down, when your father was on a bender and terrorizing you, venting was the best way for you to handle things."

"I never yelled at you." He appeared appalled at the prospect.

"No, you yelled at the universe. I just stood by helplessly and watched because I had no idea how to make things better."

"You helped me just by being there, Stormy." His face was naked with emotion. "You were the only one who understood what was happening. Part of that was because I was embarrassed for anyone else to find out. In hindsight, that seems stupid. I know about cycles of abuse, and my family was hardly the only one muddling through it at the time. I still didn't want people to know. Even now I keep it to myself."

His far-off expression made me blurt out a question that was absolutely none of my business. "Does Monica know?"

He snapped his eyes back to me, something I couldn't quite identify flashing in the depths of his eyes. "No. She doesn't know." He offered up a wan smile. "Monica is not the type of person who cares about childhood trauma."

The revelation agitated me. "Then maybe she's not the right person for you."

Hunter used his stick to poke at a small group of leaves rather than respond.

"I didn't mean anything by that," I offered lamely a few minutes later, the silence unnerving me. "I know it's not fair to cast aspersions given ... everything. I just think you could do better. I can't pretend otherwise."

Amusement curved his lips. "Oh, yeah? Do you have anyone specific in mind?"

The question caught me off guard. "No, I ... no." He didn't think I was suggesting we get together, did he? That would be mortifying when he turned me down. "I was just talking in general terms."

"In general terms, huh?" Now he really did look entertained. "Well, in general terms, I very much doubt Monica will be around much longer. While she's a perfectly nice woman, our lifestyles don't exactly mesh."

That was a relief, though I couldn't show it. "You should take some downtime," I suggested. "You know, really think about things before you date someone else."

"Is that what you're doing? Taking downtime, I mean. Tristan would've taken you to fifty fancy restaurants if you'd shown him the slightest interest."

I scowled. "Tristan is the last person I'd date. He's so full of himself. He's the star in all his stories. He looks pretty good shirtless, but that's hardly the sort of thing you can build a relationship on."

Now it was Hunter's turn to be annoyed. "When did you see him shirtless?"

I pressed my lips together at his expression. It was one part annoyance, two parts fury, and one part jealousy. It was the last part that made me feel a little better, even though I knew it was only a conditioned response. "When I went to the basketball court looking for Bobby. I found Tristan ... and he likes to flex while talking. It's pretty gross."

"Oh." Hunter relaxed, if only marginally. "I guess that makes sense. He's still a turd."

"You never liked him. That's a holdover from high school."

"You're right. Do you know why?"

I shook my head. "No. Other than he's an entitled little jerkwad who lives off his father's money rather than work for anything himself, I mean."

That was enough to elicit a true smile from Hunter, and it was devastating in its beauty. He could light up a room — or in this case an entire valley — with one expression. It almost made me think he was magical, too.

"I didn't like him because he wanted you," Hunter replied softly.

My heart skipped. "No he didn't." Honestly, that was absurd. "He didn't even notice I was alive when we were kids. He was into the rich girls, or the two well-to-do girls who lived in town. He didn't want someone who constantly smelled like French fries while wearing off-brand canvas shoes."

"No, that's what you saw," Hunter countered, eyes somber. "You never saw yourself the way you really were. You only saw the negative, never the positive. Tristan was hot for you ... and it drove me crazy."

"It drove you crazy?" I was intrigued. "Why?"

"Because I needed you." He was earnest to the point of pinching my heart. "You were all I had most of the time. You listened ... and we dreamed ... and even though none of it happened, you saved me back then. I didn't want to lose you to anyone, but especially not to him."

I found myself suddenly choked up. "You were never going to lose me. Don't you know that I was as infatuated with you as you were with me?"

"But I did lose you."

Tears pricked the back of my eyes. "I ... ."

"Don't." He waved his hand to cut me off. "Don't apologize. You didn't do anything wrong. It took me a long time to see that. I was bitter after we broke up, but even as it was happening I knew I couldn't keep you.

"You had dreams that were bigger than this place," he continued. "You wanted to see the world. It was fun to dream that I could go with you, but the realities were different. I was never going to have the money to go to college, and asking you to stay wasn't fair to you. I wasn't always the smartest boyfriend, but I knew you would come to resent me if I tried to hold you back.

"I had to let you go, so I did. I regretted it every day for a long time. It hurt to think about you. Then, one day, it didn't hurt quite as much. I still missed you, but I knew I did the right thing for you. That's what got me through it. One of us needed to be happy. I always wanted it to be you."

I thought my heart would break. "Hunter, I'm so sorry." Before I realized what was happening, tears were leaking down my cheeks.

"Don't." He looked pained as he immediately reached up to swipe at the tears. "I can't take it when you cry. You know that."

I did know it, but I was incapable of stopping now that I'd started. "No, I owe you an apology."

"You don't owe me anything."

"But I do." I was insistent. "I broke up with you because it seemed I had to. I didn't want it either, but I had this picture in my head. It was of a place I was supposed to end up."

"And I could never make it there with you," he surmised. "I know that."

"But that's not the point."

"What is the point?" He was back to being amused as he wiped away all traces of my tears with his fingers.

"The point is I thought a certain life would make me happy. I was wrong. I spent years bouncing from thing to thing, trying to find that spark of magic everyone needs to be happy ... but there's been nothing."

Spark of magic, I internally muttered. Is that was this is? Is this the spark of magic I've always been looking for? Did I somehow manage to do this to myself? It seemed ridiculous to consider, but it somehow fit.

"You can still have the life you were meant to live," Hunter insisted. "You're still figuring things out and that's okay. You're home now. You can take the time you need."

At that moment, the thing I wanted most was him. I knew without a doubt that I could never tell him that, though. I'd ruined his life once. I couldn't do it again.

"What is it you need?" I asked. "I mean ... you don't smile as often as I would like. You need to find some inspiration of your own. And I hate to break it to you, but I don't think Monica can ever be the source of that inspiration."

Rather than be offended, he barked out a laugh. "You might be right." To my surprise, he held out his hand. "Let's take a walk down memory lane, shall we?" He looked excited at the prospect, which was enough to give me pause.

"You want to hold my hand in the woods. Here?" My voice was unnaturally squeaky.

"I want to remember the good times," he clarified. "I want to talk about when we were kids ... and all the stupid stuff we used to do down here."

"Like the time we were making out and I was late for dinner and Grandpa came to find me and my shirt was inside out?"

His eyes filled with such joy at being reminded of the memory that my heart hurt just looking at him. "That would be great," he agreed. "When we're finished with that one, we're also going to talk about what you told me last night."

I froze, conflicted. "And what did I tell you last night?" Panic licked at my insides as I tried to remember if I'd said anything that could get me in trouble.

"You told me you felt as if someone was watching you behind the restaurant. I don't like the idea of you wandering around out there if you don't feel safe. We're going to talk about self-preservation — because obviously you need lessons — and then we're going to talk about whatever information you got from Bobby while he was drunk. I saw you and Alice with him, and I think he told you something."

"He did." In the aftermath of everything that had happened I'd almost forgotten. "Are you sure you want to do this?"

"Have an hour of quiet to reminisce? I'm sure."

I thought about arguing, but I needed the quiet, too. I needed to share in his warmth and revel in the familiarity of his presence. "Okay, but the Bobby story is weird and annoying."

"I would expect nothing less. I want to hear everything."

TWENTY

Hunter insisted on walking me back to my car, and we were still holding hands when we got to the parking lot.

"Well, that was nice," I said lamely. What was I supposed to say? We'd spent the afternoon holding hands in the woods like we were teenagers again. The only things missing were the fervent kisses and whispers ... and, sadly, I would've been up for that, too. The realization made me angry with myself, and I worked overtime to tamp down the emotion. He'd been nothing but a gentleman.

"It was nice," he agreed, leaning against my car.

"Just like old times."

"Well, not quite." He winked and glanced inside my vehicle, which was a mess. I was never the clean sort and that was on full display. "Although this is familiar."

"There's no one to clean my car as an adult," I explained. "I can't tell you what a disappointment it was when I reached adulthood and figured out I would have to do things like that by myself."

"Ah. That's what you missed most, huh?"

Not even close. "Um ... ."

He stared into my eyes for a long moment, the atmosphere between us practically crackling. When he raised his fingers to brush the hair from my face I thought he was going to kiss me. My blood actually rioted at the thought.

Instead, he let loose a sigh and took a step back, releasing my hand in the process. I immediately missed his proximity, which only made me angrier at myself. He had a girlfriend, for crying out loud. I wasn't the sort of person who went after other people's boyfriends ... or husbands ... or crushes, for that matter. I wasn't Alice, who got a charge out of the chase.

"I guess I should be going," I said finally, swallowing hard. "I didn't mean to stay down here so long."

"That makes two of us." His smile was rueful. "I have some things to check for work."

"I thought it was your day off."

"Technically, it is. We're a small department, though. I work seven days a week most of the time, even if it's only for an hour here or there."

"That's kind of depressing."

"Really?" He cocked an eyebrow. "Are you telling me you don't always have your head in possible story ideas?"

My mind was running to schmaltzy romance novels right now. *Stop that!* I had to get control of myself. I hadn't felt an overabundance of hormones like this since I was a teenager. The fact that the same person managed to stir me up in both decades wasn't lost on me. "That's different."

"How?"

"I'm a waitress. I don't have a single urge to serve you a cup of coffee on my day off."

"That's what you're doing right now," he corrected. "You're a writer. You always have been. That's your real job. You like spinning fantastical stories. That won't change ... and it shouldn't. You're good at what you do."

The words warmed me even as a sharp pang of regret poked my heart. "I don't feel good at it."

"I know. You feel like a failure, even though that's a stupid reaction."

"Are you calling me stupid?" I meant it as a joke, but it came out harsher than I intended.

"No. I'm calling you ... sad. Regret is a wasted emotion. You have to look forward. Yes, things didn't turn out as you thought they would. You can turn it around. As soon as you get out of your head long enough to really think about it, you're going to do great things. You just need a little faith."

"You sound like my grandfather."

"That could be the meanest thing you've ever said to me."

I laughed. "Speaking of that, I need to get going. I have to stop at the store to pick up a few things for that kitten I found. He can't keep doing his business in an old flower box."

Hunter looked amused. "I thought you weren't keeping him."

"I'm not, but the animal shelter isn't open on the weekends."

"I believe it is."

I faltered. "Oh, well ... Monday will be easier for me."

He didn't look convinced, but he didn't push further. "Well, I need to stop at the station. After that, I was thinking I would swing by the restaurant."

My heartbeat picked up a notch. "Another visit? That's quick."

"I want to see if I can find your grandfather."

I deflated. "Oh."

"I also want to see if I can find evidence of anyone hanging out by that storage building," he added. "If we can find proof someone was watching you that might be able to lead us to a suspect."

I hadn't even considered that. "You think the person I thought was watching me the other night murdered Roy?"

He shrugged. "It's a possibility."

"Unless I imagined it." I didn't want to paint myself as crazy, but it felt necessary to offer the possibility that nothing really happened. "It's possible. It was dark. It was creepy being out there alone. You just said my imagination is always firing on all cylinders. What's more likely, that a killer came back to the scene of the crime or I let my imagination run wild?"

"I'm not taking any chances." He was firm. "You should run your errands while I'm at the station. I'll meet you behind the restaurant in an hour."

There was no sense arguing with him. He'd already made up his mind. "Okay, but it's really not necessary."

"I'll be the judge of that."

I BOUGHT MORE CAT SUPPLIES THAN I intended. I meant to grab a small bag of kitten chow, a three-pack of soft food, the smallest bag of litter available, and a cheap litter box. I left with five full bags and I struggled to carry them all as I got out of my car behind the restaurant.

"Geez." Hunter was already there, leaning against his truck with his arms crossed. He hurried to help me. "Did you buy out the store?"

"I just ... didn't want him to be bored," I replied defensively when he plucked out a fishing pole toy with feathers attached to the end. "Cats need to be stimulated."

His smiled. "If you say so." He shoved the toy back and grabbed three bags from me. "But you're not keeping him, right?"

I scowled. "I can send all these things with him so he'll be set when he finds a new home."

"That's very ... pragmatic." Hunter dropped the bags at the bottom of the stairs that led to the balcony. "I'll help you carry them up after. Right now, I want you to show me where you think the person was watching you from."

I nestled the bags I was carrying next to the others and dragged a hand through my hair. All the time in the woods had made it unruly and I needed another shower to tame it. "I don't know that there was anyone here," I reminded him, feeling as if I was stuck on repeat. "I just felt I was being watched."

"Okay, then reenact it for me." His tone was so reasonable I merely nodded.

"I came down from the steps." I gestured for emphasis. "The kitten was over here, under the streetlight."

Hunter was silent as he watched me walk to the middle of the alley.

"He was right here, chasing bugs." I pointed toward the ground. "I thought he would flee because that's what feral cats do, but he wasn't afraid of me. He didn't want to be picked up, but he was so small it was easy. After I had him, I crouched here for a few minutes. I was trying to decide what to do with him."

"You were trying to talk yourself out of keeping him," Hunter countered, moving to join me. He scanned the area. "There are a lot of places someone could hide out here, Stormy. I never really thought about it before, but I'm not sure it's safe for you to stay here."

That was ludicrous. "It's Shadow Hills. There is no safer place."

"A dead body was discovered right here, by you, a few days ago." Hunter's eyes turned cold. "There's no place that's truly safe, but ... I don't think you should be coming in and out of this apartment after dark right now."

He had to be joking. "Um ... you can't possibly think I'm going to hole up in that apartment alone every night for the foreseeable future. I'll go crazy."

"Better crazy than dead."

I wasn't sure that was true. "Hunter, we have no proof that anybody was out here watching me."

"You had a feeling." His tone was accusatory. "I learned a long time ago that your feelings are usually accurate."

"When did I ever have a feeling back then?" I was honestly curious.

"How about when you were convinced that Danny Watkins was a predator and you warned Shelly Davidson?"

I'd forgotten about that. "Well ... ."

He wagged a finger, refusing to back down. "You were right. Danny was caught ... doing things ... outside of Shelly's bedroom window. You made her so nervous she made her father check when she heard a noise. And guess what he found."

"Danny," I muttered, scuffing my foot against the ground.

"Danny," he agreed. "Now, Danny was just a garden-variety Peeping Tom at that point, but it could've escalated. You made sure she was safe."

"That was just a fluke."

"It wasn't. You also knew about ... me."

My heart stuttered. "I didn't know. I suspected."

"And you were right." He cleared his throat and steadied his voice. "You recognized what nobody else in that school could. You understood about my father. You've always been ... cognizant ... of certain things. We're talking things other people can't pick up on. I trust your instincts."

I considered his words. Was he right? Had I always been more aware than others? Before I burned Monica's eyebrows off at the bonfire I would've completely disregarded the statement. Now, though ... .

My life felt more in flux than when I first arrived. I didn't like it. I was a creature of habit. Routine was my best friend. How was I supposed to get into a routine with all this going on? It seemed impossible.

"Stay there," Hunter ordered, heading in the direction of the storage building. He clearly hadn't witnessed my moment of paralyzing self-doubt.

I watched as he moved to the closest side and disappeared from view. I knew he was circling the building, so I waited. It took him longer than it should've to reappear on the other side.

"Let me guess," I said. "Nothing. I really am crazy."

"I wouldn't say that." He was grim as he motioned for me to join him. "Who smokes here?"

I wasn't expecting the question. "A lot of people smoke," I replied as I joined him.

"I need a list."

"I don't understand." He led me to the back corner of the building. There, in the spot that would've been darkest thanks to the shadows afforded by the encroaching trees, was a well-worn patch of ground. There had to be at least fifty discarded cigarette butts strewn around.

"Who smokes here?" he repeated.

"A lot of people, including Brad and Trina."

"Do they come out this far to smoke?"

I hesitated.

"Stormy, I don't suspect your aunt and uncle of trying to kill you," he said gently. "That's not what this is about. I want to know if it's reasonable for someone who works here to come out this far to smoke. It's a simple question."

"Most everyone who smokes does it by that door." I pointed toward the double doors closest to my apartment steps. "There are ashtrays right there."

"So there's no reason for anyone to smoke behind the storage building." He stroked his chin. "Unless someone was watching the inhabitant of that apartment." He gestured up, drawing my attention to the sliding glass doors that led to my kitchen.

"I'm never that far over," I reassured him, my heart lodging in my throat. "At night, I usually hang in the living room ... or my bedroom."

"It doesn't matter. Someone can still see the lights. You need to install blinds on those windows."

I nodded dumbly. "I'll talk to Grandpa."

"You don't have to talk to him. Just do it. If he doesn't like it, tell him to see me. I've been wanting to have a talk with him anyway."

"It's not that." I shifted, uncomfortable. "I don't have the money to buy them right now."

Realization sparked in his eyes. "Oh. I didn't know things were that bad." He looked apologetic. "Well, I'll go up there and measure. I'll buy the blinds."

I immediately started shaking my head. "Absolutely not."

The sympathy he'd obviously been feeling moments before evaporated, replaced by frustration. "You're getting blinds. You can pay me back once you've put some money away."

"You're not buying blinds for me. I'll just ... put a blanket over the doors or something."

"No, you're getting blinds." He started toward the bags, grabbing all five of them this time before starting up the stairs. "Don't bother arguing with me."

"Oh, I'm going to argue with you." I had to hurry to keep up with him. Even laden down, his longer legs allowed him to take two steps at a time. When he tugged on the door and it easily slid open, he gave me a look of incredulity. "What?" Frustration was positively oozing out of my pores.

"Why is this door unlocked?"

That was a very good question. "Um ... maybe Grandpa unlocked it." That seemed unlikely. He never even entered the kitchen when he invaded my personal space. He always went straight to the bathroom.

Hunter used his elbow to push the door open the rest of the way and carry in the bags, unceremoniously dropping them on the floor before looking to the windows. "Where is your tape measure?"

"You're not buying me blinds."

"Stop arguing with me and get a tape measure." Hunter's eyes fired. "I am not leaving until you have blinds and that's all there is to it."

"You are so bossy," I grumbled as I moved toward the living room. I was fairly certain there was a tape measure in the box I'd yet to unpack that I'd tucked in the corner. "That's another thing that hasn't changed since we were kids."

"Well, if you expect me to apologize, it's not going to happen. Just get the tape measure."

I rummaged in the box for a few minutes, to the point he became frustrated and moved to join me.

"Let me."

"I have it," I snapped.

"Yes, well, I think you're dragging your feet."

We were still grappling for position in front of the box when the door to the apartment opened to allow Grandpa entrance. He seemed surprised to see us, especially as we were using our hips in an effort to box each other out.

"Well, at least you're not naked," Grandpa said, once he'd wrapped his head around the situation. "Do I even want to know what you're doing?"

"Looking for a tape measure," I replied. "He's being bossy, though. Tell him to stop being bossy."

"It's like you're teenagers all over again." Grandpa shook his head and started for the bathroom. Apparently he'd forgotten that he was avoiding Hunter, because he slowed his pace before he'd gone more than a few steps. "There's a barbecue at the house this afternoon. I'm sure Stormy has forgotten — or at least wants everyone to believe that — but you're invited, Hunter. It's been a long time since you joined us for a family get-together."

Hunter looked taken aback. "Oh, well, that's really nice."

"It'll be good food."

I was surprised at Hunter's reaction. I thought for sure he would shoot Grandpa down right away.

"I would really like to go," Hunter hedged. "It's just ... I can't. I have a date with Monica in a few hours and I don't think she'll take it well if I cancel for your family."

"Probably not," Grandpa agreed, offering a small smile before turning back to his task. "I'll be awhile. Don't wait for me."

I opened my mouth to tell him to use the bathroom at his own house, but it was too late. He'd slammed the door and was apparently in his own little world. "I need to change the locks," I muttered. When Hunter didn't respond,

I turned back to see if he'd found the tape measure. Instead, he was holding up a familiar object ... and my heart dropped.

"Oh, geez. I forgot that was even in there." I felt like an absolute idiot.

Hunter stared at his old letterman's jacket so long I thought he'd lost the ability to speak. When he did find his voice, it was rusty. "I thought you said you'd lost everything you had from when you were a kid because you moved around so much."

"No, I said I'd managed to hold on to only a few important things." I pressed the heel of my hand to my forehead as he pinned me with an incredulous stare. "I figured you would want it back one day. I just forgot it was in there."

That was mostly true, and yet I never forgot to pack the jacket whenever I moved. It was the one tangible tie I had to him throughout the years, and it was one of the few things I guarded with zealous intent.

"You can have it back," I said quickly, trying to fill the silence. "I mean ... it's yours."

He clutched the jacket to his chest and looked momentarily lost. When he finally shook himself from his reverie, his voice was solid again. "We need to find that tape measure. You need those blinds as soon as possible. I also want you to make sure that door is locked at all times."

"Fine."

"Promise me." He was fervent. "Promise me that you'll do it, Stormy. It's important."

I couldn't hold back my sigh. "I promise. I'll be more careful about the door. You don't have anything to worry about."

"That would be a nice change of pace."

TWENTY-ONE

T rue to his word, Hunter measured the door for the blinds, jotting down the numbers and then warning me about leaving it unlocked again. He promised to return with the blinds as soon as possible.

"Check the locks in the restaurant when you come in," he warned, serious. "Also, make sure you check the shadows before getting out of your car. In fact ... do you have any pepper spray?"

I nodded. "I do. I bought it when I was hopping from city to city."

"Then start carrying it." There was no softness in his attitude and he reacted poorly when I rolled my eyes. "I'm serious. Do you want your grandfather to show up for work one morning and find you in the alley?"

"I ... no."

"I don't want it either. So, you're going to start being careful whether you like it or not. Do you understand?"

I was bitter about being bossed around, but I acquiesced. "I'll be careful, Hunter."

"Make sure that you are." His fingers lightly brushed against my cheek and then he headed for the door to the kitchen. "Tell your grandfather I'm still going to question him about Roy. He can't live in your bathroom forever."

I wasn't sure that was true. "He'd camp out in there all night if it meant avoiding you."

"Yes, well ... he's lucky I have other things to do today. Otherwise I would sit here and see how far he wanted to take things."

"You have a date." I bobbed my head perfunctorily. "I hope it goes well. How are Monica's eyebrows, by the way?"

He looked as if he was fighting a chuckle. "I haven't seen her today, so I can't say. They were pretty bad last night. I still don't understand why she blamed you."

I remembered the jacket just as he was about to escape through the door. "Wait." I scurried over and collected it, holding it close for a moment before handing it to him. "You don't want to forget this."

He hesitated for a second and then reached over to grab it. "I still can't believe you kept it all this time."

"Like I said, it wasn't mine to get rid of. I knew I would eventually find a way to get it back to you."

"You could've just given it to your mother. I know she visited you in a few of those cities. She told me about all of your adventures ... and then complained that you liked dirty cities. She couldn't understand what you found so fascinating about New Orleans."

"It has a certain ... appeal." I graced him with a soft smile. "The music is amazing. You would absolutely love it. The food is to die for, too. Also there's just this ... atmosphere that's hard to ignore. Creative people go there. Some perform on the streets. Others pretend they're human statues in Jackson Square."

His eyes widened. "And you think that's cool? Being a human statue, I mean."

"I think it's ... magical." There was that word again. It kept popping up today. "You should visit one day."

"If you love the city so much, why didn't you settle there?"

That was a hard question to answer. "Multiple reasons, I guess. The biggest is that I was running out of money. My only other skill is waitressing and it's impossible to live in the French Quarter if you don't make a lot of money. Er, well, unless you want to live in a one-bedroom hole. That kind of takes the fun out of it."

"So, what? Are you going to stay here, get back on your feet, write another hit book and then return to New Orleans?"

At one time, that was the plan. It seemed a distant fantasy now, though. "I don't know. I haven't written anything in months. It could be that I'm here forever."

His eyes flashed with something — hope maybe — and then his features evened out. "You can go on vacation. You can live here and still visit there."

"And that might be the path my future holds. Right now things feel ...

unsettled. I don't know what to do. I mean, the apartment is nice — and I can't complain about the price because Grandpa is doing his best to work with me — but I want someplace to call my own eventually."

"Like the Sanderson place."

I froze. I couldn't believe he remembered that. "I always did love that house. I bet it looks awful now."

He shrugged. "Nobody has lived there for about eight years. It needs a lot of work. I was inside a few years ago. It has good bones. I think, with enough money and love, it could be turned into something spectacular."

"Well, I have zero money, so I think I'm fresh out there."

"Give it time." He reached over and squeezed my hand. "I'll be in touch when I get the blinds. We'll set up a time for me to install them."

My eyebrows hopped. "You're going to do manual labor, too?"

"It's been known to happen." He focused on the kitten, who was suddenly wide awake and studying him with contemplative eyes. "As for him, you really should come up with a name."

"I was thinking Poop Factory."

He snorted. "Keep thinking. I'll be in touch."

Because I wasn't quite ready for him to go, I grappled for something to say. What I came up with was weak, to say the least. "Have fun on your date. Give Monica my condolences on her eyebrows."

He paused in the doorway. "That would require telling her how I spent my day."

I hadn't thought of that. "And you don't want to do that. Fair enough. I didn't really mean it anyway. She's kind of mean. I'm glad her eyebrows are gone." It wasn't a nice thing to say, but it was the truth.

He chuckled. "Have fun at your barbecue. I really wish I could go with you, but ... I can't."

And that was the crux of our problems. He would never be able to open his heart to me again because I'd crushed it the first time around. I couldn't even decide what I wanted to do with my future, so I would never risk telling him I still harbored feelings for him. I didn't want to hurt him more than I wanted something good for myself. We were stuck ... and I didn't see that changing.

"I'm sure the barbecue will be lovely," I said after a beat. "I haven't seen my mother since I've been back. I guarantee she's there, and it won't be pretty."

"Now I'm definitely sorry I'll miss it."

"You just like the mayhem."

"I can't argue with that."

. . .

I DRESSED IN CAPRI PANTS and a black blouse for the family barbecue. I was officially down to my last pair of clean pants, which meant a trip to the laundromat was in my future. Even though Grandpa had graciously offered the use of his machines, that would mean hanging out around his house, and the thought of that made me distinctly uncomfortable given my conversation with my grandmother earlier in the day.

The driveway was already full, so I parked on the side of the road. I could hear the younger kids in the family — the small people my cousins had already popped out — squealing and having a good time in the side yard. My grandparents went all out when it came to entertainment. They had an in-ground pool, an old-school trampoline that didn't boast those sissy nets to keep kids safe (I mean, really, the only reason to be on a trampoline is so you can bounce someone else off it), and a full tennis court that nobody but my grandmother used. Even though we were all raised with the opportunity, there wasn't one of us who became good at the sport.

I let myself in through the laundry room door, taking a moment to collect myself before coming face to face with my mother. It wasn't that she was a bad person — she had good qualities — but she was always in attack mode where I was concerned. Nothing I did was ever good enough. When my book made it on The New York Times bestseller list, her first question was why I didn't place higher.

She was simply too much, or "extra" if you will. That's the word Alice and I had started using to describe our mothers — without risking their wrath — when they were both feeling territorial. Just for the record, they always feel territorial.

"Are you hiding out here?" David asked when he happened upon me a few minutes later. He looked amused rather than worried.

I shrugged. "I was just ... thinking."

"About whether or not it would be smarter to flee and risk running into your mother another day?"

He knew me too well. We'd grown up together. He could read me better than most. "What do you think she'll do if I take off?" I was genuinely curious about what his answer would be.

"Nothing good." His expression was grim. "I believe there will be some cursing ... and then there will be some wine, because there's always wine. She'll use the wine to get my mom and Aunt Trina riled up. Then they'll track you down, no matter where you hide, and embarrass the crap out of you."

Yup. That was pretty much what I imagined them doing. "So, I should probably just suck it up and get it over with here."

"That's what I would do. You've already been embarrassed a hundred times over in front of the family. What's one more time?"

He had a point. Still, I dragged my feet as I followed him into the house. In the kitchen, I was reunited with several aunts and uncles I hadn't seen since I'd returned. They all greeted me with smiles and hugs, which I gladly returned, and then seemed to watch me with expectant gazes as I moved toward the formal dining room. That's where my mother reigned.

"There she is," Grandma called out when I appeared in the opening between the kitchen sitting area and dining room. "I was starting to wonder if you were going to show up at all. I was going to remind you about the barbecue when you stopped by earlier, but I thought it was unnecessary. Apparently not, huh?"

I glanced at the clock on the wall. I was on time, which was early given the fact that Brad's wife had made a habit of running more than an hour late since she'd been introduced to the family. Nobody gave her grief. Apparently I was the only lucky one on that front.

"I've been here for a little bit," I argued, trying to keep my temper in check. "I was talking to people in the kitchen."

"Yes, well ... ." Grandma trailed off, her eyes shrewd as she glanced between my mother and me. "Aren't you going to say hello to your mother?" she asked finally.

Now I had no choice. I'd been considering sitting at the opposite end of the table and forcing her to say something to me first. Grandma had taken that option out of my hands ... and I wasn't happy about it.

"Hello, Mother," I said darkly, my eyes finally seeking — and finding — hers. "How are you?"

There was a catch in her chest as she regarded me and I braced myself for an onslaught of passive-aggressive statements. Instead, she sucked in three steadying breaths and flashed a smile that was faker than Grandma's bottle-blond hair. "Hello, Stormy. It's so good to see you." She didn't get up and offer a hug, for which I was thankful.

"It's good to see you, too." I sat in a chair that was far from her reach should she decide to wrap her hands around my neck. She was playing a game — probably because Grandma had warned her about acting out — and she expected me to be the first to crumble. That wasn't going to happen this time. I was older now, wiser. I had infinite patience.

Okay, the only part of that statement that was true is the older part. I felt like an idiot and snakes writhed in my stomach. She would definitely win whatever game she was playing. The only option I had was putting up a valiant fight.

"How is the apartment?" Mom's tone was clipped. "I wanted to come and help you set it up, but I never received an invitation."

Like that had ever stopped her before. "It's fine." I matched her tone, going for a breezy demeanor that I knew would drive her around the bend. "I don't own anything, so there's really nothing I need help with."

"That's not true," Grandpa countered, shuffling into the room. He was dressed in bright red shorts, a pale-yellow polo shirt, and a black belt. When I glanced at his feet, I found he was wearing black socks and a pair of Crocs. Yup. His outfit matched the chaos in his brain. "Hunter was over measuring for blinds. It sounds like you're going to do some decorating."

Well, that was a thorny subject ... and not just because Hunter was the last person I wanted to talk about. I couldn't very well admit to feeling as if someone was watching me. It would turn into a thing, and my mother might well insist that I move in with her as a precautionary measure until Roy's killer was caught. I'd rather live in my car than share a roof with my mother.

"He was just helping because I think blinds are a good idea if Grandpa is going to keep using my apartment for his afternoon bathroom breaks," I replied coolly. "It's not a big deal."

"Yeah, that's not what was going on." Grandpa shook the side of my chair and raised an eyebrow, an unspoken message being sent.

I scowled as I got up from his chair — he had a regular stool in the restaurant and two regular chairs in his own house. Nobody was allowed to usurp his territory. I moved to the spot to his left. "You could've just asked," I grumbled. "Or, I don't know, you could've sat in a different chair."

"No, I couldn't." He was blasé as he shifted his eyes between my mother and me. It was obvious he was trying to read the temperature of the room. "You and Hunter seemed to be getting along — other than that pushing and shoving thing you were doing of course — so I'm surprised he didn't come to the barbecue with you."

He was just talking to hear himself talk now. He wanted my mother to be aware that Hunter and I had been spending time together so she could have something fresh to complain about. She was never happy when we took off for the woods for hours as teenagers.

"He was just helping me," I repeated. "It's not a big deal. We're ... friends."

"Friends?" Mom's perfectly manicured eyebrow arched. "I don't remember you two ever being friends. I remember lots of groping and pawing and wistful looks that made me want to vomit."

Ah, yes, there she was. Despite her best efforts, she couldn't stop being herself. "Well, we're just friends now. I don't know what you want me to say. I needed help measuring for blinds and he volunteered." That sounded plausible, right?

"And what about his girlfriend?" Mom asked. "Is she all right with him helping you?"

I avoided eye contact and reached for the coffee carafe. "I don't see why she would be upset. It's not as if anything is going on."

"Yet," Grandpa clarified. "Nothing is going on yet. It's only a matter of time. I'm hopeful the boy isn't stupid and ends things with the whiny girl before giving in to his baser urges with you. That would be the polite thing to do."

The conversation was quickly spiraling out of control. "Let's talk about something else," I suggested, glancing around the table. "Like Dad. Where is he?" Seeing my father right now would be a blessing. He always stood up for me when Mom got her panties in a bunch.

"Your father is on a sales trip and won't be back until next week. He sends his regards."

Well, crap. There went that idea. "And everyone else?" I glanced around, hopeful something — I would take anything at this point — would steal the spotlight currently fixed on me.

"Everyone who is coming is already here," Grandma replied. "Your grandfather will start barbecuing in a few minutes, right, Charles?"

Grandpa absently nodded. "Sure. Sure." The man was a great cook but a terrible griller. His steaks were always burnt on the outside and raw on the inside. Even ruined steak would be better than this conversation, though.

"I can help," I offered.

He shook his head. "Oh, no. You should catch up with your mother. It's been a long time since the two of you were together."

Not long enough. I just knew she would start grilling me about my writing plans. She wanted me to succeed more than anyone else because then she had bragging rights over her sisters about which of them had raised the most successful child. She had that title sewn up for years ... until things fell apart and I failed her. Now I was no different from anybody else, and she took it as a personal affront.

"Yes, Stormy and I will spend hours catching up," Mom agreed, her smile more evil than welcoming. "For starters, I thought we would discuss why she was questioning Mom about Grandma's witch history ... and then we'll turn things to Hunter and her plans for getting back on her feet financially. I think, between those three topics, we should be able to eat up a few hours."

My stomach twisted and I wished I would've risked running. How could the outcome have been any worse?

"How does that sound?" Mom asked brightly.

Like my worst nightmare. "It sounds great," I lied, flicking my accusatory eyes to Grandma. She'd ratted me out. I would have to pay her back somehow. "All those topics sound amazing. I can't wait to talk about them."

I was still playing the game. It was all I had left.

TWENTY-TWO

"That was fun, huh?"

Alice appeared at the end of the driveway and gave me a sidelong look as I collected myself for the drive back to the restaurant three hours later. I thought I was safe to have a private moment out in the open.

Apparently I was wrong.

"Every meal spent with our family is a true joy," I drawled, fumbling for my keys.

"You know she did it on purpose, right?"

"Who?"

"Your mother. She's trying to teach you a lesson."

"Oh, I know she did it on purpose." I thought back to the dinner, to the ten times she brought up the book, and blew out a sigh. "Grandpa says she doesn't understand what happened and that's why she keeps doing it."

"I don't think any of us truly understand what happened." Alice's voice was softer than usual. She was trying to console me, though that was well out of the realm of possibility at this point. "Maybe you should sit us all down and explain it."

That sounded like pure torture. "Or maybe I'll just go back to my job as a waitress and muddle through until the rest of you realize that you can't control my life. How does that sound?"

"As if you're crabby." Alice smiled. "I don't blame you. That dinner was ...

brutal. She really doesn't realize what she's doing. In her mind, you're throwing away something great and she can't get behind that."

"I'm not throwing it away. They threw me away."

"I get that, but I don't quite understand why after that first book."

"You're only as good as your most recent book My first book did well. My second book bombed. You don't get a second chance after a bomb like that."

"But ... I thought you were supposed to write three books for them. That's what you said."

"They cancelled the contract for the third book after losing so much money on the second."

"How can they do that if you have a contract?"

"They just can." I stared at the bush across the street for a long time, lost in thought. Finally, I shook my head and returned to the here and now. "It's not my job to hold her hand through this. I'm doing the best I can. I can't bolster her and myself at the same time."

Alice pursed her lips and nodded. She was oddly pragmatic at times and she had that look about her now. "I think the true problem is that she's worried about you and Hunter. If you two get together again, I don't think anything will drag you apart. That means you'll never have another shot at a hit book."

A sudden rush of anger coursed through. "Really? Hunter again?"

"You spent the afternoon with him. People say you were together at Deadman's Hill."

I was stunned. "How can anyone know that? We were alone."

"Ha!" Alice jabbed out her finger and did a hip-wiggling dance that made me want to kick her into a bush. "I knew it! When I couldn't find you at the restaurant I figured you were off somewhere with Hunter. I played a hunch and said Deadman's Hill because you guys used to hang out there." She pumped her fist and looked to the sky. "I've still got it."

I faltered, unsure how to proceed. "You were just guessing?" I asked.

She nodded and grinned. "Don't worry about it. I promise not to tell anyone. Your secret is safe with me."

Alice had a price when it came to information. I had no doubt she would dangle it over the head of anyone she thought would pay ... and right now the only person who might be interested was my mother. If she thought she was fooling me, she was sadly mistaken.

"Don't tell my mother." I was firm.

Alice adopted an air of innocence. "Would I do that?"

Oh, she would definitely do that. I knew she would be scampering inside to do just that the moment I left. The notion made me tired. "You know what? Do whatever you want. I'm exhausted. You think this is all a game, but it's my life. You guys wonder why I was so anxious to get out of here. This is why. Stuff like this."

Alice looked taken aback. "There's no reason to be such a baby."

"No? I just want five minutes of peace, Alice. I'll never get that here." I stormed around the front of the car and tugged on the door, my mind going to the afternoon in the woods with Hunter. I'd been at peace then — well, except for the way my lips wanted to throw a party whenever he was close — but that was the only time my mind had been quiet since I'd returned to Shadow Hills.

"I think you're overreacting," Alice said as I slid into the driver's seat. "This is just the way family is. We're all up in each other's business."

"I'm sick of it. I just want a little quiet ... and privacy ... and contentment. At my age, that shouldn't be too much to ask." I slammed the door before she could answer and brought the car to life.

What she had to add didn't matter. She was right. This was the nature of family. It was also the main reason I'd run. I had no choice but to put up with it now, but what would be the ultimate price?

I SPENT THE NEXT TWO HOURS on the couch in my living room playing with the kitten. I'd spent a small fortune on items for him, and as I stared at my banking app, old reruns of *Friends* playing in the background, I knew I was in real trouble.

"You're very cute, but expensive," I said to the kitten as I scratched behind his ear.

For his part, he didn't look bothered by the statement. He had a pink feather stuck in his fur from one of the toys and I had no doubt he'd been having a grand time playing while I was at the barbecue.

"I should've stayed home with you," I muttered as the kitten kneaded his claws on my lap. He looked intelligent, as if he understood every word I said. "Or maybe I should just run now," I murmured. "I could take off tonight, find a job somewhere in the state, and not tell anyone where I'm going. At least then it would be quiet."

The kitten looked as if he was frowning.

"We both know I don't have the guts to do that," I offered. "I think we're stuck here ... for a long while."

The kitten went back to kneading.

"I guess it's not so bad," I murmured as I went back to stroking his soft head. My eyes drifted back to the television. I'd only had half an ear on the show since I sat down. It was mindless, not hard to keep up on, and I sank back into the flow of the episode.

A few minutes later, a soft scraping sound had me lifting my chin and glancing around. The cat was on my lap, staring at the kitchen. As far as I knew, there was nothing in the restaurant below me that could make that sound. The only equipment, the refrigerators and freezers, emitted a low hum.

I listened for a moment, but the sound didn't repeat. I managed to push it out of my head and refocus on the television when it happened a second time. I hit the mute button on the remote and stared at the kitchen. I was almost certain that the noise had originated from the back balcony, and given the discussion Hunter and I had had this afternoon, the realization was enough to make my stomach clench.

I risked a glance at the kitten and found he was alert and staring in the direction of the sound. That indicated I wasn't imagining the phenomenon. Sure, he was a cat, but he was a compelling witness as far as I was concerned.

My fingers shook as I closed out of the banking app and scrolled for Hunter's name on my contact list. He'd insisted on programming his number into my phone earlier so I had someone to call in an emergency. That was looking fortuitous.

"Hello?" He sounded confused on the other end of the call.

"It's me." My mouth was dry.

"I figured that out when I saw your name pop up on the screen." He waited a beat. "Do you need something?"

"Who is that?" a female voice asked in the background. She sounded agitated.

He was still with Monica. A quick glance at the clock on the wall told me it was barely ten. Of course he was still with her. They were probably spending the night together.

"Is something wrong?" he repeated, drawing my attention back to the call.

"I ... ." What was I supposed to say here? Sure, he'd told me to call if I was afraid or ran into trouble. That wasn't fair to him, though. He had a life. I wasn't his responsibility. I hadn't been for a really long time.

"It's nothing," I said finally, feeling like an idiot. "I'm probably imagining it. I'm sorry to ruin your evening. Tell Monica ... tell her whatever you think she should know. I really am sorry."

He didn't let me hang up. "Hold on." I could hear him murmuring in the background, the sound muffled as if he had his hand over the phone. He returned to the call within a few seconds. "Is something happening?" His voice stronger this time.

"I don't know."

"Tell me what's happening," he growled.

"I thought I heard something by the sliding glass doors," I admitted. There was no going back now. "The cat heard it, too."

"What is it?"

"I'm too afraid to look," I said. "What if there really is someone out there?"

He was silent for several seconds. When he spoke again, it was in a determined voice. "Don't go to the door. Wait there. I'm about eight minutes from you. I'll come up through the back alley with my lights going to scare whoever it is away."

Eight minutes seemed a long time. "Maybe I should get a knife from the kitchen."

"Or maybe you should go down into the restaurant and lock yourself in a bathroom on the main floor."

That sounded like a terrible idea. "I ... ."

"Just stay where you are as long as you can," he instructed. "I'm on my way. If someone tries coming through that door, I want you to escape into the restaurant. Don't try to be a hero."

What he said made sense and the fear coursing through me was real. "Hunter ... ."

"I won't let anything happen to you." He was insistent. "Just ... hold on. I'm on my way."

FOR FOUR MINUTES AFTER WE disconnected I sat on the couch and stared at the dark kitchen. I didn't hear a single noise, and the kitten went to sleep. I was starting to feel a bit foolish because I hadn't heard the sound again — how was I supposed to explain that to Hunter? — when I heard it again.

This time the kitten hopped off my lap and stalked toward the kitchen. It was as if he intended to protect me even though he weighed less than a pound and had to struggle to climb the single step that led to the elevated room.

"Where are you going?" I hissed, hopping onto shaking legs as I found my voice. I couldn't let the kitten cross to the sliding glass doors. Something bad could happen to him if somebody really did decide they were coming through. "Come back here."

I felt as if I was walking on legs that had been somehow affixed to my body through shoddy means. My feet felt alien as they slapped against the linoleum and it was awkward every time I bent down in an attempt to scoop up the kitten. I couldn't see him in the darkness, but occasionally I felt his tail brushing against my legs.

"Stop messing around," I hissed. "I don't have time for this. In fact ... ." I froze when I saw a hint of movement on the other side of the glass. I'd almost forgotten the fear until that moment ... and then it came roaring back with a vengeance.

I stared at the spot where I saw the movement and tried to will myself to come up with a rational explanation for what I was seeing. It was a plastic bag that had somehow gotten away from the grocery store and was blowing in the wind. It was one of my cousins — probably Alice — messing with me. It was my mother coming to tell me what a failure I was again.

There was someone else out there. Someone who could very well be a killer. And as I stared at the silhouette, I realized the noise I was hearing was someone trying to open the door. There was nowhere for the slider to go, though, because of the broom handle in the track.

The figure moved closer and beat a hand on the glass, causing me to fall back on my rear end. My heart hammered so hard I thought it might actually pop out of my chest and flee. I let loose a strangled sound that caused the cat to screech as the figure on the other side of the door doubled his or her efforts to get inside.

"Go away!" I bellowed in an attempt to scare my uninvited guest, but despite my best attempt, my voice came out in a squeak.

The figure started tugging again.

"Go away." I didn't know what to do other than search for the cat. If I could find him, we could flee downstairs. Hunter was only a few minutes away. He would scare away whoever it was. "Where are you?" I asked helplessly as I felt around for the kitten. Even though I wanted to run, I couldn't leave him.

The figure on the other side of the door used both hands now to try to beat through the glass. The noise was enough to have my throat clogging. "Stop it!" I shouted. The feeling I'd had the night before, the sensation that something was trapped inside of me and was trying to get out, returned. This time the thing that escaped was a huge bolt of light ... and it barreled directly for the figure on the balcony.

I was so surprised I didn't bother staring at the individual's features. Instead I simply watched the light fly through the window unimpeded and collide with the silhouette.

There was a sound — a cry of pain maybe — and then the figure was staggering down the stairs. I remained rooted to my spot, watching with dumbfounded disbelief. After a few seconds, I crept closer to the door so I could look out. I could feel the stairs vibrating as my late-night visitor made his escape, and as soon as he cleared the stairs the figure bolted across the alley and toward the woods. That was the last thing I saw as the alley exploded in a sea of red and blue light.

It was Hunter. He'd arrived, just as he said.

His left the cruiser running in the alley as he threw open the door. He was too far away to see his face, but from the way he stared I was almost positive he'd seen someone flee into the woods. I thought he might follow, but instead he bolted up the stairs toward my balcony.

My fingers shook as I messed with the light switch, trying to flip it on. When I finally did, Hunter was at the top of the stairs. He looked relieved to see me.

It took me two tries to get the broomstick out of the track and open the door. When I did, I practically tumbled through the opening as Hunter pulled me in for a hug.

"Are you okay?" he whispered, stroking the back of my head.

"Someone was out there."

"I know. I saw a shadow when I was pulling up. I was going to chase him, but ... I had to check on you." He didn't release his grip, instead rubbing his cheek against mine as he held me tight. "I don't know what you did to get that big light to come on like that, but it was smart. It scared him away."

I kept my eyes closed. I didn't want to talk about the light. "Did you see who it was?"

"No. You don't have to worry, though. I won't let anything happen to you. I promise."

I believed him and yet he couldn't fix everything. He couldn't explain what was happening. Things were spiraling now, and I wasn't certain I would ever be able to get back to the way things used to be.

What was happening?

TWENTY-THREE

Hunter checked the woods, but by the time he got there the shadow was long gone. He prowled my apartment after, checking the sliding glass door at least ten times before declaring he was spending the night on the couch.

I was dumbfounded. "Do you think that's really necessary?"

"Yes." The tilt of his chin told me that there was no changing his mind, so I grabbed a blanket and pillow from the closet and made sure he was settled before retiring to my bedroom.

I couldn't decide if knowing he was in the apartment was better or worse. I felt safer with him serving as a barrier should someone try to break in again. But all I could think about was the fact that he was in my apartment, right outside the door, close enough to touch.

I tossed for hours, finally dragging myself from the bed to stand at the edge of the living room and stare at him. The light from outside was dim, but it illuminated his face. As if sensing me, he shifted and looked up. We shared a long, mournful stare. Then, wordlessly, he lifted the blanket and shifted to make room.

I had a decision to make, and it wasn't hard. I crawled in next to him, shivering as he tucked the blanket around us and held me tight.

"I won't let anything happen to you," he murmured, his breath hot on my ear. "I promise. We'll ... figure it out."

I wanted to ask exactly what he thought we were going to figure out, but this was not the time for a heavy discussion. "I'm sorry for all of this. It's not your job to take care of me."

"I'm a police officer. It is my job." His body was warm next to mine. "Go to sleep, Stormy. In addition to getting you blinds, I'll upgrade the security system on that door tomorrow. I don't want to hear any arguments."

"Okay." Something occurred to me. "Do you still snore?"

He chuckled, the sound low and throaty. "Does it matter?"

"No, but I'm actually looking forward to it."

"Then batten the hatches. I think you're going to be happy."

HE DID INDEED STILL SNORE. I slept harder than I had in years, though, despite the upheaval of the previous night. When I woke, the sun was just beginning to peek over the horizon. I felt warm and safe and happy.

And then he shifted.

"You're awake," I realized. The lack of snores should've been a giveaway.

"I am."

I rolled so I could see his face, almost sighing when I caught sight of the morning stubble and lazy smile. "Did you sleep okay?"

"Surprisingly, yeah. I didn't even stir once I went down."

"Me either. I didn't dream. I can't remember the last time that happened."

"You used to say that you got your story ideas from dreams." He pushed my hair from my eyes, making me realize it was probably standing on end in a hundred different directions. He didn't seem to care, so I didn't either.

"I haven't gotten story inspiration in a long time." Even though I was ridiculously comfortable, I strained to a sitting position and studied the clock. "I have to be downstairs in thirty minutes."

"Morning shift again?" His lips curved into a smirk. "I take it from that look on your face that you're still not a morning person."

"I hate mornings. Grandpa is making me stay on them until he's convinced I don't need supervision. He's a mean dude when he wants to be."

Hunter barked out a laugh. "He's a pretty decent guy."

"Then why is he making me work mornings when he knows I hate them?"

"Have you ever considered that he wants you close? You've been gone a long time. You're one of his favorites, though he'd never admit to having favorites."

"The boys are his favorites."

"On the surface, yes. He's closer with the boys, like David, because he thinks he should be. But he favors you."

"He has a funny way of showing it."

Hunter's hand moved to my back so he could lightly rub. "I still think he loves you."

"Of course he loves me. We're family. You have to love family, even when you don't like them."

"Fine. I think he likes you, too. You're just determined to be hard on yourself right now, so there's no point in continuing this conversation. Hopefully, when things settle a bit, you'll realize what a pain you're being and get over it."

I shot him a look. "I'm not being a pain."

"Oh, you're being a pain." He poked my side and grinned. "You've always been this way. You're a crab in the morning, but I think there's more going on here than just that."

He was right. "Do you ever think things are so bad there's no way they can ever get better?"

It was a serious question, and the way the smile slid from his face told me he was going to give it a serious answer. "Only once."

"With your dad?" I felt like an idiot. He'd gone through so much. Of course he felt that way as a kid.

"No. I knew I would get away from my father if I could somehow survive for a few years. When you and I got together, the escapes were easier. The dreams were easier, too. I saw the way your family was and knew there was more out there."

The reaction was so earnest it shocked me into silence.

"The only time I felt like there was no way out was when I lost you." He shimmied to the end of the couch and refused to meet my gaze. "It took a long time to crawl out from that hole. I did, though. Eventually. You'll do the same. You just need to ... breathe. I don't think you're allowing yourself to relax even a little bit."

"How can I when there are strange people trying to get into my apartment?"

"I plan to make sure that's impossible after today, so you can't continue to use that as an excuse."

I decided to remind him one more time that I wasn't his responsibility. "You don't have to. I'm sure you have things that need to be done in your own life." Like Monica, who was probably spitting mad.

"Don't start." He pinned me with a look. "This is going to happen. I'm not leaving this apartment until I'm sure you'll be safe. Just ... stop arguing about it."

Another glance at the clock told me I had no choice in that matter. "Well, thank you." I grunted as I found my footing. "I think I might be too old to sleep on the couch like we just did."

That was enough to earn another smile. "Yes, you're old and decrepit."

"Sometimes I feel that way."

"Well, get over it." He was firm. "Your life is still at the beginning. Once you realize that, you'll start looking forward instead of back. That will be a great day."

"I certainly hope so."

GRANDPA WAS BEHIND THE GRILL. The look he shot me was unreadable.

"I'm on time," I said automatically. Sure, my hair was still wet and I'd whipped it back in a braid to keep it out of my face, but I wasn't late.

"I'm well aware." His eyes returned to the stairs, as if waiting for someone else to come down.

"What are you looking for?" I asked, confused.

"You know *who* I'm looking for."

My stomach did a jittery jig. "I don't know what you're talking about." I was never the smoothest of liars.

"Oh, geez." Grandpa rolled his eyes until they landed on me. "His car is in the alley. I've already heard from the grocery store people that it was there all night. Don't bother denying it. Everyone in town already knows."

The blood started rushing through my ears as I tried to wrap my brain around what he was saying. "But ... ." On wooden legs, I moved to the back door and looked out. Sure enough, Hunter's cruiser was parked exactly where he'd left it. I'd completely forgotten about it.

"The Sysco deliveryman is coming in twenty minutes," Grandpa noted. "He needs to park there. If Hunter is planning on sneaking out via the back steps, you might ask him to get a move on."

My mouth was unnaturally dry. "I ... nothing happened." I blurted it out before thinking. "He was just helping me with something."

"I know exactly what he was helping you with." Grandpa didn't boast even a hint of a smile. "Did he at least break up with his girlfriend?"

"Nothing happened," I repeated, panic starting to creep in. "You can't tell anyone about this."

"No? I thought nothing happened. If it's so innocent, why are you so worked up?"

"Because it's not fair to Hunter." I didn't care about my reputation. His was

181

a different story. "If people in this town start talking ... ." I trailed off, horrified at the prospect.

"Don't worry about it, Stormy," Hunter announced, appearing in the opening that led to the stairs. He was focused on Grandpa, not me. "People in this town have been talking about me my entire life. After what went down with my father, this is minor."

Grandpa pursed his lips. "The girlfriend is no more, right? That will make this easier."

Hunter hesitated. "Nothing happened last night. Stormy called because someone was trying to get into her apartment. Don't give her a hard time about it."

"That's not what I asked." Grandpa shifted his eyes to me. "What does he mean? Why would someone try to get into your apartment?"

I shrugged. "I don't know. It happened late and I panicked. That's why I called Hunter."

"But ... that makes no sense."

"It does if you consider the fact that a body was found in the alley right under her apartment a few days ago," Hunter challenged. "Speaking of that, you and I are going to have a talk. You can keep hiding all you want, but it's going to happen."

Grandpa straightened. "I don't hide."

"Whatever." Hunter flicked his eyes to me. "I'm going to get the things I need to upgrade your security system from the hardware store. I need the keys so I can get in and out without interrupting your shift."

I nodded and reached into my apron, handing over the keys without a word.

"How are you going to upgrade the security up there?" Grandpa challenged. "There are only two ways to get in."

"And I'm upgrading both of them." Hunter was firm. "I might change the back locks on this restaurant, too, so be prepared for that."

Grandpa opened his mouth, I'm sure to argue, but then snapped it shut. "Make sure she's safe," he said finally.

"That's the plan. As for the other thing ... don't worry about it. I'll handle Monica."

"She's an unpleasant girl, son, but I don't want my granddaughter earning a reputation that isn't warranted. It's not fair."

"I don't care about my reputation," I argued.

"Shush, you." Grandpa wagged a finger. "This is a small town. You need to handle your business."

"I'm going to handle my business," Hunter reassured him. "You need to make yourself available for questions later. I'm going to be ticked if I have to hunt you down this afternoon."

"I haven't been hiding," Grandpa protested.

"Yeah, yeah, yeah." Hunter shook his head. "Just be available. I'm sick of your crap ... and I am going out of my way to keep your granddaughter safe. You owe me."

Grandpa was resigned. "Let's not pretend that you're doing this for me. You're doing it for her ... and yourself."

Hunter remained silent.

"I'll be around if you need to talk later," Grandpa relented. "You have to wait until I'm done on the grill. We'll be slammed through the breakfast rush."

THE MORNING SHIFT SEEMED TO DRAG on forever. And ever, and ever and ever.

Grandpa watched me like a hawk, perhaps thinking I was going to run upstairs to hang out with Hunter the second he turned his back.

For his part, Hunter walked in and out through the back door, ignoring everyone but David, who dropped in from the gas station to see what the fuss was about. Hunter moved his car to one of the employee parking spots and set about his tasks.

Occasionally he met my gaze when I was placing orders or picking up plates, but he only offered an encouraging smile. We didn't talk, and eventually I managed to push him out of my mind when he set up shop in my apartment. Every once in a while I heard hammering upstairs, but he didn't come back down and I lost myself in my work.

After a few hours, I managed to convince myself — mostly — that the only people who knew Hunter had spent the night were Grandpa and the grocery store manager. That notion went straight out the window when the door flew open shortly after ten and Monica stormed in. The look on her face told me that the gossip train in Shadow Hills was still chugging along.

"*You.*" Her eyes were narrow slits of hate.

I swallowed hard, glancing around to see if anybody was watching. Every set of eyes in the restaurant had turned in our direction. There was so little to do in town that meal theater was a regular occurrence, and it was obvious everyone in the cafe section was ready for some entertainment.

"Hey, Monica." I tried not to focus on her eyebrows. They'd clearly been drawn on with pencil ... and unevenly at that. I reminded myself that she had every right to be angry. From her perspective, her boyfriend had spent the night with another woman. She couldn't possibly be aware of the circumstances surrounding the act itself, so she'd filled in the gaps herself. "You look nice today."

Her expression darkened. "Do you think that's going to work on me?" She stalked over to the coffee counter, her hands clenched into fists at her sides.

"Maybe we should take this outside?" I suggested, hating the eyes I felt watching us. "It might be better if we keep this private."

"Better for whom?" Monica's tone was icy. "Do you think they don't already know? Are you really that stupid? Or don't you care? I'm guessing it's that you don't care."

I pressed my tongue to the top of my mouth and remained focused on the coffee pot. "Nothing happened."

"Oh, don't even." I had no doubt that if Monica thought she could get away with it she would launch herself over the counter and start beating me over the head with the coffee pot.

I found the strength to raise my chin and meet her gaze head on. "There was an incident last night and Hunter came to help. Someone tried to break into my apartment. That's all it was."

"So he had to spend the night with you?" There was fury in her eyes. She hated me. There was no doubt about it. To be fair, she'd probably hated me before we even met. My history with Hunter would've ensured that.

"He slept on the couch." Sure, I ended up sleeping with him, but she didn't need to know that. "He was being a good friend."

"He's not your friend," she screeched. "He's my boyfriend ... or was. If he thinks I'm going to sit back and let him make a fool of me, he's got another thing coming."

I felt bad. Like ... *really* bad. I'd cost Hunter something more than just a letterman's jacket this time. "I swear nothing happened." The words felt empty coming out of my mouth.

"I don't believe you!" If it was possible to shoot fire from eyes, like in movies, I would be a charred mess. "I knew when I heard you were coming back that it was going to be bad. I told him. But he reassured me. He said he would never have feelings for you again because of what happened.

"I wanted to believe him, so I did," she continued. "He was lying. I think I always knew that. Still, I thought you would at least show me a modicum of respect and not go after him the first week. I guess I know what sort of person you are now."

I searched for the right words — any words would do at this point — to placate her. There was nothing. There was no justification that would suffice.

"Is there a problem here?" Grandpa demanded from between the swinging doors, causing me to jolt. I hadn't noticed him sneaking up to check out the show.

"Is there a problem?" Monica's voice was like razor blades on glass. "Are you kidding me? There's a big freaking problem. Your granddaughter is a whore."

Grandpa slid his eyes to me and I read the disappointment there. He knew this would happen. I'd managed to convince myself otherwise, but it was too late to backtrack and do things the right way. I'd managed to hurt Hunter and myself. Heck, I'd managed to disappoint my grandfather. Life couldn't get much worse.

"I'm sorry you're upset," Grandpa said blandly, "but this conversation is not for public consumption. If you want to continue, then you'll have to take it someplace else."

Monica was incredulous. "Are you kicking me out?"

"I'm asking you to take this conversation elsewhere."

"And what if I refuse?"

"Then I'm kicking you out." Grandpa was matter-of-fact. "I'm not going to sit here and listen to you attack Stormy. She's not your problem. If you have issues with Hunter's behavior, take them up with him. He's the one you're in a relationship with."

Monica puffed out her chest. "I'm going to tell everyone exactly what sort of person your granddaughter is. I don't think anyone will be surprised, though."

"You might want to check your attitude at the door," Grandpa warned. "People already know what type of person she is."

"Oh, they're going to know even more about her now. Mark my words." Before I could say anything, Monica spun on her heel and stormed toward the door. "I'm going to make you pay, Stormy. This is nowhere near over."

I heaved out a breath when she disappeared through the door, and turned toward my grandfather to thank him for stepping in. He was already gone, though, disappeared back into the kitchen.

"That kind of sucked, huh?"

I jerked my head to a nearby booth and found Roy's secretary, Erin, drinking coffee with another woman I didn't recognize. She looked positively thrilled with the turn of events, as if she'd been waiting hours for a show and had finally been rewarded.

"It totally sucked," I agreed, rolling my neck. I still had a shift to finish, and I was determined to do it with as much dignity as I could muster. "Do you need more coffee?"

"Sure."

"I'll be right over. Just give me a minute."

TWENTY-FOUR

I refused to run cowering into the kitchen. That would simply reinforce the town's assumption that Hunter and I had done something wrong. Instead, I held my shoulders square and finished my shift even as a voice whispered in the back of my head: *You did do something wrong.*

I didn't want to think about Monica as a victim, but now she'd been hurt by me twice. Yes, Hunter and I had only slept together on the couch. There had been no wandering hands or tongues. There hadn't been as much as a hint of a chaste kiss (or a dirty one, for that matter). That didn't change the fact that I was more than willing to cuddle up to Hunter all night, and that was a betrayal of whatever he had with Monica. If the roles had been reversed and I was the one with a boyfriend sleeping on the couch with another woman, I would've been just as loud as Monica, maybe more so.

"What are you thinking about?" Grandpa asked from the coffee counter twenty minutes before the end of my shift. I was anxious to get off my feet — and out of the public eye — but also determined to stand strong in the face of all the whispers.

"I'm just ... thinking." I forced a smile that I didn't really feel. "You don't think this will blow back on Hunter and hurt him, do you?"

Grandpa arched an amused eyebrow. He didn't respond, though.

"I get the feeling that it's been difficult for him given what went down with his parents. I don't want to add to that."

"Good grief." Grandpa tilted his head back and pinched the bridge of his nose so he could stare at the ceiling. "You are unbelievable."

"It's a serious question." I refused to back down. "I don't want to cost him more than I already have."

Grandpa's eyes were incredulous when they traveled back to mine. "You cannot be serious."

"Why wouldn't I be serious?"

"Because ... it's the most ridiculous thing I've ever heard. What is it you think you've taken from Hunter?"

I thought back to what he'd said about being broken-hearted after our breakup. "More than you're capable of understanding."

"Oh, I'm capable of understanding quite a bit," Grandpa countered. "I'm not an idiot. You and Hunter aren't so complex that nobody can figure you out. You're actually an open book."

"Oh, really?" I rolled my eyes. My grandfather wasn't known for being particularly observant about things that didn't involve him. "And what do you see when you look at us?"

"Two people who will never get over one another." He was matter-of-fact ... and full of himself. "I don't know that I believe in love at first sight. I never did. Lust is another thing ... as long as you're over eighteen, which you and Hunter weren't when this all started." He sent me a pointed look.

"Everybody was afraid when you were a kid that you would throw your life away and never experience anything if you stayed with him," he continued. "Now, the opposite is true. You went out into the world but you weren't happy. I'm starting to believe you need him to be happy."

I was shocked. "I don't believe a woman needs a man to be happy."

"I don't either. I might've twenty years or so ago, but I know better now. This isn't about a woman needing a man. This is about you needing Hunter."

I didn't know what to say.

"I'd already come to the conclusion that he needed you years ago," Grandpa offered. "I tried to reach out to him, offer him the family he so desperately craved, but he didn't want to be around us without you. That's when I knew you were the key."

Tears pricked the backs of my eyes. "He's with Monica."

Grandpa rolled his eyes. "Don't kid yourself, Stormy. That relationship is already over. Heck, he let it continue longer than he should have simply because he wanted a way to keep you at arm's length. I think he realizes that was a wasted effort. Monica will be gone by the end of the day — if she doesn't break up with him first because she sees the writing on the wall."

"She's still his girlfriend," I persisted, refusing to give in to hope.

Grandpa clucked his tongue and shook his head. "Do you want to know what your problem is?"

"Not really."

He barreled forward as if I hadn't said anything. "Your problem is that you have to experience every wrong emotion before you can embrace the right one. You've always been that way. You weren't a kid who could learn the easy way. It always had to be hard."

I shook my head. I had to get him off this subject. "I need to talk about Roy Axe," I started, earning a glare. "You can be as angry as you want, but Hunter is convinced that whoever tried to get into the apartment last night is tied to Roy's death. We need to figure out who did this."

"Why do you think I would know anything about Roy?"

"You used to be friends. Somewhere along the way you had a falling out. I want to know what it was about."

"He was an ass."

"That seems to be the general consensus," I agreed. "That didn't stop you from being friends with him years ago. I remember you two hanging out."

"We weren't friends."

I waited, folding my arms over my chest. I refused to let him escape from this conversation again.

"I guess the most you could say is we were friendly," Grandpa continued. "We golfed together for a time. We had coffee together. Heck, he still had coffee here every morning even though everybody hated him."

"You're avoiding the question," I pressed. "That's not like you. The more you sidestep this, the more I think you have something to hide."

He glared. "I didn't kill him."

"I know you didn't." That was mostly true. "That's not who you are. You're far more likely to annoy him to death. That doesn't change the fact that you've been avoiding Hunter. I want to know why."

"I haven't been avoiding Hunter. He simply has bad timing."

I waited.

"This is none of your business." He threw his hands in the air. "I'm only telling you this to get you to shut up. You're giving me a headache. Do you know who you learned that from? Your mother."

He was trying to derail me, but I had no intention of letting that happen. "Tell me what happened between you and Roy."

He let loose a sigh, the sound long and drawn out. It was almost as if he was being tortured. "So, it's not a big deal, but ... well ... Roy cheated on his wife."

I waited for him to continue. When he didn't, I hiked an eyebrow. "You're kidding. I never would've guessed."

"Nobody needs the sarcasm, young lady," he shot back.

"How do you know that was sarcastic?" I challenged. "I might be in the dark regarding Roy's penchant for cheating on his wife."

"Nobody is in the dark regarding Roy's crap. That's simply not how it works. He liked being brash and bold because he thought people would respect him if he acted like a buffoon. He didn't realize how much people hated him. Or, maybe he did. It's possible he acted that way because he was desperate for attention. Some people need the attention no matter what, and Roy was always one of those people."

"You still haven't told me what he did," I pointed out.

Grandpa's scowl only grew more pronounced. "There was this girl. Tina Thompkins. She was in your grade when you graduated from high school."

Now it was my turn to frown. "I remember her."

"Yeah? Well, she went to work for Roy about three years ago. She worked for me before that, but she was having trouble being on her feet all day. She was a good girl. I didn't want to see her fall by the wayside."

I didn't say anything, instead allowing the space between sentences to fill with silence. I had the feeling I was about to learn something terrible.

"I suggested she work for Roy as a secretary," Grandpa continued, refusing to meet my gaze. "He already had one secretary, but he was making noise about needing another. I suggested Tina and he agreed to hire her.

"At first it seemed like a good fit," he continued. "Tina was happy and not having the same physical problems she had at the restaurant. I didn't think much of it until I ran into Tina at the store in Gaylord one day. She was crying and we got to talking and ... well ... she mentioned she'd lost her job."

The feeling of dread grew, but I remained silent.

"I asked her what happened and it all came spilling out." Grandpa's expression turned dark. "She said Roy pressured her for sex if she wanted to keep her job. She didn't have any other options so she gave in. Then, after all that, Vera became suspicious, so he fired her anyway."

I thought back to the story Bobby had told while drunk at the party. "She's the reason Vera was talking to a divorce attorney. Roy was paying her off, draining the retirement fund he'd set up with Vera. There had to be a reason. Did she threaten to sue?"

Grandpa's face was blank. "I don't know. I didn't even know Roy was paying her off. That's not the way Tina made it sound."

"I'm still confused about why you were hiding from Hunter," I said. "Helping a young woman get a job is not illegal."

"No, but I figured if I talked to him I would let it slip that Tina had a motive to kill Roy. I didn't want to make things worse for her. We both know I can't keep my mouth shut, no matter how hard I try."

That was the truth ... and it kind of made sense. Still, there was a hint of doubt playing through my mind. "You didn't go out of your way to help Tina because you were doing anything with her, did you?"

Grandpa looked scandalized. "I'm a married man!"

"So was Roy. That didn't stop him from cheating."

"Maybe not, but I'm not Roy."

There was something he wasn't telling me. I knew from studying the obstinate tilt of his chin that he was done opening up. If I wanted more information, I was going to have to find it myself.

"Just out of curiosity, what did Roy say when you called him on his actions?" I asked as I grabbed the coffee pot so I could make my rounds.

"He said that his needs were more important than hers, that she should've thought better about sleeping with her boss if she wanted to keep her job. He insinuated she chased him, but we all know that wasn't true."

My stomach twisted. "Yeah. He was the sort of guy who bragged, even if there was nothing to brag about."

"Exactly." Grandpa's eyes narrowed as he regarded me. "What are you going to do with this information?"

"Probably pass it on to Hunter. Don't worry. I won't tell him where I heard it."

"I appreciate it."

"It's the least I can do."

HUNTER WAS KNEE-DEEP IN A NEW security system when I bolted upstairs to change clothes after my shift. He barely looked up as he sat cross-legged on the kitchen floor and paged through a thick instruction manual. The kitten was nestled on his lap and seemed intrigued by the action.

"How was work?" he asked absently.

I briefly wondered if I should tell him about the scene Monica made. It would be an uncomfortable conversation and I didn't want to get into it when

I had a lead to track down. "It was work. I'm going to change clothes and then I'll help."

That was enough to get him to look at me. "No offense, Stormy, but I don't need your help."

I dubiously regarded the various pieces of the security system strewn about the floor. "Are you sure? I've grown to be pretty good with electronics."

He looked haughty. "I've got it."

I watched him a long moment and then nodded. "Okay. I'm going to change my clothes and run out. I have a few errands."

Hunter didn't look interested in my errands. Instead he waved off the statement and went back to the instructions. Apparently he planned to sit there until he climbed that particular mountain and beat it into submission. That was so like him.

"Good luck," I called out before dashing into the bedroom. I was out of clean clothes, so I had to dig something out of the hamper. I now had no choice but to go to the laundromat or I was going to have to spring for more clothes. I wasn't sure which was worse.

Once I exited the restaurant and hopped in my car, I plugged Tina's name into Google. After a couple of clicks, I found what I thought was probably her house, and drove in that direction. It was on the outskirts of Shadow Hills, in a not unpleasant neighborhood. In fact, the closer I drew to her street, the more impressed I became. Compared to the rest of the town, which contained rundown homes and overgrown lawns in certain areas, everything here was neat and tidy. I wasn't an expert on real estate, but the houses looked more expensive, too.

It took me three times around the block to find the house I was looking for because some of them weren't properly marked. When I did, I was pleasantly surprised to find a pretty redbrick ranch with an abundance of flowers in the front garden. If Tina was hurting for money, I couldn't see how she could afford this house. Perhaps she'd managed to find another job after all and was thriving.

I parked on the street and exited my car, giving the house a long once-over before starting up the sidewalk. I wasn't sure how I was going to approach Tina — it would be difficult no matter what tack I chose — and my mind was already on what I was going to say when I noticed a hint of movement out of the corner of my eye.

"Can I help you?"

I widened my eyes when I saw Tina. She was dressed in ratty shorts and a

T-shirt and looked to have a small garden hoe clutched in her hand. She appeared as surprised to see me as I was her.

"Hey, Tina." As far as greetings go, it was the lamest of the lame. Still, I'd been caught off guard and it was going to take me a moment to recover.

"Hello." Tina looked wary, furrowing her brow as she looked me up and down. "I don't want to buy anything."

"I'm not selling anything," I reassured her quickly. "I just ... um ... ."

She narrowed her eyes. "Stormy Morgan?"

Relief washed over me. That was one less problem. "Yeah. It's me. I'm back in town."

"I guess so." The mistrust that had been on her face only moments before evaporated as she smiled. "What's going on? When did you get back?"

"Two weeks ago, but I was moving back and forth between Harsens Island and here, so I've only been back at the restaurant full time for a few days."

"You're back at the restaurant?" Tina looked surprised. "I thought you were writing books."

It took monumental effort to keep my smile in place. "Yeah, well, that's a work in progress. So ... um ... I hear you used to work for my grandfather."

She nodded. "It didn't work out because I have bad circulation and my feet always swelled after a shift. Your grandfather was helpful, though, and went out of his way to help me find another job."

"He might've mentioned it. In fact ... ." Whatever I was going to say died on my lips as a toddler moved from a spot behind Tina and plopped on the ground. The little boy had a clump of grass in his hand. He looked to be having a grand time with it, barely noticing me.

"Mommy, look. Look!"

Tina smiled fondly at the boy. "Yes. Grass."

That's when things coalesced for me, the thing Grandpa didn't want to spread around becoming clear. "Oh, geez," I muttered. "That's Roy's kid, isn't it?"

Her lips curved down. "How did you know that?"

"It makes sense."

She looked as if she wanted to bolt. I didn't blame her.

"We need to talk."

She didn't look convinced. "What if I don't want to talk?"

"You're either talking to me or the cops. Which do you prefer?"

She sighed. "I guess I prefer you, but that's not saying much."

In her position, I'd feel the same way.

TWENTY-FIVE

Tina blanked her face. "I don't know what you mean." She refused to make eye contact.

"Roy is his father." I gestured toward the toddler. "That's why my grandfather was going out of his way to protect you. He didn't want news getting out."

Tina hesitated and then nodded. "Your grandfather is one of the few people who know."

"This is a small town," I pointed out. "People had to ask where you got him."

"Dakota." Tina smiled fondly at the boy, who offered her a wide grin as he grabbed more grass in his grubby hands. "That's his name."

"Obviously his last name isn't Axe."

"No." She turned solemn. "He has my last name."

"And nobody ever asked about him?"

"People asked. I just said it was a guy I met at a bar in Gaylord. People accepted that. We have a lot of unexpected pregnancies here. I'm hardly the first single woman to show up with a baby in Shadow Hills."

I remembered that well from high school. "I think twenty people in our graduating class were pregnant before the commencement speech."

"Which is why so many people are desperate to get out of here." The look she gave me was long. "You got out, but you came back. That has to be a first."

"The story is long and boring. You don't want to hear it."

"I could say the same about my story."

"Except Dakota's father was found dead behind the restaurant several days ago," I pointed out. "There are no dead bodies in my story ... at least none that aren't fictional."

"Yeah." She exhaled heavily and then pointed toward a pair of lawn chairs in the shade of a large maple tree. "I'll tell you the story, but I don't want it getting out. It's not about me. It's about Dakota. People would treat him differently if they knew."

"Because Roy is somehow worse than some random bar hookup?"

"You met him. Of course he was."

I couldn't argue with that.

She grabbed Dakota around the waist and carried him to the shade. Once there, he seemed perfectly content playing with the grass and leaves, occasionally lifting his treasures to show his mother. Tina made a big deal out of each thing he showed her, making me believe she was a good mother. I wanted to protect her.

"In a nutshell, your grandfather helped me get the job with Roy, and I was really grateful. It was the perfect job for me — until he started making suggestions."

My lip curled. I could just imagine the suggestions Roy made. "Everyone in town knows he was a dirty pervert. There's nothing you could say that would surprise me."

"But I didn't know that," Tina admitted ruefully. "I guess I was just out of the loop. I thought he was a nice old man because your grandfather is a nice old man."

I had to bite back a laugh. If my grandfather heard himself being referred to as "old" he would have a meltdown. "Yeah, I've never heard anyone refer to Roy as nice."

"I just didn't realize. He started pressuring me within weeks of me taking the job. The money was good and the workload was tolerable. I didn't want to lose the opportunity."

"You also didn't want to disappoint Grandpa," I surmised. "In your mind, he'd gone out of his way for you."

"He did."

"Except Roy was so desperate to be seen as an equal where Grandpa was concerned he would've done it regardless." I rubbed my forehead. "How long before he threatened your job if you didn't sleep with him?"

"Six weeks."

I felt sick to my stomach. "What an Axehole. You should've reported him to the police. That's sexual harassment. Hunter would've helped you."

"I didn't want anyone to know. I was embarrassed."

I couldn't blame her. It was doubtful I would've acted differently in her situation, no matter how much I wanted to believe I was above it all. "What did he do when he found out you were pregnant?"

"He freaked out. He was desperate that Vera not find out. He wanted me to have an abortion, which I flatly refused."

"Did you shake him down for money?"

"Why would I do that? He didn't want Dakota, but I did. I didn't expect anything from him."

I was surprised. "Wait ... are you saying that you didn't get child support from Roy?" It was bad enough that the guy was a lecherous old goat, but to not take care of his child was a new low.

"I took money. I wish I could say it wasn't necessary. He wanted to pay me in one lump sum, because it would be easier to explain to his wife. I agreed, with the stipulation that he help with Dakota's college education when it was time."

I pursed my lips. "How did you know he would survive that long?"

"I didn't, but I had no interest in upending lives. I just wanted to be able to live my life away from gossip and prying eyes. It's worked out well so far. I found a job doing medical transcriptions online, and with the money Roy gave me I'm doing pretty well."

She was doing better than me. I couldn't very well afford to throw stones. "So, you had no motive to kill Roy."

She arched an eyebrow, clearly amused. "Did you think I did?"

I shrugged. "I guess maybe I was hoping it was you ... not on a personal level or anything," I added hurriedly. "The idea that there's a killer running around out there has me unnerved." As did the fact that I'd managed to burn a woman's eyebrows off with my mind and my ex-boyfriend slept on my couch the previous evening. "Can you think of anyone who would've wanted to kill Roy?"

She shook her head. "It's possible multiple people wanted to kill Roy. I didn't harbor any ill will toward him. He wasn't exactly my favorite person, but he gave me what he could for Dakota. He stayed out of our lives. He's worth nothing to me dead. I don't gain anything."

She was better off if he'd lived long enough to see Dakota go to college. "So ... I guess it's back to square one for me."

"Sorry I couldn't be more help." She seemed genuine. "I'm pretty sure this has nothing to do with me."

"Unless it was Vera and she was angry over the money that went missing from their accounts," I muttered, causing her to widen her eyes. "That still wouldn't be your fault, though," I reassured her. "You're clean in this."

"I don't feel clean where Roy is concerned. He makes it worth it, though." She grinned at Dakota, who handed a rock to me. The small Petoskey stone made me smile.

"Thank you." I beamed at him. "I'll cherish it for life."

I WAS STILL ANTSY FOR ANSWERS, SO MY next stop was Barry Buttons. I wanted to know if Vera's attorney had any insight.

Barry's secretary seemed confused when I said I merely wanted to talk to her boss, not enlist his services. She stalled, but when I refused to leave she finally placed a call to his office. If her expression was any indication, she was surprised when Barry readily agreed to see me.

He was the smarmy sort. I could tell that the second I invaded his personal space. He was a big guy, gut hanging over the belt of his pants, and there were photos of him and various women splashed all over his office. There were also trophies declaring him the "World's Best Divorce Attorney," which I found tacky and unnecessary.

"Stormy Morgan." He grinned at me as if we were old friends. "It's been a long time."

"It has," I agreed, forcing a smile for his benefit. "I saw you in the restaurant the other day."

"The restaurant?" His forehead wrinkled. "You will have to be more specific."

That was weird. Shadow Hills had exactly one full restaurant, one lunch cafe and one pizza shop. "Two Broomsticks."

"Oh, right." He bobbed his head. "Duh. I forgot Charlie was your grandfather. Were you in there eating lunch?"

"No. I filled your coffee."

"Oh." He seemed perplexed. "I didn't know you were back and working for your grandfather."

"I'm back, at least for the foreseeable future."

"That's so sad." He made a clucking sound. "I'm sorry things have gone so poorly for you."

I was fairly certain I hadn't mentioned anything going poorly. He was just being a condescending jerk. I bit back a series of uncomfortable words to tell him exactly what I thought about his false sympathy and remained on task — though it took monumental effort. He definitely wouldn't answer my questions if I started with a verbal attack.

"I'm a work in progress," I said blandly. "I'm actually here about Roy Axe. Did you know I was the one who found his body?"

"I knew one of Charlie's grandchildren found him. I didn't know it was you. That's a terrible business. You must be traumatized."

He looked as if he wanted to console me. "I've managed to muddle through," I said dryly. "I'm more interested in who would want to kill him ... and why he was dumped behind the restaurant."

"I don't know the who, but the why is relatively easy. He parked in that back lot a good hour before your grandfather opened every day."

That was news to me. "Why did he do that?"

"Because he wanted to hang out with your grandfather."

"But ... why?"

"Even though it defies reason, people love Charlie. He has a way about him. He's rude and he likes messing with people, but he does it in a charming manner. Roy desperately wanted to be liked by everyone, yet very few people could tolerate him. He wasn't the most observant sort, but he picked up on things like that."

In a weird way, that made sense. Everything I knew about Roy indicated that he was desperate for affection. It was obvious that Vera didn't much care for him — not that she had reason to — and he was hungry for approval. I'd seen people like that in the book world. Validation, no matter what form, was more important than anything else to some authors. I'd been one of them at the start. Now I knew better. There were more important things than being thought of as a big shot.

"So, you're saying that his regular routine included parking in the lot behind the restaurant every morning. Did everyone know that, or was it something only a few people were aware of?"

He shrugged, noncommittal. "It's a small town. Almost all the information you could possibly want is readily available if you care enough to look."

"Did Vera know?"

"I would have to think she did. They were married a really long time. She knew him better than most."

"Did she know everything about him?" I was fishing. This was a delicate topic, but I'd already come this far.

"Like what?"

"I don't know. Like ... did she know that Roy basically hit on anyone with boobs?"

Barry snorted, amusement evident on his round face. "Vera isn't blind. She was well aware of Roy's rather unsavory appetites."

"And yet she stayed married to him."

"Women of a certain generation aren't as willing to risk losing everything, even if it means gaining peace of mind."

"Was Vera planning to divorce Roy before he died? Is that why you were spending time together?"

"I can't discuss private client details with you."

It was a well-rehearsed answer. It was also true. That didn't mean I was going to simply abandon my search for information.

"What about Roy's will?" I asked. "Is Vera better off with him dead than she was with him alive?"

"You'll have to ask her."

"What about in a general sense?"

"Meaning?"

"Meaning you can't talk about the specifics of the work you do for Vera. What if I ask you generic questions? Can you answer those?"

"I ... suppose." His eyes narrowed, as if he expected a trap. He was wise to be wary. I was too tired to play an extended game, though. This would have to be quick.

"So, say I'm married to a man for more than thirty years and I find out that all the money he said would be waiting for our retirement was suddenly gone," I started. "Would I be better off with that man continuing to bring in money, or dying and leaving me his Social Security and a potential life insurance policy?"

"That's a very specific question."

"I'm a curious soul."

"You're definitely that." He let out an exaggerated grunt and leaned back in his chair, extending his legs in front of him. He didn't look annoyed by my persistence as much as intrigued. "Without having specifics, in general, I would say someone would be better off with a dead spouse in those circumstances. That doesn't mean I condone murder."

"Of course not." I waved off the statement. "Did Roy have a life insurance policy?"

"I have no idea."

"Has Vera expressed sadness at his death?"

"You'll have to talk to her about that."

"What would happen to an estate if it was proven there were children sired outside of the marriage?"

He sat up straight. "What are you suggesting?"

Now it was my turn to play coy. "I'm not suggesting anything. I'm merely asking a hypothetical question."

Barry didn't look convinced, but now he was fully engaged in the conversation. "It depends on multiple things."

"What are those multiple things?"

"There are ... variables. For instance, if the child's mother struck an agreement with the father then the child might be in line to inherit nothing."

I thought about Tina. She would be the type to sit back and do nothing even though she was owed money for her son's future. "What other variables?"

"An unborn child would be a completely different scenario. In that instance, the child would have to go through DNA testing after birth and any money that might go to the child's mother, or in a trust, would be delayed."

"Is that it?"

"In a nutshell."

I wasn't sure what to make of the information. "What do you think happened to Roy?" I asked. "Who do you think hated him enough to kill him?"

"If you're asking me if I think Vera is capable of killing her husband, I don't. She put up with a lot from the man, but she wouldn't have killed him. Part of her loved him, despite everything that he did to her over the years.

"I think Roy loved Vera, too," he continued. "It was in a careless way, but he still loved her. The things he did weren't designed to hurt her. He just craved the attention."

"Yeah, but how many people did Roy hurt in other ways over the years?" I persisted. "Nobody had anything nice to say about him. There's a reason for that."

"There is, but if you're focused on Vera — and I don't understand why you're even here asking these questions since you're not a police officer — you're barking up the wrong tree. Vera wouldn't kill Roy. As for everybody else in town, I'm not an expert.

"The thing about a place like Shadow Hills is that everybody knows everybody, but that doesn't mean secrets are always out in the open," he said. "People work overtime in an environment like this to hide their true motivations, especially if those motivations are anything other than altruistic. In my opinion, whoever killed Roy is good at hiding who they are. That could be anyone, because no matter how well you think you know someone, it's never as well as you might think."

That was also true. "You've given me a lot to think about. Thank you for your time."

TWENTY-SIX

H unter was finishing up his security overhaul when I returned. He looked proud of himself, his chest puffed out, as he displayed the new wall mount.

"Well?"

My mind was busy with a million possibilities, but I nodded. "It's pretty cool." I stepped closer to give it a solid once-over. "It looks expensive."

He let lose an exasperated sigh. "Don't worry about that. I hardly went broke buying it. Check out these." He tugged on the string to pull the blinds closed. "Now you can walk around naked and not worry about anyone watching you from outside."

That was enough to earn a smirk. "I'm usually only naked in the bathroom and my bedroom."

"That's because you're a prude." He poked my side, his grin expanding. "Tell me how manly I look after finishing this. I've earned it."

"You're a god among men," I reassured him, my mind drifting back to my conversation with Barry.

"Okay, you're not praising me nearly enough." Hunter turned serious. "What's bothering you?"

There were so many things I wasn't sure where to start. "I found out some things about Roy, but I'm not sure I should tell you. Someone could get hurt in the process."

"Is that someone Tina?"

"How did you know?"

"I make it my business to keep my ear to the ground. When Tina turned up pregnant, she told a story about picking up a guy in a Gaylord bar. The thing is, anyone who has ever spent more than five minutes with her knows that Tina is the last person who would ever have sex with a random guy."

"People get drunk," I pointed out.

"Not Tina. She was never a partier. She was one of those kids who always worried about her future. She wouldn't risk something like that."

He had a point, which only served to fill my head with more questions. "If she was always so careful, how did she allow herself to get knocked up by Roy?"

He held out his hands. "I don't know. I questioned that myself. She was always ... really careful. She wasn't like us. You and I were probably lucky there wasn't an accident back when we were young and dumb."

"I was on birth control."

"Yes, but accidents still happen ... especially when partying in a field is involved. Tina probably thought she was safe — right up until the point she wasn't."

"How did you figure out who the father was?" I was genuinely curious.

"It wasn't difficult. I wondered if there would be trouble when she started working for Roy." He sank down onto one of the dining room chairs. "We all know Roy's reputation. It's an open secret in this town. Everybody commented on it, but nobody did anything about it."

"What could you do?"

He shrugged. "I don't know. I thought about having a talk with him about the time Tina lost her job. I didn't know she was pregnant at that point, but it was obvious she was upset. I tried to talk to her, but she refused to open up.

"I had no doubt Roy sexually harassed her, but as long as she didn't file a complaint, my hands were tied," he continued. "I was dealing with my father then. He was making noise about suing me because he was convinced I was the reason he'd lost his job, so I was distracted. Tina's situation sort of fell through the cracks."

"And you feel guilty about it." I sat across from him and studied his rugged features. "My grandfather mentioned what happened with your father. I'm sorry that things turned out that way. I know you were always hoping you could somehow navigate a better relationship with him. I guess you've probably given up on that."

"I've definitely given up on it. The thing is, by the time he was finally removed from his position he was like a stranger to me. I moved out of that house the second I could. There weren't many options because I was only making minimum wage, but Ted Lansky offered me the room above his automotive shop. The rent was cheap, practically free, and all he asked in return was that I keep an eye on the place. I jumped at the chance."

"I remember." I nodded in understanding as my mind drifted back to those first few months of freedom. "I was still home that summer. We had a lot of fun in that apartment, but whenever my dad was in town he would always track me down there and threaten you with castration."

Hunter chuckled. "That was funny. I think that was the happiest summer of my life. High school was over, so that was behind me, and my father was pretty much out of my life. I had you ... and work ... and sunny days down by the river. Nothing ever quite seemed that happy again."

My heart pinged. "I'm sorry."

He shook himself out of his reverie. "What are you sorry for? You didn't do anything wrong."

"Maybe if I'd tried harder ... ."

He shook his head. "We were too young. It wasn't going to work then. I needed to figure out my life and you had dreams to chase."

"Well, one of us managed to accomplish what was necessary." I sent him a smile. "You've obviously figured out your life. You seem to be thriving."

"In some ways my life is better than I imagined. In other ways ... well, let's just say there are things to work on."

"That makes sense." I focused on the security system. "I don't think Tina killed Roy."

"I sincerely doubt it. If things drag out too long, though, I'll have to question her all the same."

"She doesn't want news getting around because of Dakota. She thinks he'll be treated badly if people figure it out."

"I think more people know than she realizes. If I could put it together so easily, I'm sure others have."

"Vera?"

He shrugged. "I plan to have another talk with her this afternoon. She's been difficult to pin down. She talked to me that first day, but she's pulled a disappearing act since. If I'd known how much trouble she was going to be, I would've interrogated her in the restaurant that day."

"Yeah, speaking of that ... ." I licked my lips and debated how I wanted to broach the next subject. "So, I think I figured out why my grandfather is dodging you. It didn't seem normal, so I was curious. I asked him about it this morning and he owned up to part of it, but he was still hiding something from me. I'm pretty sure that something was Dakota."

Realization dawned on his face. "He feels guilty because he suggested that Tina work for Roy, doesn't he?"

"I think he feels really guilty. I also think he knows who Dakota's father is. He didn't want to tell me because he was afraid I would tell you."

"I already knew, so you didn't spill secrets out of turn."

"Yeah, but it was bothering me that he was hiding from you that way. I didn't want to believe he was capable of killing Roy, but he was acting really weird."

"He doesn't care about protecting himself. He cares about protecting Tina. I'll tread lightly, but I still need to talk to him."

I shifted my eyes to the small employee parking section. "I was talking to Barry Buttons a bit ago. I had questions about what would happen to Roy's estate if there was a claim from a child."

"Did you find anything interesting?"

"He would only talk in hypothetical terms. He said that if the mother — in this case Tina, but we weren't really talking about Tina because he refused to get into specifics — signed off on child support with the father, it's likely that Dakota would have no claim on Roy's estate."

"Do you think Tina signed off?"

"She didn't say as much, but I think she just wanted to forget about what happened with Roy. He paid her a lump sum not long after Dakota was born. He told her that it would be easier to explain away than having to come up with multiple lies to placate Vera over an extended period."

"That makes sense." Hunter rubbed his chin. "Did she mention anything else?"

"Just that she made Roy promise to revisit the money situation when it came time for Dakota to go to college. I think she wants him to have more options than she had. She said that she wanted peace of mind when it came to raising Dakota."

"She's a good mother," Hunter noted. "I've seen them together at the park. He's a bright kid, easygoing. She's doing a great job with him."

"And he might not be the same kid if Roy had a hand in raising him," I surmised. "I get it."

"Did you find anything else of interest?"

"Barry also mentioned that Roy was known to park in the employee lot most mornings because he wanted to hang out with Grandpa. He was apparently there an hour early almost every day."

"That's true. I've seen him there myself a time or two."

I focused my full attention on him. "Was his vehicle found here that morning?"

"No."

"Where was it?"

"At the real estate office."

"So how did his body end up here?"

"That's one of the many questions I need answered." He looked at the clock. "It's later than I realized. Do you want to go downstairs and have a late lunch? I'm guessing you haven't eaten other than a bit of nibbling during your shift."

"How did you know that?"

"I remember what it was like when you worked here the first time. You said that grazing calories didn't count."

"I never was very bright."

He laughed. "So lunch?"

I hesitated. "I'm hungry, but ... there's something else I should tell you." I couldn't put it off any longer.

He narrowed his eyes. "You didn't do anything to screw up my investigation, did you?"

"No. At least I don't think I did. This is about Monica."

His expression was neutral. "What did she do?"

I told him about her appearance in the restaurant earlier, cringing at the way his expression darkened. "I should've told you then, but I was afraid of making things worse. That's no excuse. I just ... I'm so sorry. People are gossiping about you because of me. You don't deserve it.

"We know that nothing happened, but everyone else thinks that something did," I continued. "I am ... forever sorry to have hurt you again."

When I found the courage to meet his gaze, I found amusement rather than fury waiting for me. "This isn't funny," I said, straightening.

"It's not funny," he agreed. "But that prudish streak of yours always did make me laugh. You're not to blame for this. I am. I knew after the first date that things weren't going to work out with Monica. I kept her dangling despite everything, and that wasn't fair to anyone concerned."

I wasn't sure what to say. "If you didn't like her, why did you stay with her?"

He pinned me with an incredulous look. "Seriously? I should think that would be rather obvious."

"You did it because of me." It was a statement, not a question. "You wanted to send a clear message so I would stay away from you."

"No, I wanted to send a clear message that I wasn't pining for you," he clarified. "I knew keeping distance between us probably wasn't going to happen. I just felt like I couldn't breathe when I heard you were coming back."

"You acted surprised when you first saw me."

"I was surprised that you were barely back and had already found trouble. I wasn't surprised to see you, but I kind of wish it were under different circumstances. As for Monica ... I feel bad because I don't feel anything for her. I don't even like her, but I kept her around. That doesn't exactly make me a good person."

"You're the best person I know." I meant it. "Everybody makes mistakes. You need to talk to Monica. However this goes, she deserves your honesty. She's a terrible person as far as I can tell — and her eyebrows look absolutely hilarious — but it's not okay to purposely hurt her."

"I agree. Your safety took priority for the morning. Now I'm going to carb up and handle her the way I should've weeks ago. I won't leave her twisting in the wind."

I wanted to ask what would come after, if there was a chance for something to happen between us. Now was not the time. Once the dust settled and Roy's killer was found we could think about other things ... if either of us even wanted that. My emotions were so tangled I could barely see straight.

"So ... lunch."

"Lunch," he agreed, getting to his feet. "By the way, I put that gross flower box on the balcony. The fact that you were letting the cat go in that is beyond disgusting. I scooped his litter, too, and made sure he had a bowls of food and water."

"You really have been industrious."

"I'm a man of many talents," he agreed.

He showed me the new lock on the stairway door as we headed down. He'd gone all out, spared no expense, and I was grateful. Grandpa was sitting in a booth when we entered the café. Hunter headed directly for him.

"This is a fortuitous turn of events," he said, sliding into the seat across from Grandpa, who was buried in his newspaper.

Grandpa's scowl was evident when he looked up from the day's headlines. "I thought you left hours ago."

"Just to pick up the blinds for the doors upstairs. I ordered them yesterday and they came in today. You'll be happy to know that your granddaughter now has a state-of-the-art security system. Nobody can get to her upstairs."

"Those doors are glass, son. If someone truly wants to go after her, they will." Grandpa stared at him for a moment and then sighed. "Thank you for taking care of her. It never occurred to me there was something to worry about."

"I just want her safe." Hunter patted the booth seat next to him and I slid into the spot, holding my breath as he and Grandpa stared each other down. "Now we need to talk about serious matters."

"Because the potential murder of my granddaughter isn't serious?"

"You know why I'm here," Hunter pressed. "More importantly, I know why you've been hiding from me."

Grandpa scorched me with a dark look. "Really? And why do you think I've been hiding from you? I haven't, by the way. I don't hide from anybody."

Hunter lowered his voice. "I know about Tina. I know she had Roy's baby. I know you feel guilty for suggesting she take the job. Before you go crazy and start yelling at Stormy, you should know that I knew about Roy being Dakota's father before she even gave birth. I never said anything because it wasn't my business."

Grandpa leaned back in his seat and pinned Hunter with a pointed look. "That girl has been through enough. She doesn't need you asking her invasive questions."

"I'm hoping it doesn't get to that point," Hunter agreed. "I still have to find Roy's killer. He might've been a terrible human being, but he didn't deserve to die that way."

"Tina isn't a viable suspect," Grandpa insisted. "She has health issues. Even though Roy was older, she wouldn't be able to take him out. Besides, she wouldn't leave Dakota long enough to do it and there's no way she would take that boy to watch her kill his father."

"I don't think it's Tina," Hunter insisted. "Chill out. I'm not looking at her. That doesn't mean I'm not looking at other women who were in that office. If Roy did that to Tina, what's to say he didn't do the same with someone else?"

That hadn't occurred to me, but it made sense. "Can we put together a list of the people who have worked for Roy throughout the years?"

"That's the plan," Hunter confirmed. "And because he hid from me for days, your grandfather is going to help ... just as soon as we have lunch. It's going to be on him, too, because I spent the entire morning protecting his granddaughter."

"I didn't agree to that," Grandpa said stubbornly. "In fact ... ." He was interrupted by the front door banging open.

I shouldn't have been surprised to see Monica. She'd probably spent the better part of the morning searching the town for Hunter. Circling back only made sense. The look on her face when she saw us sitting together made my blood run cold.

"Oh, crap," Hunter muttered.

"This won't be good," Grandpa groused. "She's about to make a scene. You know how I feel about other people making a scene. I'm the only one allowed to make a scene in my restaurant."

TWENTY-SEVEN

Even before I'd accidentally burned off her eyebrows, Monica had one of those faces best described as "angry Kardashian after finding out cameras have been banned for life." She was beautiful, in an over-processed way, and it occurred to me that I'd never seen her without makeup. To be fair, I had spent very little time with her. She was always "on," though, and that was never truer than today.

"Aren't you going to say anything?" Her gaze was furious, and it was directed at Hunter.

"We should go outside," he said as he started to push himself to his feet. He didn't look like a man about to go before a firing squad, but he certainly didn't look happy.

"Why should we go outside?" Monica planted her hands on her hips. "Is there something you want to say that everybody who knows what's going on can't hear?"

"This is a private matter." Hunter was firm. "I don't want my life spread all over this town for obvious reasons."

"Your private business has already been spread all over this town," Monica hissed. "Everyone knows that you spent last night making a fool of me."

"Nothing happened," I volunteered. "I swear ... he was just helping me because I was afraid."

When her eyes turned to me, there was more than anger there. Outright hatred was reflected back. I sucked in a breath. I never thought it was possible to have someone look at me that way.

"I'm not an idiot." Monica practically spit the words and I shrank back into my booth seat. "He spent the night."

"On the couch," I protested.

"Oh, nobody believes that! Do you have any idea the looks I've gotten since word started spreading that you were coming back? People pity me. Me!" She thumped her chest like a wrestler, which made me wonder if she could hold her own in a fight if it came to it. She looked as if she did Pilates regularly, which meant she was strong. I was essentially a third-string bench-warmer on the powder puff team.

"I didn't even know you existed until we ran into your mother at a festival," she continued, oblivious to the ears taking in her diatribe. "She greeted Hunter like she was his mother — and for a moment I thought she was — but then, when she was introduced to me, she made a big show of acting really sad and saying that she was disappointed he was dating and always wanted him for her daughter."

I felt the need to say something, but what could I say? Even though I had no idea where I might end up, I spoke anyway. "My mother has issues. She doesn't think before speaking."

"Oh, she knew what she was saying," Monica shot back. "Her aim was to make me as uncomfortable as possible ... and it worked. After that, I started asking Hunter questions about you. He didn't want to answer them. That's when I knew I had something to fear.

"If he'd been forthcoming and said, 'Oh, she's just a girl I dated in high school and her mother should live in a nut barn,' it would've been okay," she continued. "But he didn't want to talk about you at all, so I started asking around."

Hunter, who had given up trying to leave, shifted on his seat. "You asked around?"

"Of course I did." Her eyes flashed. "I thought we were going somewhere. I thought we had a future. I went to Sebastian, because he seemed to know everything about everyone in this town. I thought for sure he would tell me I was crazy. Do you know what he told me?"

I could only imagine — and it wasn't good.

"He told me that you two were joined at the hip. That he assumed you would get married right out of high school," she barreled forward, barely taking a breath. "I said that never works, and he said it would've worked with you two. I asked him if he thought there was a chance you would get back together. I expected him to say that it was far too late for that. He told me that Stormy broke your heart. You're the type of guy who won't put up with that, except here you are. You're putting up with it again."

Hunter pressed the heel of his hand to his forehead. "We were kids, Monica. I don't hold any ill will toward Stormy. We really need to take this conversation outside."

"She won't let that happen," Grandpa said in a low voice, his back still to Monica as he drank his coffee. "The only way out of this for her is to play the victim. I knew this would happen." His eyes landed on me. "People all over town are talking about Hunter's squad car being here all night. I wasn't exaggerating."

"It's hard to tell," I shot back. "It's like the grandpa who cried wolf."

"This won't die down," Grandpa warned sternly.

I had no doubt that was true. "Just ... shut it." I slid my gaze to Hunter. "I am so sorry for this."

"It's not your fault." He sent me a reassuring smile and then focused on Monica. "I don't know what you want me to say. Nothing happened last night. Stormy was in trouble. It's my job as a police officer to make sure she's safe. That's it. End of story."

"Uh-huh." Monica remained understandably dubious. "Do you spend the night on the couches of every resident in need? No? I guess that means Stormy is a special case."

"This isn't about Stormy." Hunter sounded tired. "This is about me. We really need to go outside and talk."

"Why? So you can break up with me?" When he didn't immediately respond, Monica narrowed her eyes. "Wait ... are you seriously going to break up with me? That is so ... I can't believe it!" She stomped her foot. "Well, I'm not going to let you break up with me. How do you like that? I'm breaking up with you." Before he could respond, she turned on her heel and stormed out the door.

I glanced back at Hunter. Only now did he seem upset, and it was annoyance fueling him more than regret. "I guess I'm going to have to take a raincheck on that lunch."

"That's probably best," Grandpa agreed.

"You and I need to talk later," he said, and it took me a moment to realize he was talking to me, not Grandpa.

"We do?" I swallowed hard, fear bubbling up.

My reaction elicited a smile, however small. "We definitely need to talk. Don't go getting crazy or anything. I have to deal with Monica right now. I owe her an apology, even if she is downright evil eighty percent of the time."

Grandpa smirked. "Good luck, son."

"Yeah." Hunter dragged a hand through his hair. "I'm going to need it."

Grandpa smirked as he watched Hunter exit. Then he focused on me. "One door opens as another closes."

I didn't like what he was insinuating. "Nothing happened."

"Oh, Dolly, you always were a bad liar."

"I don't have sex with other people's boyfriends."

His brow furrowed. "Can you not say that word so loudly?"

"What? Sex?" I glanced around and found ten sets of eyes planted firmly on me. "Well, it's true. We didn't have sex."

"There are more ways to have an affair than just sex," Grandpa pointed out. "Some ways, emotional ways, are even more devastating."

There was nothing I could say.

"It doesn't matter." He was calm, something I wasn't used to seeing from him. "Things have been set in motion. What will be, will be."

"Oh, you're so profound." I struggled to a standing position. I'd lost my appetite and needed air. "I'm going for a walk."

"I wouldn't use the front door unless you want to draw the attention of every passing motorist within a fifty-mile radius."

He had a point. "I'll use the back door."

I trudged toward the swinging doors that led to the kitchen, and freedom, stopping when he called out to me. "What?"

His eyes twinkled when I met them. "Some things are meant to be, kid. You might want to consider this was always going to happen and accept it before your big conversation with Hunter."

That was not what I wanted to hear. "Nothing happened!"

"As long as you keep telling yourself that, you're doomed for disappointment. Suck it up. Life is about to change for you. It's time you accept it. Those dreams you've been grappling with? I have a feeling some of them are about to come true."

And that was the most terrifying thought of all.

SNEAKING AWAY AND LEAVING HUNTER TO deal with the fallout seemed cowardly, but it was his relationship. There was nothing I could offer except further drama if I tried to intervene on his behalf. What happened seemed as much my fault as his, but I couldn't involve myself. He had to do what he felt was right, and if that meant staying with Monica, that was his choice.

Except that I wanted him free. It was hard to admit, especially after I'd fought everyone else saying it, but if he was unencumbered by a girlfriend we might actually be able to figure out if there were remnants of real feelings or just hormones zipping about the room when we were together. It felt real, but it could've been something else entirely.

For lack of anything better to do, I headed downtown. Yes, I was likely to run into someone who would ask questions about the previous evening, but I didn't feel like being alone. I wanted to disappear in a crowd. Shadow Hills wasn't known for crowds, but being alone felt like the wrong choice given the almost break-in of the night before.

The coffee shop was half empty. One of the few faces I recognized was Erin's. She sat at a table alone, looking at her phone. After ordering my drink, I hesitated, and then timidly approached her table.

"Um ... want some company?"

Amusement was evident on her face. "I'm guessing *you* want some company." She gestured to the chair across from her. "Sit down."

"Thanks." I got comfortable.

"Rough day, huh?" She didn't look gleeful at the prospect of gossip, but she didn't appear averse to hearing whatever I had to offer.

"It's been ... a day." I sipped my coffee. "I'm assuming you've heard gossip. What are people saying?"

She gave a slight shrug. "I wouldn't get worked up about it. This town thrives on gossip. People have been spreading stuff about me for as long as I can remember. You have to learn to deal with it."

"Nothing happened." I had no idea why I felt the need to keep reiterating that point. It was more for Hunter's benefit than mine. "I swear he was just there because I was freaking out."

"I'm afraid I don't know the full story," she said. "What were you freaking out about?"

"Someone was trying to get into my apartment."

"Really?" Her eyebrows hopped. "That's freaky. How did they get into the restaurant?"

"Not from inside, from the sliding glass doors on the balcony."

"Wow. Did you see who it was?"

I shook my head. "I panicked and called Hunter. That's how this whole mess started."

Rather than sympathize, she snickered. "Honey, this whole mess started when you were a teenager and saw him shirtless. Some people just get under your skin and you can never shake them."

"I guess." I rubbed my forehead. "Have you ever had someone get under your skin?"

"Sure."

"Anyone good?"

She shook her head. "Just Bobby Buttons."

I couldn't hide my surprise. "No way. Are you guys dating?"

"We're more ... intermittent," she explained. "I think we've dated, like, eight times. I always break up with him because he's not motivated. I do not want to be stuck renting a house like my mother for the rest of my life. But there's something about him I can't shake."

I wasn't sure how to respond. Bobby seemed a drain on society. That probably wasn't what she wanted to hear. "Have you considered giving him an ultimatum? Maybe if you say you'll never date him again unless he gets a real job he'll do as you want."

Her snort was disdainful. "Yeah, I've never found ultimatums work in relationships. I've tried several times. The last guy laughed at me like I was an idiot. I guess that's what I get for trying to date old guys these days."

It was a strange statement. "You tried to date an old guy?"

She nodded and sipped her drink. "Yeah. I thought an older man might be more ... grounded. I guess that's the word I'm looking for. I don't think I'm that hard to please. I want a man who is willing to take care of me, provide a good house, and allow me to remain at home. That's it."

That sounded like a lot. "So ... you want to be a homemaker? Like, have a bunch of kids or something?"

She shrugged. "I could take or leave the kids."

Apparently she just didn't want to work. "Where did you find this old guy?" There didn't seem many options for dating in that particular pool in Shadow Hills. If you were a good guy, made a decent living, and weren't a complete tool, odds were you were already married.

"It wasn't easy, and I had to lower my standards like you wouldn't believe," she replied. "The thing is, I asked myself a very serious question when it came time to define my future needs. That's a thing on all these talk shows, defining future needs.

"I wanted financial stability more than I wanted sexual chemistry," she continued. "That's most important to me, so that forced me to adjust my expectations. I had tons of sexual chemistry with Bobby, but he might be the most unmotivated man in the world. I can't deal with that."

I could see that. Still, sacrificing the chemistry seemed unfathomable. "Have you ever considered there's someone out there who can check the boxes in both the financial and chemistry columns?"

"Not in Shadow Hills."

"You're still young," I reminded her. "You have plenty of time to find someone."

"I'll be thirty in a few years. Everybody knows that you start losing your looks at thirty."

I didn't know that. "But ... ."

She kept talking as if she hadn't heard me. "If I want to get the future I deserve, then I have to stop messing around. Bobby is a menace. The only way he'll fulfill those needs is if he somehow gets hit in the head, comes down with amnesia, and develops a work ethic. I have tons of chemistry with him, but he can't give me what I want. That's why I told him we needed a clean break this last time. He's not happy about it — he caused several scenes in the office demanding to know who I was dating — but he's going to have to learn to deal with it. I need a strong man."

I thought of the drunken man I'd spent time with a few nights before. "He seems to have a few issues," I hedged.

"He's an idiot."

"His father is kind of a jerk, too," I continued. "I went in to ask him questions about Roy and he gave me a really creepy feeling."

Her forehead wrinkled in surprise. "You went to see Barry? Why?"

"Oh, um ... I had some hypothetical questions about what would happen to Roy's estate should it be revealed that he had a child out of wedlock. I wanted to know if that would affect what Vera was due to inherit."

"What did he say?"

I shrugged. "He said there were a lot of factors, including whether or not the other woman signed off on a financial stake."

"I didn't know that." She straightened in her chair. "Is an agreement signed before a death still legal in a case like this?"

I nodded. "Apparently so."

"I ... well ... huh." She looked conflicted. "Do you think someone killed Roy because of money?"

"It's possible."

"I bet it was Vera." Erin's expression darkened. "She refused to let that poor man go even though it was obvious he didn't love her. The more he tried to escape, the tighter she clung to him. It was pretty sickening."

The vehemence pooling off her made me distinctly uncomfortable. "I think she's just frightened. She's never been on her own. I don't know that she's broken-hearted about his death but I don't think she wished him ill."

"No, she's evil."

"Well, Barry said that Roy's estate is probably going to be a nightmare to unravel if there are other children out there." I thought of Dakota. "Someone will have to put in a claim and go through a DNA test if it comes to that."

"Can you even do a DNA test when someone is pregnant?"

I shrugged. "I was thinking more along the lines of children who already exist. Vera said there might be one or two running around ... and even if Roy managed to get the mother to sign off, there's still the possibility of battling over the estate in court."

"But ... that doesn't seem right. I mean, if you sign off, you sign off."

"I don't think anything is simple when you're dealing with law enforcement," I replied. "Either way, I don't look for Roy's murder to be solved anytime soon. The money would likely be held up until Vera is cleared as a suspect. The insurance company won't pay out to a murder suspect."

Erin rubbed her chin. "I'm surprised that she hasn't been arrested yet. She's the one with the most to gain from his death."

"There are questions about the logistics of the murder."

"What do you mean?"

"Roy was killed behind the restaurant, but his vehicle was found over here. Hunter said they're checking it for prints and he expects a hit. I guess we'll see."

"I guess." Erin's expression was momentarily cloudy and then she forced a smile. "So ... what's going on with you and Hunter? Once he dumps Monica, is it smooth sailing back to one another?"

Ugh. That was a question I didn't — and couldn't — answer. "Nothing is going on with Hunter," I repeated. "As for me ... ." I trailed off, my gaze drifting to the funeral home across the street. "I just remembered, I have to talk to Sebastian about something. It was nice talking to you."

I was eager to make my escape.

"Okay, but the questions about Hunter aren't going anywhere," she said mischievously. "The fact that he spent the night with you on your couch is going to come up at some point."

"Not today." I headed for the door. "Good luck on the job search ... and I hope things work out well with your old guy."

"You and me both, honey."

TWENTY-EIGHT

S ebastian reclined on one of the settees, flipping through a heavy book. He straightened, pasted a businesslike welcoming smile on his face, and then deflated when he saw it was me.

"It's nice to see you, too," I snickered.

He held up a placating hand. "Nothing personal. I thought you might be a customer."

"Sorry. I don't plan to die anytime soon. Although, if Monica has her way, my mother might be in here soon pulling a Vera and picking out everything I hate."

Sebastian's expression changed from disappointment to amusement in an instant. "I heard the big gossip." He shifted so there was an open spot on the settee and patted the cushion. "Sit down and tell me absolutely everything."

I scowled. "There's nothing to tell."

"Don't be ridiculous. You two spent the night together. There's definitely something to tell."

Defeat washed over me. There was no way this gossip would die down anytime soon. "He slept on the couch." I was morose when I plopped into one of the chairs. I didn't want to sit next to Sebastian in case he tried to wrestle me down and demand answers. He was built, strong enough that it wouldn't take much effort to hold me in place.

"But I heard you slept with him," Sebastian countered. "That's more than just friendship."

"I ... ." Something occurred to me. "Wait ... how do you know we slept on the couch together?"

He shrugged. "That's what everyone is saying."

"Yeah, but ... how can they possibly know that?"

"Honey, gossip runs faster in this town than the mayor when he has the trots," he deadpanned. "Once one person knows, everybody knows."

"Except the only two people who should know we slept on the couch together are Hunter and me. There was nobody else there."

Sebastian faltered. "Well, maybe he told someone."

I shot him a "get real" look. "Really? You think that came up in random conversation, do you? Besides, he spent the entire morning at my apartment installing a security system. The only time he left was to get blinds and a few tools. He went to the store and immediately came back. There's no way he just volunteered that information out of nowhere."

"I guess." Sebastian turned pensive. "Maybe someone made it up and just got lucky. Stranger things have happened."

"If you were making up that story, wouldn't it make more sense to say we were in my bedroom? That's more likely. Sleeping together on the couch — and nothing more happened than that, gutter mind — isn't the assumption most people would jump to."

"I guess that's true." He studied my face. "What are you thinking?"

"That someone saw us." That was the only thing that made sense. "The sliding glass doors give an open view of the entire living room if you're on the balcony looking in." A small shudder ran through me at the thought of someone watching us sleep. "Who told you Hunter and I were on the couch together?"

"Let me think." Sebastian chewed his bottom lip. "I know I heard it this morning. I was getting coffee at the shop. Dana Sandusky was in there getting her usual white chocolate decaf mocha, but she wasn't talking about you. She was talking about being constipated. She's pregnant, and apparently that's a thing."

I made a face. "Thanks so much for that visual."

He chuckled. "It was Erin Higgins." He bobbed his head after a moment's contemplation. "She was in there getting tea. She seemed upset, looked pale. She said she was feeling sick to her stomach and didn't sleep most of the night. She told me."

I thought back to the conversation I'd had with Erin only minutes earlier. "I just ran into her at the coffee shop. Now that you mention it, she brought up Hunter and me being on the couch, too. It didn't click at the time. Does she live there or something? At the coffee shop, I mean."

Sebastian chuckled. "No, but Roy's office is just down the street. She made regular runs because it was her job to keep the agents caffeinated. She's a big fan of the peppermint tea. Janice — she's one of the workers there — said she heard Erin was pregnant and that's why she liked the tea. It settles her stomach."

"Pregnant?"

He shrugged. "It's probably Bobby Buttons. Those two can't stay away from one another. It's a little disgusting."

It sounded plenty disgusting. "But ... she didn't mention being pregnant."

"Why would she? No offense, but you're barely back in town. It's not as if you two know each other all that well."

"No, but ... ." Something clicked into place. "She said she was dating an old guy."

His eyes widened. "Okay, maybe she would open up to you."

"She said that she and Bobby had sexual chemistry but that he refused to get a job." My mind was working at a fantastic rate. "She said that she decided to go after a man who could take care of her financially. She didn't care that he was old."

Realization dawned in Sebastian's keen eyes. "You think she was messing around with Roy."

It made sense, and yet there was something off about the assumption. "When I first questioned the workers about Roy's death, Erin was out front. She seemed genuinely broken up. She said that he was a good boss as she sobbed. Sandy Gellar was there, but she said that Roy regularly gave Erin disappointed looks. She was really snarky about it, as if she knew something but wasn't sharing."

"Well, Sandy is excellent with gossip," Sebastian agreed. "If Erin was pregnant by Roy, though, everybody in town would know about it. Nobody in Shadow Hills can keep a secret."

"What if it's more than that?" I asked. "You said that everyone in town was mad at Roy for borrowing things and not returning them. When Hunter went to his house, he found a pristine garage that had recently been cleaned. What if Roy had something really gross going on in his garage?"

"Like what?"

"Like ... ." What? I was a fiction writer and my mind immediately went to the preposterous. I felt as if I was on to something, though.

"Like an underground adult film enterprise," a voice volunteered from the rear door, causing us both to jolt.

When I turned to see who had entered the building, my heart lodged in my throat. Erin stared at us with unreadable eyes. "You just couldn't leave it alone, could you, Stormy?"

"I ... ." It felt as if something big was about to happen, but I couldn't wrap my head around what it could possibly be.

"This is all your fault," Erin muttered, scraping her foot against Sebastian's pristine hardwood floors. "None of this would've happened if you'd just kept your nose out of my business."

I was confused. "I didn't stick my nose into your business."

She rolled her eyes. "If you weren't digging, if you didn't know, then why did you ask me all those questions about the guy I was seeing? Why did you tell me what Barry had said?"

I struggled to catch up. I considered myself relatively astute when it came to reading people and figuring things out, but I was at a genuine loss. "I was just talking out loud."

She shook her head and heaved out a sigh. "You know. You know because Barry told you. He covered for Vera and Roy for years, but when Vera decided it was time to get out, he saw an opportunity. I knew he couldn't be trusted."

I swallowed hard and slid my eyes to Sebastian. He looked as confused as I felt. "Do you know what she's talking about?" I asked.

He shook his head, but there was something about his stare that told me he was ahead of me on this one. "There were rumors," he said. "They've been going around for years."

"Rumors about Roy knocking up his employees?"

"Well, yes, but those weren't the rumors I mean. Roy didn't exactly hide his proclivities. Vera was better about it, but in a town this size even she couldn't keep a secret."

"So ... Vera did what?"

"Vera came up with an idea to make movies," Erin answered for him, her tone bitter. "She conducted research online and found there was a niche for films featuring older men and young women. Roy could never keep it in his pants, so she thought they might as well make money off his impulses."

"Did you know about this?" I demanded of Sebastian.

"I heard some things," he hedged, distinctly uncomfortable. "I thought it was made up. You know how this town is. There are people still spouting that rumor that Maude Jenkins is really a man because she's been able to sprout a full beard since menopause. I didn't think it was real."

221

I wanted to kick him. If he'd shared that bit of gossip from the start it might not have taken us so long to realize what was happening. "You are unbelievable," I hissed. "I'm taking your gossip card away as soon as this is over."

"It won't be long until it's over," Erin promised, her eyes — once so full of life — somber and dead. "I can't afford for this story to get out. I have to silence you."

"Silence us?" Sebastian's voice hopped. "How are you going to do that? Do you have a gun? Or a knife? I once saw a horror movie where the killer used a fire poker to carry out a bunch of murders."

"Stop giving her ideas," I hissed.

"I'm not going to do anything," Erin promised. "But they ... ." She inclined her head toward the front door. While we'd been distracted by Erin, two people had entered through the front door without a sound.

"Vera," I said on a note of disgust.

"And Barry," Sebastian added. "This is quite the gathering of minds."

"It's a waste is what it is," Barry snapped, shaking his head. He had a hand in his coat, making me think he had a weapon stashed. Erin was acting the same way, so we'd gone from outnumbering her to being outnumbered — and that didn't take into account the potential weapons. We had to distract them until we came up with a plan ... or someone came looking for us ... or we could find a way to escape. There had to be a way.

"I don't understand what's happening," I said, opting for honesty. At the very least I needed answers. "What is all of this?"

"It was a business plan," Vera replied blandly. "Roy was a terrible husband, but he was great when it came to money-making ideas. He also had a porn fetish, which is how I knew what sort of disgusting scenario would sell. He was always buying it, so we decided to turn it into a financial investment. You know, old guy mows lawn naked and pretty young thing comes over to help ... and gets so hot she just has to have him."

The images she stirred in my mind were disgusting. "So Roy and Erin filmed a bunch of movies and you sold them?"

"Not just Erin," Vera countered. "You need variety if you're going to pull off something like this. You need props and professional lighting with pink gel bulbs to soften the wrinkles."

"I think I'm going to be sick," Sebastian complained.

He wasn't the only one. "How many women did Roy do this with?"

"Knowingly, only Erin. Unknowingly, ..." Vera trailed off, mustering a demented smile.

"I think I've got you beat on feeling sick," I said to Sebastian, grim.

"This whole thing is absolutely disgusting."

"You're saying that Roy had sex with anyone who would fall for his crap and filmed them without their knowledge," I volunteered. "You guys made money off the backs of innocent young women."

Vera's eyes narrowed. "They were hardly innocent. Each woman who was with him knew that he was married. That didn't stop a single one of them. They were all trying to trap him, get pregnant, and take his money. They earned what they got."

"And Tina?" Even though I knew it was wrong to out her, I desperately needed to understand. "She didn't seduce Roy. She was blackmailed into having sex with him or risk losing her job."

"Tina ended up with all of my money," Vera fired back. "She lives in a better house than I do. She has money in the bank, unlike me. That little brat of hers has a future. I couldn't even have children. She should consider herself lucky."

"Yes, I'm sure she feels grateful to have been used for your disgusting practice," I muttered.

"Nobody got hurt," Barry argued. "It was a quiet operation. None of the women filmed even knew until Erin opened her big mouth." He glared at the younger woman. "She set all of this in motion. Unfortunately, you're going to suffer the fallout. There isn't much I can do about that.

"I knew when you came to the office asking questions that you were going to be a problem," he continued. "I compared notes with Vera. She said you'd been poking your nose into her business when she was here making arrangements for Roy's funeral. When Erin called and told us about the conversation the two of you had this afternoon it became apparent we had to silence you."

"But I didn't know anything," I argued. "Until right now, I had no idea what you guys were doing."

"So you say," Vera said. "We can't take the risk. We're at the end of an odyssey now. We have to make sure that things play out as they were meant to."

"What odyssey?" I snapped. "You killed Roy. Why? He was the reason you were making money."

"He was also the reason we lost all the money," Vera shot back. "Tina was hardly the first woman to come up pregnant by Roy. There were two payouts before her. By the time she got her cut, we had almost nothing left. The nest egg we'd managed to put together with the movies was gone.

"I only agreed to the movies for the money," she continued. "I figured he owed me after the years of betrayal. He swore up and down that the movies were a great idea. They would keep him busy and allow us to survive. We were surviving, and building, and then this one turned up pregnant." She extended a finger in Erin's direction.

"Don't blame this on me," Erin hissed. "It would've been fine if he didn't want to add yet another woman to the mix. He was supposed to stop with me."

This kept getting more convoluted. "So ... you were in love with him?"

Erin snorted. "Oh, please. I already told you that I love Bobby, even though he's a total loser."

"He is," Barry agreed, ruthlessly bad-talking his own son. "He's as lazy as they come. Erin had a plan to get the money for them to live on. Bobby couldn't know how she managed to come by it because he never would've forgiven her. We had a lie ready for that. He's not very bright. He would've believed she inherited from a dead relative. Everything was going along smoothly and then ... baby."

Erin pinned him with a dark glare. "It's not my fault. Roy said he'd had a vasectomy."

"He told every woman that," Vera argued. "He just preferred riding bare-back. You were supposed to be on birth control."

"It makes me bloat before my period! I can't be naked on camera if I'm bloated."

"Well, now you're going to be bloated for another six months," Vera said with satisfaction. "Congratulations."

I was starting to feel dizzy from the rapid-fire conversation. I needed to redirect the participants. "Why did you kill Roy?"

"Because he lied," Erin shot back. "He knocked me up after he said it wasn't possible. When I told him, he said that I couldn't be in the movies any longer because no one wants to see a fat girl in porn."

"He really was a pig," I groused.

"Totally," Vera agreed.

"I suggested we try pregnancy porn, but he said he couldn't agree to that because he needed to feel inspired before a shoot and the very idea grossed him out," Erin explained. "I was trying to talk to him outside the restaurant when he told me that the money was going to stop coming in because he had his eye on someone new. I think it was one of your cousins. He said that I would have to raise the baby with Bobby because he had no money to give me.

"I couldn't live with that." Her voice had gone shrill. "He dragged me into this whole mess. Bobby might be an idiot, but he knows we didn't have sex in the last three months. He'd never believe this baby is his. I needed that freaking money to convince Bobby to stay."

Things finally slipped into place. "You tried to blackmail Roy in the parking lot, but he had nothing to offer. So you stabbed him."

Erin didn't look sorry in the least. "I stabbed him and then I had to drag him out of the truck. He was still alive when I started hauling him out, but he didn't last long.

"I saw you upstairs that morning," she continued. "You were at the window. I was certain you saw me."

"I didn't."

"I had to be sure. You were acting strange when you started asking questions at the real estate office the next day. I was certain you were playing a game."

"I wasn't."

"Erin did absolutely everything wrong that day," Barry explained. "She should've left Roy's truck and taken off on foot, but she didn't think that far ahead. She panicked and drove to the real estate office, where Vera and I met her. By that time, the police had already been alerted. We couldn't very well drive the truck back."

"No," I agreed. "It was too late."

"I watched you," Barry explained. "I was out there every night watching you. I saw you and your cousin snooping around the storage shed one night."

We were hiding a Ouija board because we'd freaked each other out while drunk. "And last night? Which one of you tried to get into my apartment last night?"

"That was me again," Barry said. "I was going to make it quick. Really, if you had just minded your own business. I thought that if we took you out of the equation Hunter would turn his attention to that investigation and forget about Roy. There would be no reason for him to look at me because I have no ties to you."

"Hunter isn't an idiot," I pointed out. "Two murders in essentially the same spot would have to be tied together."

"Not necessarily."

Oh, geez. They were all idiots. All three of them. "And what happens now?" I demanded. "Are you going to split Roy's life insurance three ways and live forever?"

"We're going to do what we have to do," Vera replied, matter-of-fact. "We may not like each other sometimes — most of the time when it comes to Erin

— but we're tied together in blood now. Unfortunately, some of that blood will be yours."

My heart began slamming against my rib cage. "If you kill us, Hunter will never stop chasing you."

"He won't know it was us," Barry replied. "We'll set it up to look like a murder-suicide. Most people will believe that Sebastian has been pining for you since high school and once word got out that you might get back together with Hunter he snapped. It's fairly straightforward."

"I really am sorry," Vera said. "I hoped it wouldn't come to this. I have nothing against either of you. It's just ... I can't go to prison. This is the only way to ensure that doesn't happen."

"You could've stopped short of covering up a murder," Sebastian shot back. "That's one way to avoid prison."

"It's far too late for that." She turned to Barry. "Shoot them."

He scowled. "Why do I have to shoot them? Why can't you shoot them?"

"I don't think you guys have thought this through," Erin said to nobody in particular, her eyes on us. "I mean ... I'm pretty sure this guy is gay."

"Who says I'm gay?" Sebastian practically exploded.

"This is not the time," I hissed, pinning him with a look. "It doesn't matter what they think. What matters is that we get out of this."

"Fine, but I'm not gay." He smoothed the front of his shirt and huffed.

"Later," I gritted out, my eyes going to the door behind Erin. That seemed our best bet. "We need to make a break for it. We'll get only one chance."

He nodded. "Let's go."

Vera and Barry were still arguing, so I figured we were okay to move. We'd barely made it two steps before Erin started flapping her arms.

"They're running! Shoot them!"

I risked a glance over my shoulder and saw Barry reaching into his pocket, Erin's words serving as a verbal cattle prod.

Things started happening in slow motion after that. I shoved Sebastian as hard as I could even as the strange bubbling sensation I'd felt the night I burned Monica's eyebrows off started again. It was as if I could no longer hear in real time. Voices were drawn out, and unnaturally deep.

I willed myself to keep it together, but it was too late to stop what was about to happen. Instinctively, I recognized that. Still, I wanted to protect Sebastian. "Get. Down." Even my voice sounded alien.

Sebastian didn't argue with the order. Perhaps he sensed something big was about to happen, too. He'd barely dropped to the floor when a light formed out of nowhere. It reminded me of what had happened the previous night as I waited for Hunter to arrive. This time, the explosion that accompanied the wave of sunny light was deafening.

If you asked me where the origin point was, I wouldn't be able to say. All I know is that we were surrounded by a cloud of light. When the explosion came, it shook the funeral home.

Erin screamed.

Barry yelled.

Vera ran for the door.

Before any of them could take more than two steps, the barrage of magic ripped free and slammed into them, rocking them backward. The blow knocked me back, and my head just missed an end table as I smacked against the floor.

The noise ceased.

Erin's scream was cut off.

Barry's bellow of warning ceased after the second word.

Vera never made it to the door.

As the world started spinning at normal speed again, I took stock from my position on the floor. I saw three bodies on the floor, none of them moving. They were either dead or unconscious. I wasn't sure which was better.

Sebastian stirred. Still breathless, he rolled over to look directly into my eyes. "Are you okay?"

I nodded, disbelief over what had just happened causing my heart to continue galloping, even as my ears began to clear. "Yeah. Are you?"

"Yeah."

I looked back toward the bodies, uncertainty tapping out a new rhythm via my heart. "What do we do?"

"We call Hunter," he replied. "And then, girlfriend, when it's just you and me, we're going to have a really long talk."

I swallowed hard. I wasn't looking forward to the conversation.

TWENTY-NINE

"**W**hat happened?"

Hunter's face was red with worry when he charged through the door several minutes later. He zeroed in on me immediately.

"Are you okay?"

"I'm fine," Sebastian offered drolly. "Not that you care or anything."

Hunter didn't bother giving him side eye, instead brushing my hair out of my face as he knelt in front of me. "Are you okay?"

"I'm fine," I reassured him, although I was feeling anything but fine. "You should check on them." I indicated the three bodies on the floor.

He stared at me for another second and then nodded, moving toward Barry first. He kicked the gun that was near his hand to the far side of the room and then pressed his fingers to the man's neck. I was almost afraid of what he would find. "His pulse seems strong."

I let out a shaky breath and darted a glance toward Sebastian. He looked more curious than worried.

"What happened?" Hunter asked, moving to check on Vera.

I hadn't given much thought to what I was going to say. How was I going to explain a magical explosion that knocked out three people while leaving Sebastian and me unscathed? "Um ... ."

Sebastian grabbed my arm and gave me an almost imperceptible shake of his head before answering. "I don't know what it was. There was a loud ... bang. It was almost like an explosion. I have no idea where it came from."

"An explosion?" Hunter jerked up his chin and looked around the room. "Some of the furniture looks as if it's been moved. Do you think it could've been an earthquake?"

"Maybe." Sebastian held out his hands and shrugged. "I was so frightened that I didn't pay much attention. I thought they somehow managed it until ... well ... now. I'm really jittery, man. This is the freakiest thing that's ever happened to me."

"You look okay," Hunter offered, his eyes traveling back to me. "But you look as if you're about to throw up."

He wasn't far off with his observation. "I feel a little shaky," I admitted.

"Neither of us has ever been threatened by crazy people before," Sebastian supplied. "I think she needs a hug to feel better." He immediately moved closer to me and slid his arm around my back. "They were going to kill us."

"That's what you said on the phone," Hunter acknowledged. "You didn't say why, though."

"It's kind of a long story."

"I appear to have time." Hunter moved to Erin and checked her pulse. "They're all alive. I see no wounds. I'll call for the paramedics."

"You might want to check Erin for a gun," I said as he yanked out his phone. "She was acting like she had one."

His eyebrows knitting, Hunter felt around the young woman's clothing, grimacing when he came back with a small handgun. "You two wait right there. I'm calling this in, cuffing Barry, and then I'll be right over."

"Take your time," I offered lamely.

Sebastian shot me a look. "You need to start acting like a normal person," he whispered, keeping as close to me as humanly possible as he navigated me toward one of the settees. "If you don't get it together, he'll figure out something is going on."

That was the most ludicrous thing I'd heard all day ... and given what we'd gone through, that was saying something. "You don't think he'll figure it out anyway? There's no way to explain this."

"Then we don't explain it." Sebastian's voice was low but firm. "He doesn't need to know it was you ... at least not right now."

"But ... ."

"No." His eyes were deadly serious. "You need to keep it quiet, at least until we can break things down. When we get a chance — and it probably won't happen today — you and I will have a long talk. I wasn't kidding about that. For now, keep your trap shut. I know that's basically unheard of in your family, but you need to start learning about discretion."

I shut my mouth and nodded. What he said made sense. Still, it was Hunter. I couldn't keep this secret from him forever. But as I glanced back at the bodies strewn about the room, I realized Sebastian was right. For now, claiming we didn't know what had happened was the only reasonable solution to our predicament.

"Okay." Hunter slapped the cuffs on Barry and moved in our direction. "The paramedics are on their way. Tell me what happened."

Sebastian launched into the tale, leaving nothing out but my magical intervention, and when he was finished Hunter looked stunned.

"I can't believe it." He scrubbed his cheek and shook his head. "I knew something weird was going on in Roy's garage, but ... porn." The horrified expression on his face would've made me laugh under different circumstances. "I can't believe this."

"Well, believe it." Sebastian had recovered most of his bravado and was relishing being the center of attention. "Erin is supposedly pregnant by Roy because he lied about having a vasectomy. You might want to inform the paramedics about that little detail."

"I will." Hunter seemed baffled by the information we'd laid out. The disheveled room added to his unease. "It must have been an earthquake, right?"

"I don't know," Sebastian replied. "Whatever it was, it knocked Stormy and me down. We both covered our heads. It probably wasn't smart because they had guns, but ... it was freaky, man."

Hunter's eyes sought — and found — mine. "You're really okay?"

I nodded. "I'm okay. Just really shaky."

"I don't blame you." He cracked a slight smile. "I'll have the paramedics check you over, too. After that, I'll get you home. It'll be morning before these three are ready for questioning."

Home. For once, the word wasn't frightening. "I can live with that."

IT WAS ALMOST TEN BEFORE HUNTER could leave the funeral home. I offered to call my grandfather to pick me up, but he insisted I wait. He wanted to take me home, and because I didn't want to deal with myriad invasive questions I was willing to hang out and watch the emergency responders work.

"These locks are new," I said dumbly when we got to the back door of my apartment. "Grandpa must've changed the locks and not given me a key."

"I changed the locks," Hunter reminded me, his voice weary. He sounded as if he was ready to pass out on his feet. "I put copies on your keyring."

"Oh." I rummaged in my pocket until I came up with my keys. "I guess it was a waste for you to spend half your day upgrading my security system. Turns out it wasn't necessary."

"It was necessary." He held open the door so I could step inside and followed me after turning the bolt to lock us in. "Now I don't have to worry about you."

"I'll pay you back for the security system just as soon as I can," I promised. "I don't know how much it cost, but I bet it was plenty."

"Don't worry about it."

"That doesn't seem fair."

"Don't worry about it," he repeated, trudging up the stairs behind me. "You're safe. That's the most important thing."

"Yeah, well ... ." I found the correct key for the new lock on my apartment door, and when I stepped inside I was surprised that Hunter remained on the other side of the threshold. "Are you coming in?"

He didn't immediately answer, instead biting his lower lip.

Here it comes. He's going to let me down easy now. He's going to tell me that he was here only to keep me safe and now he wants to put distance between us. I should've seen this coming.

"Monica and I are over," he stated after a moment. I could tell he was trying to arrange his thoughts. He had a certain look about him when mired in deep thought. "She wasn't happy. In fact, she kind of begged me to change my mind. She had a lot of not-so-nice things to say about you when I told her it was over. She might go after you again."

"I'm sure she will." That was a worry for another day. After what had happened in the funeral home, Monica didn't frighten me in the least.

"I tried to tell her that it wasn't your fault, that you had nothing to do with it, but she could see it was a lie."

Was I supposed to say something here?

"It was a lie," he said softly. "She and I were never going to make it, but that doesn't mean there's nothing between us. I didn't want to still have these feelings for you. More than anything, I didn't want to try to survive having my heart broken again."

"I don't want to break your heart again." My voice caught. "I don't want my heart broken again either."

"We're both leery of certain things. Pretending there's nothing here will be bad for both of us, though. I don't think we'll be able to stay away from one another."

"Probably not." I offered a half smile. "There is something chemical that happens to me whenever I see you. I have no idea what it is, but ... it leaves me feeling warm all over and kind of like an idiot."

He grinned. "Well, at least we're in the same boat there."

"So, what do we do?" It was an honest question. I felt stranded in the ocean with no rescue boat in sight.

"We date."

"Date?" That seemed too simple of an answer for feelings as complex as the ones roiling inside me.

He nodded, his grin widening. "In two weeks."

"Two weeks? You're putting us on a schedule?"

That made him laugh. "I have to clean up this case, and the town will be in an uproar over what happened at the funeral home. That's on top of the fact that they were already buzzing about you and I spending the night together."

"Nothing happened!"

He snorted. "Something happened. I came to a realization. I don't want to pretend that you don't make my head fuzzy ... or my heart race ... or my shoulders feel lighter just by being close to me."

That was possibly the most romantic thing anyone had ever said to me. My mouth went dry. "I ... ."

"We have to wait." His tone was no-nonsense. "If we show up holding hands tomorrow, Monica will fly off the handle and make our lives miserable. I'm not saying she won't be just as bad in two weeks, but all the chatter with the townsfolk will have died down by then. They'll be off gossiping about someone else if we wait."

"And you won't have to disclose our relationship in your report if we wait," I surmised. It made sense. "That's a very rational approach."

"Yeah?" He looked hopeful. "I'm not saying this will work out. We're both older and we've been through a lot. We're not the same kids that we used to be."

"No," I agreed. "That fact might make things better."

"It might make them worse."

The statement grated. "If you're going to start with a defeatist attitude what's the point of even trying?"

"Because I can't not try. Also, I'm not being a defeatist. I'm a realist. This won't be easy."

"No."

"We've both been through far harder things. Heck, you just survived three crazy people trying to kill you and a flash earthquake that no one can explain."

Did he have to mention the earthquake? Suddenly, I was itchy. "Yeah."

"You've also survived your dreams crashing down around you," he said. "We've both survived that. This would be a new beginning. We can't just pretend the past decade didn't happen and jump right back to where we were. We have to start slow and get to know one another as adults."

He was offering me the world. His world. "That's a smart idea."

"Good." He brushed his fingers over my cheek. "I'll call tomorrow to make sure you're okay. Even though we can't date for two weeks, I can still see you. I'll have more questions for you tomorrow."

My mouth dropped open when he turned to descend the stairs. "That's it? You're not even going to kiss me?"

He chuckled and glanced over his shoulder. "Anticipation is half the fun. You should remember that from when we were kids. I'm pretty sure you made me wait two weeks back then."

"Oh, so this is payback."

He winked. "It's the right thing to do. You've had a long day and I'm freaking exhausted. I want to be at my full strength when I finally take you out."

Ugh. Why did he have to sound so reasonable? "Okay, but I bet it'll be harder to go two weeks without kissing me than you think."

"It's going to be pure torture. I'm still up to the challenge."

"I guess we'll see who cracks first."

The dimple in his cheek came out to play. "You're on ... for all of it."

For the first time in, well, years, I felt like a complete person. I was still puzzled over my newfound magical abilities, but the rest of it felt right and comfortable. "Right back at you."

Made in the USA
Las Vegas, NV
17 October 2023

79248372R00142